A TWIST OF FATE

#1 *NEW YORK TIMES* BESTSELLING AUTHOR

LISA JACKSON

Recycling programs
for this product may
not exist in your area.

ISBN-13: 978-1-335-40590-6

A Twist of Fate
First published in 1983. This edition published in 2021.
Copyright © 1983 by Lisa Jackson

This edition published by arrangement with Harlequin Books S.A.

For questions and comments about the quality of this book,
please contact us at CustomerService@Harlequin.com.

Harlequin Enterprises ULC
22 Adelaide St. West, 40th Floor
Toronto, Ontario M5H 4E3, Canada
www.Harlequin.com

Printed in U.S.A.

Chapter 1

The telephone receiver was slammed back into its cradle with such force that the paperweight sitting next to the phone slipped off the desk. Two framed pictures of a round-eyed, blond-haired girl rattled and then dropped onto the corner of the desk. The tall man who had slammed the telephone so violently righted the portraits with care, clasped his hands behind his back and resumed his pacing. *Would it ever be possible to communicate with Krista again,* he wondered. His shoulders were slightly slumped, and there was a pained darkness just beneath the anger in his eyes. He swore an oath, aimed for the most part at himself, and continued pacing in front of the wide plate-glass window.

For a moment he paused to look out the window and try and control his rage. A fading California sun was dispersing the final rays of daylight inland as it settled peacefully into the tranquil Pacific Ocean. Long lavender shadows had begun to deepen against the white sand of the beach, and the first cool hint of autumn hung crisply on the air. Kane closed his eyes tightly, as if to shut out the serene view. Turbulent emotions stormed through his body. He kept telling himself that he couldn't change the past, that he couldn't blame a dead woman for his daughter's condition, and yet he did.

A solid rap on the door interrupted his black thoughts, and automatically Kane called out a terse acknowledgment. A moment later Jim Haney marched through the door carrying an ungainly sheaf of papers and a long manila envelope. Jim's tired face held a genuine smile, although he also noted the severe lines of stress that contorted Kane's body. Kane's normally impeccable wool suit was wrinkled and his expensive silk tie askew. Harsh creases webbed from the corners of Kane's deep-set gray eyes and there was a cold, hard determination in the set of his jaw. It wasn't hard for Jim to surmise the reason for Kane's obvious annoyance. Jim knew Kane well enough to recognize that Kane was angry and concerned over his eleven-year-old daughter. The guilt that Kane bore silently was beginning to show. Kane needed to think about something else—anything else—and Jim hoped that he had found the solution to Kane's studious disinterest in anything other than the near-fatal accident that had left his daughter disabled.

Jim's smile remained intact as he met Kane's annoyed gaze. "I guess this about wraps it up," Jim announced, fanning the air with a smooth sheaf of computer print-outs. Kane's cool eyes followed the green and white pages with only feeble interest while Jim continued. "The Seattle sale—it's final—and all of the loose ends are tied up…except for one."

"So quickly?" Kane asked skeptically as he settled into the worn leather chair behind his desk and began scanning the printout.

"For once it looks like we may have gotten lucky."

"Good!" There was a note of finality to Kane's words. He looked up at Jim with a grim smile. "Then there's really no reason for me to wait, is there?"

Jim coughed nervously before meeting Kane's unwavering gray stare. "Are you sure that you're making the right decision?"

Involuntarily a muscle in Kane's jaw tightened. "Let's just say that I'm making the only decision possible."

"But to just pack up and leave all of this…" Jim's voice trailed off as he waved expansively. The gesture encompassed the entire gray concrete office building of Consolidated Finances, the understated but costly furnishings and the calm ocean view.

Kane's eyes swept the office, noting the leather furniture, the thick plush carpet, the book-lined cherry-wood walls, and then fell back on his friend. "Think of it as a prolonged leave of absence, if you like."

"Then you will be back?" Jim asked guardedly.

"When I have to be," Kane agreed, with an expression of distaste. "No doubt the board of directors will insist that I come back and oversee the operation from time to time." Kane returned his attention to the computer sheets before him. Quickly shuffling through the smooth, flat pages, he located the report that he sought. A dark furrow etched its way across his forehead as he reread the printout. "Still losing money in the legal department?" he asked, almost to himself. "I thought that we had cleared up that embezzling scam last week and had gotten rid of Cameron—or whatever his name was. Didn't we?" He turned his sharp eyes on Jim.

"That's the one loose end that's still dangling. It looks as if Cameron has an accomplice."

"What?"

"I had a hunch from the beginning that someone was working with him, but I couldn't prove it until I made sure that Cameron was out of commission. I'm not sure who the culprit is—haven't been able to dig up any tangible proof—but I've narrowed it down to a few possibilities." Jim handed Kane the manila envelope. "Here's some personnel information on some of the suspects."

Kane reached for the envelope. "Well, whoever he is, he must be a damned fool! You would think that with all of the hubbub about Cameron, anyone else involved would be busy covering his tracks rather than taking any further risks. This guy must get his kicks by flirting with danger."

"It may not be a man," Jim suggested.

Kane cocked an interested dark eyebrow. "A woman?" A satisfied, almost wicked smile crept over his lips.

"Like I said before, I'm not sure, but it looks as if Cameron has always been…fond of the ladies. He's had a reputation for promoting women."

"Whether they're qualified or not?"

Jim shrugged. He didn't like the glint of inquisitive interest that had stolen over Kane's features. "I haven't had Cameron arrested as yet, but he's being watched. Hopefully his colleague will surface soon."

"So you're telling me that Cameron is still on the payroll and that although you're sure he hasn't taken any more funds, someone near to him has." Kane Webster was beginning to show his anger.

Jim squirmed only slightly as he went on to explain. "That's about the size of it. We're watching Cameron round the clock, night and day. We know that he hasn't pocketed the funds himself, because we've kept him tied up with auditors and the like ever since it became apparent that he was embezzling trust funds. So far he hasn't become suspicious."

Kane wasn't convinced. "And his *friend*?"

"Somehow she's still manipulating the accounts and taking money." Jim shook his head and grimaced. "I haven't been able to trace it to her as yet. She's very clever."

Kane sat thoughtfully in his chair and pulled out the personnel files that Jim had handed him. He didn't doubt Jim's assumption that Cameron had a woman accomplice. He'd worked with Jim too many years not to respect the younger man's opinion. Jim's suspicions had always paid off in the end for Consolidated Finances.

The names on the personnel reports meant nothing to Kane, and at first glance, all of the files seemed to hold nothing out of the ordinary. "You're sure that the thief is one of these people?"

Jim nodded his head in affirmation. "No one else has the authority to move bank funds so freely."

"But couldn't someone else forge a superior's order?"

"I thought about that, too. I had it checked out, but the auditing system of the bank is too complete. No, our misguided embezzler is sitting right there in that envelope. All we have to do is figure out who she is."

Kane puzzled over Jim's recent discoveries

in what had appeared to be a sleepy little Seattle bank. His eyes narrowed as he thought about the trap that he would set for Cameron and his accomplice. The fact that it was a woman interested Kane. He had learned several years ago that women could be a devious lot, and it only reinforced his bitter opinion of the opposite sex to learn of the female embezzler.

Jim Haney watched the play of emotions that traversed Kane's dark features. He had worked with Kane for over ten years and had come to know his boss as well as anyone. Kane was a fair employer, but Jim knew from past experience that Kane could be ruthless if crossed. Right now, as Kane's lips thinned, Jim was thankful that his name wasn't Mitchell Cameron. And he couldn't help but feel pity for the unfortunate woman who had gotten tangled up with Cameron. Jim had his own opinion about the accomplice's identity, and he had met the woman. It was damned hard to believe that such an intelligent, sophisticated woman would be involved with the likes of Cameron. Oh, well—that was Kane's problem. "Did you want me to have the police go to work on Cameron?" he asked.

"No." Kane shook his head, still immersed

in his thoughts. "I'll see to it personally. I'm leaving for Seattle tonight." A satisfied grin moved over Kane's features.

"You're really going to enjoy throwing the book at Cameron, aren't you?"

"And the woman! I don't like any thief—especially when she's got her hands in my pockets!" Kane retorted. "This just gives me one more reason to head north as soon as possible."

"That's something I don't understand at all," Jim admitted. "Why you bought that miserable excuse of a bank—it's been losing money for years—just so you can freeze your tail off in Seattle."

"California lost its sparkle for me quite a while ago," Kane muttered tersely, then softened his tone as he caught the wounded look in Jim's eyes. "You know of course about Krista. The doctor thinks a change of climate would be good for her. As soon as I have a permanent residence, I'll send for her."

A personal question died on Jim's lips as he noticed the sober tone of Kane's final words. He hadn't gotten to be vice-president of Consolidated Finances by asking questions that were none of his business. He'd heard the rumors associated with Kane: a glamorous ex-wife, a sticky divorce and an unfortunate accident. But Jim had never pried. He was too interested in self-preservation to open doors that Kane preferred locked.

Kane pushed the manila envelope into his briefcase along with a small portrait of his daughter. He paused for a minute and looked at the eager young face before tucking the picture into a side pocket in the leather case. That accomplished, he snapped the briefcase closed.

"The moving company will take care of the rest of this litter," Kane observed, looking around his office for one last time. "If you need to get in touch with me, Carla has the number of my hotel in Seattle."

"Good luck," Jim said, clasping Kane's hand warmly.

"Let's hope I don't have to rely on luck!" With a smile that didn't reach his eyes, Kane walked out of his office for the last time.

The early-model Volkswagen Rabbit skidded to an abrupt halt, splashing dirty rainwater from the street up onto the sidewalk. The driver of the little yellow car was a slim, striking woman who pulled the emergency brake, slung her purse over her shoulder and slammed the car door shut without taking the time to lock it. She hastened through the damp September evening toward the cozy Irish bar.

There was a determined and slightly mysterious gleam in her large eyes as she hiked her raincoat up and clutched the collar tightly to her throat. Sidestepping a puddle of water as if it were second nature, she pushed her way through the stained-glass door of the restaurant.

The familiar interior was dark, but Erin's eyes became quickly accustomed to the dim lighting and the air thick with cigarette smoke. Loud, tinny music was coming from a rather bedraggled-looking band reminiscent of the late fifties.

Unconsciously Erin wiped away a few drops of rain that still lingered on her cheeks, while she moved her gaze over the Friday night throng of customers that was heralding the beginning of what promised to be another rainy Seattle weekend.

Appreciative glances and admiring smiles followed her movements, but she ignored everyone other than the distinguished man of about fifty sitting before the polished bottles and the mirrored backdrop of the bar. Erin's eyes met his in the reflection, and for a moment a dark, guarded look crossed over his distracted blue eyes. Finally he smiled tightly and motioned for her to take the vacant stool at his side.

"Mitch," Erin sighed almost gratefully. "What on earth are you doing here?"

He hesitated, and in that instant, any warmth in his eyes faded. "How did you know where to find me?"

"Olivia Parsons thought you might be here," Erin replied. Her smile disappeared at the thought of the leggy brunette.

"Oh, I see. Dear old Livvie," Mitch mumbled sarcastically. "Your friend and mine! Here's to friendship." He waved his glass theatrically in the air and signaled to the bartender for another drink. "What can I get you, Erin?"

"Nothing," Erin whispered, trying to keep the conversation as quiet as possible and yet be heard over the din of the band.

"Nothing?" he echoed, mimicking her. "Not going to join me for old times' sake?"

"What are you talking about and why are you here?" she asked, confused by his cynical attitude. Where was the kind man with the soft voice and the dry sense of humor whom she had known for over eight years? Mitch didn't bother to answer her questions. He seemed intent on evading the issue, but she persisted. "Mitch, what are you doing here?"

"What does it look like?"

"It looks suspiciously like you're getting smashed," she replied honestly.

"Very astute, young lady. I always did say that you were a smart girl, Erin." Mitch drained his old drink and reached for the new one. "Are you sure you won't join me? The Scotch is excellent!" Erin shook her head, but Mitch accosted the bartender. "Bring the lady a glass of Chablis," he commanded over Erin's protests.

Erin was having trouble hiding her annoyance with her boss and his unpredictable mood swings, but she kept her temper in check and tried a more subtle approach with him. "Why did you leave the bank early today?" A glass of chilled white wine appeared on the bar before her.

"You haven't heard?"

"Heard what?" Erin asked uneasily. There was a menacing quality about Mitch that she wasn't accustomed to and didn't like.

Mitch shrugged and Erin noticed that his

shoulders drooped. "Why don't you ask Kane Webster, if you're so interested."

"Webster? The new president of the bank? What does he have to do with the fact that you left the office and your clients in order to promote a hangover?" she inquired. Mitch had changed dramatically in the last several months. His behavior had become erratic, almost secretive, and his work had suffered. However, until today Erin had never had to cover for him with a client or track him down in some bar. Erin counted Mitch as one of the few close friends she had in the world, and it pained her to witness his deterioration.

She couldn't forget that Mitch had helped her through an agonizing period in her life by offering her a challenging job and a chance to bury herself in her work. He had encouraged her to do postgraduate work in law and keep busy in order to forget about Lee and the embarrassment and heartache she had suffered while she was married to him. Mitch had helped Erin realize that when Lee had left her eight years before, it hadn't been the end of the world. When she had needed a friend, Mitchell Cameron had been there. And now, if Mitch had a problem, Erin vowed to return the favor.

"Mrs. Anderson was in today," Erin stated, and took the glass of wine from the bar. "She was very disappointed that you weren't able to meet with her yourself. Somehow she didn't really think that I was a suitable replacement for the head of the legal department, and I can't say that I blame her. I certainly wasn't very knowledgeable about her grandfather's will or the estate..."

"That's her problem," Mitch stated blandly and again focused his attention on the bottom of his glass.

"It's not Mrs. Anderson's problem," Erin corrected.

"Well, it certainly isn't mine!"

"But the bank..."

"To hell with the bank," Mitch spat out and slammed his glass on the polished counter. Several of the patrons close by turned interested eyes on Erin and Mitch. Erin felt herself shrink. The last thing she wanted to do was cause a scene.

"I don't understand what's gotten into you lately," Erin began in a low whisper. "And I don't know what Kane Webster has to do with you coming down here to drown your sorrows, but if there's anything I can do—or if there's something you want to talk about..."

"I don't want to talk about anything! You're the one who came looking for me," he reminded her crossly. "I didn't invite you!"

"I was worried about you."

"Well, don't worry over me. I can take care of myself!" Mitch's voice was bitter.

"Mitch, what in the world is going on?" she asked. Erin was stung by his acrid words, but compassion held back the sharp retort that had entered her mind as she watched Mitch order another drink. It was apparent that something was eating him, and because of the kindness he had shown her in the past, she held her tongue. She reached for his sleeve and in a quieter voice asked, "Won't you please tell me what's wrong?"

"Wrong?" The word ricocheted back at her followed by Mitch's mirthless laugh. "What could possibly be wrong?" His blue eyes glittered like ice. "Unless, of course, you think that being fired from a bank that you've given twenty years of your life to is a problem."

The meaning of his words struck her like an arctic blast. "Fired? Webster fired you? But why?"

"Like I said, ask him—if you've still got a job. Who knows, you could be next!"

"But he hasn't even come up from California yet."

"Oh, he's here all right, and mark my words, all of the employees at First Puget—oh, excuse me—Consolidated First Bank better be ready!" he pointed out sarcastically.

Erin sat for a moment in numbed silence. The thought of Mitch being fired was absurd, ludicrous. Mitch had been prominent in building the legal department of First Puget to one of the most prestigious in the city. It was true that for the first time in over a decade the legal department had lost money, but certainly the new president wouldn't hold Mitch solely responsible, would he? Nothing made any sense to her anymore. Mitch caught the look of confusion and pity in her eyes. His attitude softened momentarily.

"Look, Erin. Don't waste your sympathy on me. And it's really not a good idea for you to be seen with me. Believe me, it would be in your best interests to just leave me alone."

"You look like you could use a friend," Erin suggested.

"What I need now is a good attorney, not a friend."

"But you are an attorney," Erin replied, still completely perplexed.

Mitch looked her squarely in the eyes. "I'm a lawyer, yes, but I specialize in civil law. What I need now is a criminal lawyer."

"I don't understand...."

"You don't have to," Mitch answered abruptly and stood up. "I told you before, I don't need your sympathy or any of your self-righteous friendship!" He turned his back on Erin, fumbled in his pocket for a moment and threw a wad of crumpled bills onto the bar. "See ya around," he called over his shoulder, but Erin didn't think he directed his words at her.

"Mitch...wait," she began, but his long uneven strides carried him out of the door and into the night. As she watched him leave she was still recovering from the shock of his dismissal. Why would he have been fired? It was hard to believe that she wouldn't see him on Monday morning, sitting behind his large oak desk, puffing on a slim cigar and perusing *The Wall Street Journal*.

"Looks like you've been stranded," a smooth male voice suggested intimately. "How about a drink with me?"

Erin turned in the direction of the voice and murmured a firm "No, thanks" to the young man with the clipped mustache. He shrugged his shoulders at her denial, as if it was her loss, and manipulated his attention to a lanky blonde sitting near the dance floor.

Erin made her way back to the car. The drizzle had turned into a downpour and the late-afternoon sky had blackened. The drive home was automatic, and as the windshield wipers slapped the rain off the glass, Erin thought about Mitch and what it would be like without his presence in the bank.

She had suspected for several months that Mitch was in the throes of some personal problem. At least it had appeared that way. He had seemed tired and worried—no, more than that—tense, tightly coiled. The closer the final date for the imminent bank sale had drawn, the more tightly wound Mitch had become. Erin had told herself at the time that it was only her imagination, that all of the employees of First Puget were bound to be a little anxious about the new management. But now, as she drove through the dark, slick side streets, she chided herself for not seeing and acknowledging what had been so transparent: Mitchell Cameron was in deep trouble. Its exact nature she couldn't guess, but it was serious enough to have cost him his job.

Without thinking, she killed the motor of

the car as she pulled up in front of the Victorian apartment house. Closing her eyes and rotating her head, Erin tried to relieve the tension in her neck and shoulders. She wondered about Kane Webster. What kind of a man was he? What did she really know about the man, other than the few neatly typed memos with the bold signature that had crossed her desk?

She hadn't heard much about his personal life. Apparently he preferred his privacy. Occasionally Erin had seen his name in print—in the financial pages. If she had read anything about him in the social pages, it usually had to do with his ex-wife, a gorgeous model who had made an unsuccessful attempt at becoming an actress. But that was several years ago, before an accident that had killed Jana and left the daughter disabled, or so it was rumored.

Erin frowned to herself as she thought about her new employer. One thing was certain: Kane Webster had made his fortune on his own, spending the last decade purchasing failing financial institutions and transforming them from operating in the red to operating in the black. He had gained a reputation in financial circles for being something of a rogue because of his unorthodox methods of operation. But if results were the measure of success, Kane Webster was prosperous. It was as if King Midas had reached out and touched the ailing banks himself.

Wearily Erin got out of the car and locked the door. She started up the short shrub-lined walk to her home and smiled at the elegant old house. It was a lovely Victorian manor, perched on a hill overlooking the city. The front porch was comfortable and trimmed in ornate gingerbread. The turn-of-the-century home had been fashioned into apartments twenty years before, and the contractor had taken care to accentuate the nineteenth-century charm of the house. Erin had fallen in love with it the first time she had laid eyes on it. Ignoring opposing arguments from just about everyone she knew, she had used her small inheritance as a down payment and purchased the building two years ago. Or to be more precise, she and First Puget Bank had purchased it; there was still a sizeable mortgage against it.

Even in the drizzle of early twilight the old manor looked warm and inviting. The white three-story building with its gently sloping roof and deep gables had a picturesque aura that was distinctly "Old Seattle." Upon close inspection it was obvious that the house was in sad need of many repairs, but tonight Erin overlooked the chipped paint and the rusty drainpipes. She had applied for an employee loan with the bank to make the needed improvements, but she knew as well as anyone that her loan would be a very low priority to Kane Webster. With a bank that was already losing money, how could he possibly make any low-interest employee loans?

Erin's own apartment, located on the uppermost floor of the stately house, was an attic converted into a cozy loft with a bird's-eye view of the city. She climbed the stairs slowly, sifting through the various pieces of junk mail and complaints from her tenants. Her mind was only half on the stack of mail in her hands, when she heard the telephone ringing. Racing up the final steps, she hurriedly unlocked the door, threw the mail on the table and grabbed the phone.

"Hello?" she inquired, breathless from her dash up the stairs.

"Erin, honey, it's good to hear your voice. Where have you been? I've been calling for hours," a friendly male voice said.

"Lee?" Erin asked hesitantly.

A good-natured laugh bellowed from the other end. "Hi! How've you been?"

"Fine, Lee," she managed, wondering why he persisted in calling her. After the last call two weeks ago, she thought he understood that she didn't want to see him again.

"What do you say we get together? You know, have a couple of drinks and a few laughs. I'll come by and pick you up in a half-hour," he suggested.

Erin was tempted. There had always been something seductive about Lee, not in the sexual sense, but in the fact that he was such an outgoing, likable kind of guy. The same qualities that made him great fun at a party made him an immature husband. Erin could almost picture Lee's college-boy good looks—thick blond hair with just the right amount of wave and laughing blue eyes.

"I don't think so," she replied, trying to take a firm stand with him and failing.

"Why not? Don't tell me you've got other plans?"

"No…" Erin responded, and wondered why she hadn't lied and just gotten rid of him. After all these years and all of the heartache, why couldn't she just slam the receiver down and end the conversation?

"Then, let's have a night on the town…"

"I can't, Lee. I'm sorry. I've got a pile of work to catch up on before Monday."

"But it's the weekend," he coaxed in a honeyed voice. "You know what they say, 'All work and no play makes Erin a dull girl.'"

Lee chuckled, but something in his words brought Erin crashing back to reality. Suddenly she remembered just how little she had in common with a boy who refused to grow up. She recalled the shame and humiliation she had suffered while playing the role of dutiful wife.

"No, Lee. That's not what *they* say at all. That's what you said eight years ago."

"Hey, baby, that's all water under the bridge. Come on, what would a drink hurt?"

Erin sighed audibly. "Look, Lee, I'm not in the mood. Not tonight—not ever. I thought I made that clear to you a couple of weeks ago."

There was a pause in the conversation and Erin could almost hear the wheels turning in Lee's mind.

"Just what is it that you want from me?" she asked.

"I told you—we could have a few laughs."

"Why not just turn on the television and catch reruns of *Gilligan's Island*," she suggested and immediately regretted the sarcasm in her words. Nervously she began tapping her fingernails on the tabletop.

"I have to see you," he pleaded.

"Why? It didn't matter eight years ago. Why the sudden interest?" Erin's voice had begun to shake. Memories began to wash over her.

"You really want to do this the hard way, don't you?" Lee accused.

"I don't even know what you're talking about," Erin sputtered, but an uneasy feeling was growing in the pit of her stomach. This wasn't just a friendly call. He wanted money from her—again. Suddenly Erin felt a deep pang of pity for the man who was once her husband.

"Look, honey," Lee cajoled with only a trace of uncertainty in his voice. "You know I lost the job in Spokane, and well, since I've been back here, my luck hasn't been all that great. I thought that…you could loan me a few bucks, just until I get back on my feet."

Erin swallowed hard before answering. "You haven't paid me back from the last time that I helped you 'get back on your feet.'" Erin's voice was flat. She hoped she sounded unshakable.

"Things just didn't turn out in Spokane. You know how it is, what with the lousy economy and all. It's just hard to get started."

"Oh, Lee," Erin sighed, and felt herself wavering.

He sensed the change in her voice. "I just need a few hundred to get started…"

"Spare me the sad story, Lee," Erin interrupted. "I can't loan you any money right now. I just don't have it."

"Don't have it—or won't lend it?" Lee asked desperately.

"I'm sorry, Lee."

"I doubt it!"

"I don't think that you and I have anything more to discuss. You were the one who made that decision several years ago. Good night."

Erin hung up and noticed that her hands were trembling. Why did he always affect her this way? It was as if she was reliving those last few months before the divorce had become final all over again. Why didn't Lee just disappear from her life completely? Was it her fault? Did he notice her hesitation and somehow construe it as an invitation? While they were married, he had wanted his freedom so desperately. And yet, since the divorce had become final, he kept showing up, trying to rekindle the dead flames. When he finally moved to Spokane, Erin had breathed a sigh of relief. She thought that finally he would make a life away from her.

That was why she had made the mistake of loaning him fifteen hundred dollars, hoping that he would establish himself in Spokane. But his plans had backfired, and he was back in Seattle. It hadn't lasted six months.

Erin shook off her raincoat and started taking the pins from her hair. She couldn't worry about Lee right now. She had too many other pressing problems, the first of which was to get up early in the morning and straighten out the mess that Mitch had made of the Anderson will. That meant that she would have to go back to the bank on a Saturday, but she saw no other solution. With the new boss in town, it wouldn't do to have him walk in on Monday morning and face an angry beneficiary.

Erin shook her hair down to her shoulders and made her way to the bathroom for a long hot bath. It had been a tiring and disturbing day.

Chapter 2

In the silent city, the stark marble building knifed upward through the early-morning fog. Workmen were already removing the old lettering to announce formally that First Puget Bank had become one more cog in the banking machine known as Consolidated Finances. Erin felt a surge of sadness as the final gold letter was lifted off its marble support. It was disheartening to realize that an institution with eighty-year-old roots on the banks of Puget Sound could be so easily transformed into a new, slick piece of financial machinery. Erin couldn't help but feel that some of the personality of the bank would be lost in the transition. Quietly she let herself into the building with her own key and waved to the security guard near the door.

The large foyer of the bank was conspicuously quiet without the usual din of customers, tellers and ringing telephones. It was an eerie, tomblike feeling, and usually gave Erin a feeling of peaceful tranquillity, but today she felt somber.

The elevator was waiting for her, and with a vibrating groan, it whirred into motion and lifted her to the twenty-third floor and the maze of offices that comprised the legal department. She walked in the glow of the security lights, not bothering to turn on the bright iridescence of the outer office fixtures. As she passed Mitch's office she lingered for a moment, experiencing a stab of regret and bitterness. Why couldn't things have worked out better for him? Why did Webster let him go? She wondered about the circumstances surrounding his departure. Was Kane Webster really on a witch hunt of sorts, or was there more to the story? She touched the brass doorknob but released it quickly. What good would it do to go snooping in Mitch's office—it would only stir up unwelcome feelings. The best idea would be to do her work and leave the building before depression really did settle on her shoulders.

Erin's office was dark, but she clicked on the brass desk lamp rather than the overhead fluorescent fixture. The lamp bathed the desk area in a gentle warm glow and gave the room a more intimate and less businesslike atmosphere. She adjusted her reading glasses and pulled out Mitch's dog-eared copy of the Anderson will. As she began to read the verbose and tangled document, Erin became totally consumed by her work. She pulled out several large volumes and unconsciously began humming to the airy notes of the piped-in music. Within minutes she settled herself comfortably on the carpeted floor of her office and became oblivious to anything other than the interesting terms of the document.

Kane stepped out of the cab and handed the driver a healthy tip. He stood for a moment on the curb and squinted up at the tall building he had purchased. With stern satisfaction he watched while the new sign for Consolidated Finances was put into place. He couldn't help but wonder if, as Jim had suggested, he had made a mistake in purchasing this particular bank. It had lost money for nearly two years through terrible mismanagement and was teetering on the brink of bankruptcy. It would take a great deal of finesse on his part to avoid the collapse of the entire organization. Perhaps he had been rash in his decision to acquire the bank. In his eagerness to get away from a glittery lifestyle in California, and in hopes of favorably relocating his daughter, it was possible that he had been too hasty in his decision.

It was too late to start second-guessing himself at this point. With a determined grimace he let himself into the newest in a series of West Coast branches of Consolidated Finances.

As the elevator took him upward he reflected on the position of the bank. Certainly it was salvageable. The first order of business was to plug the embezzling leak. Kane smiled to himself. Nothing would give him greater satisfaction than to deal with the woman who was attempting to steal money from the account holders of the bank. He'd already dealt with Cameron, just yesterday, and fired the bastard. Unfortunately Cameron hadn't given Kane any clues as to the identity of his accomplice. Kane had underestimated the man. He had expected Cameron to crumble into a thousand pieces and give him any information he required in return for immunity from prosecution. But Cameron was made of sturdier stuff, it seemed.

Cameron's attitude had reinforced Jim's opinion—the accomplice had to be a woman, someone Cameron cared enough about to try and protect. Kane hoped that there might be a clue in Mitch's office, just one tiny shred of evidence as to the identity of the woman.

The steel doors opened and Kane stepped into the dimly lit reception area of the legal department. As he was about to snap on the lights, he paused. Was it his imagination or was someone actually humming? His eyes swept the reception area and the adjoining offices until he saw the golden glow of a desk lamp illuminating a partially opened door. The humming continued, a soft womanly quality in its melodic tones. Kane's mind speculated about the woman. Who would be here alone on a Saturday, early in the morning, when the bank was closed? Security personnel? A custodian? Unlikely.

Kane smiled almost evilly to himself and left the hallway in darkness. Maybe for once he had gotten lucky. It was about time for his luck to change. Perhaps the job of finding

Cameron's accomplice was going to be much easier than he had first supposed. Stealthily he strode onward toward the beckoning doorway. His jaw tightened and he cautioned himself to be wary. It would be easy for a thief to cover her tracks if she was smart enough to realize that he could be suspicious of her. He would have to tread lightly. Silently he made his way to the door, unprepared for the scene that met his eyes.

A small woman with thick black hair brushed loosely over her shoulders was sitting on the floor of the office. She sat cross-legged with her back to the door, and she was poring over an enormous pile of open-faced legal documents and books. The office itself was an incredible tangle of notes, books and loose papers. The object of his inspection wasn't what he had imagined. Wearing tight-fitting jeans and a bulky violet sweater that hid none of her soft curves, she was so absorbed in her work that she didn't hear his entrance. A pair of reading glasses perched tentatively on the end of an upturned nose and a pencil caught behind one ear kept her hair from falling in her face. Absently, to herself, she continued humming. To Kane she appeared more like a college student preparing for final exams

than a businesswoman, and she hardly looked
the type who stole. There was a tranquil but
nevertheless faintly disturbing beauty about
the young woman.

Kane's reflexes hardened. No matter who
this woman was, he had to force himself to
keep his objectivity about her. Right now she
had unwittingly assumed position number
one on the list of embezzling suspects, and
Kane couldn't forget that fact. No matter how
innocent or vulnerable she seemed, she was
most likely to be the snag in the legal department. It didn't matter that the elegant curve
of her jaw conformed to her regal bearing, or
that her obsidian hair shimmered with streaks
of indigo.... Before he let his thoughts wander any further, he caught himself. The last
thing he could afford at this point was to feel
any interest in her whatsoever.

He coughed to get her attention, and immediately she swung her startled head in his
direction. Her eyes met his, and just for a moment he felt as if he was slipping into their
lilac depths. Even over the top of her reading
glasses, he could see that there was a tremor
of fear in those luminous eyes, and involuntarily he wanted to reach out and comfort

her. But he forced himself to remain standing, unwavering.

Erin had been completely oblivious to anything other than her work, but a soft cough interrupted her thoughts. She whirled to face the intruding noise, half expecting to see a familiar face.

"Mitch?" she called from habit.

The man standing in the doorway was a stranger and a ripple of alarm broke over her. Her surprise was revealed by the barely concealed gasp. Whoever the tall man was, he had evidently been standing in the doorway for several minutes. He had been right over her, silently appraising her. The thought of his eyes traveling unrestricted over her made her uneasy, tense.

"Were you expecting someone?" he asked.

"Yes…no…you surprised me."

He cocked an eyebrow and leaned against the doorjamb, still watching her intently. He was a tall man, and even in his casual clothes Erin could tell that he was well-proportioned and lean. Strong, broad shoulders supported the expensive weave of his open sport coat. As he stood somewhat insolently, his supple legs strained against the light weight of his tan corduroy slacks. His hair was thick, burnished auburn, laced with traces of gold that gleamed in the warm light of the room. His face was tanned and angular to the point of being harsh, and his gray eyes held hers in a severe gaze that spoke of power and hinted at arrogance. For a moment neither spoke, and Erin felt the spark of electricity in the air.

"May I help you?" Erin inquired in her most coolly professional voice. She guessed at the identity of the intruder and tried to present a calm and efficient demeanor to her new superior. It wasn't an easy task, considering the fact that she was sitting cross-legged in a semicircle of legal documents. She rose as gracefully as possible, without letting her eyes waver from the calculating face of the man who just last night had fired Mitch.

"You're Miss O'Toole?" he continued his inquiry, not answering her question, and only breaking the power of his gaze by a glance at the carved nameplate on her desk.

"That's correct," she agreed, for some reason unable to smile. "I assume you're... Mr. Webster?"

"Kane," he suggested. His silvery eyes drove more deeply into hers and she could feel that he was watching her response, almost anticipating her reaction. "You were expecting me?"

"No, of course not."

"Then…you were waiting for Mitchell Cameron?"

"I told you before, no."

"Then what exactly are you doing here?"

She paused for a moment. It had to be evident that she was busy with legal work, didn't it? Perhaps it was the way that he asked the question that made her feel a need for caution. "I was working."

"I can see that," he scoffed, and for a minute a smile threatened to creep over his face. "But I guess my question should be more specific. Why are you working—" his eyes scanned the office "—seemingly alone, on a Saturday?"

"I am alone!" Was he relieved? "And the reason that I'm here is that there has been a tremendous increase in my workload with the conversion to Consolidated," she replied, but he didn't seem to be listening. To her consternation he came into the room and casually hooked one leg over the desk corner, as if to remind her that he owned the place—literally.

She felt a need to back away from him— to put a little space between his body and hers, but she ignored the temptation. Intuitively she knew that she couldn't show him the least sign of vulnerability or weakness. The harshness in his attitude and his tight-lipped questions made her stiffen and become increasingly wary.

"I see," he mused as if he really didn't. He tented his hands under his chin in a thoughtful and, in Erin's opinion, overly dramatic pose. "Then you're saying that you're overworked?"

"No..."

"No?" He smiled broadly, but the grin didn't light the cold depths of his eyes. "Then you must be inefficient," he suggested.

"I beg your pardon!" Erin blurted, the color draining from her face. What was he doing to her with all of these insane questions and inaccurate accusations?

"Well, it has to be one or the other, doesn't it?"

"Of course not!" she rifled back at him, and suddenly felt as if she had just swallowed a well-placed morsel of bait. He was toying with her for some reason, and it frightened her. To hide her nervousness she began stacking the legal volumes back on the shelf and tidying the scattered papers. She started to arrange her desk in brisk, sure movements, all the while aware that his eyes touched her face, her hands, her neck, her breasts....

She pulled her attention back to him. "I explained that I had a little extra work to finish up. For some reason, that apparently irritates you. I had no intention of offending you so...."

"You haven't offended me." His voice was softer.

"Then what is it with you? I'm just trying to do a decent job, for your bank, I might add, and you march in here unannounced and start an interrogation!"

"Have I been interrogating you?" he asked gently, and reached for her wrist.

"You still are!" she retorted as his hand captured hers. His fingers were a warm, soothing manacle and her pulse began to heat with his touch. Her eyes flew to her wrist, to his eyes, to his fingers and back to his eyes. Then, as abruptly as he had reached for her, he let the hand drop. The intimate gesture had startled Erin, but the release was a disappointment. Unconsciously she drew away from him. He was too commanding, too powerful, and her response to him was too violent.

"I'm sorry," he apologized, and his dark

brows drew together. "I didn't mean to make our first meeting an inquisition. I didn't expect to find anyone here today."

"Neither did I," she breathed. "And that's precisely why I came in—to work without interruption—from the telephone or…anything else." Her breathing was still uneven; the man made her nervous. She tried to control herself and avoid overreacting.

"Do you come in after hours often, Miss O'Toole?" Another question!

"Only when I feel it's necessary!" she responded cuttingly, and then feeling immediately contrite, added, "Please call me Erin. Everyone else does."

"Fair enough. I like to keep things on a personal level."

Erin's black eyebrows shot skyward with his last remark, but she decided it would be wiser not to comment. She had only to remember his grip on her wrist and the storm of emotions that had seized her with his touch. She didn't understand why she was overreacting to him, but she knew that it would be best to put distance between them.

He rose to leave, and Erin felt the air slowly escape from her lungs. She needed time to collect herself, to be alone. However, before reaching the door he paused.

"What was your relationship with Mitchell Cameron?" he asked.

Erin swallowed hard and met the chill in Kane's eyes. "He was my boss," she replied curtly.

"That's all?" Kane's angular face was tense, his jawline firm.

Erin narrowed her eyes. "No…that isn't all!" she said defiantly, watching his gray eyes grow a shade more calculating.

"Somehow I didn't think so."

"Mitchell Cameron is my friend. That fact won't change, even if you did fire him!"

"So you know about that," he thought aloud. "Did Cameron tell you?"

"That's right."

"Did he explain why?"

"I thought maybe you could answer that one." Now she goaded him.

Kane slammed the door closed, reversed his stride and came back to Erin's desk. He planted his hands firmly on the polished surface and pushed his face to within inches of hers.

"What exactly did he tell you, and when?"

"I don't really know if it's any of your business," she shot back at him. Why was he so angry with her? She didn't understand it, but she felt her temper rise with his.

As quickly as a cat springing, he reached out for her and pulled her face nearer to his. "Anything about this bank is my business!"

"But Mitch doesn't have anything to do with the bank anymore, does he?" she asked rhetorically. "You took care of that!"

She felt his closeness, the warmth of his hand against her chin, the light pulse in the tip of his fingers, the heat and magnetism that seemed to radiate from him.

"Why don't you tell me about 'your friend,' Mitch," he coaxed, and suddenly the fingers that had been rough became gentle. His thumb persuaded her to relax as it moved sensually along the line of her chin and jaw, stopping just short of her throat.

"There's nothing to tell," she whispered, trying to think coherently and disregard the intimate persuasion of his hand.

His eyes, flooded with passion, cooled. "Just how good friends are you?"

"Good friends—just that," she managed, and seeing the clinical hardness on his face, pushed his hand away, adding, "Nothing more. And I resent the implication."

"Implication?" he mocked.

"That I sleep with him. That is what you were getting at, isn't it?" she asked with a bitterness she couldn't conceal. "Not all successful women sleep their way to the top!"

"I didn't mean to imply…"

"You certainly did! I really don't understand what all of these suggestive questions are about. I came in here to get some work done!" Erin began gathering the loose papers on her desk as she attempted to stem her anger. She knew it wouldn't do anyone any good to let her temper surface, but she couldn't help but feel a deep-seated resentment toward the man who had fired Mitch. She wondered fleetingly about her conflicting reactions to the man—his touch, his words— but she pushed those provocative thoughts aside as she snapped the desk drawer shut, locked it and retrieved her car keys from her purse.

"I'm only trying to find out firsthand how the staff of this bank works," he explained.

"So that you can fire us all?" she rifled back at him.

A twinkle lighted his steel-colored eyes. "Is that what you're so upset over? You're angry because I let Cameron go?"

How could she explain that everything about him upset her, threw her off balance. "It's really none of my business," she admitted, her poise and professionalism back in place.

"If it makes any difference to you, I have no immediate plans for—how shall I phrase it—restructuring the personnel of the bank. At least not until I see firsthand exactly how efficiently each department runs."

"Except in Mitch's case," Erin prodded, still confused.

"Cameron was different, and as you so aptly stated, 'it's none of your business.'"

Kane pressed his hands together and his lips thinned. "Do you make a practice of working here alone?"

He prepared to analyze her response, but it seemed innocent. "Not usually. But as you must realize, Mitch had been wrapped up with your auditors and computer people."

"And you had to assume his duties alone?" Kane guessed.

"Not entirely," Erin conceded. "Olivia took over a few of Mitch's clients..."

"Olivia? Parsons? The executive secretary?"

"She's more than that. Actually an assistant officer," Erin explained, thinking about the sultry woman who had once so openly flaunted her affair with Lee before the divorce was final.

Kane's eyes never left Erin's face. He noticed the embarrassed burn on her cheeks, the furrowed brows and the slight droop of her shoulders. Something was definitely bothering Miss O'Toole, and he meant to find out exactly what it was. He noticed that she picked up her purse, a gesture that indicated she intended to leave. She couldn't, not yet.

"If you'll excuse me, Mr.... Kane," she requested. She started to walk past him, but his hand reached for her arm.

"You're leaving?"

"That's right," she agreed but remained standing still, conscious only of the warm touch of his hand on her arm.

He grimaced. "I was looking forward to having someone here while I set up my desk."

"But you didn't expect anyone, did you?" she reminded him.

"No, I didn't. But since you're here, you might as well give me a rundown on exactly how this department functions—or at least the way it did in the past."

"Sorry—I've got plans this afternoon," she

lied. He was still touching her and the feeling was delicious, warm, inviting. The dimly lit room was beginning to close in on her, and she knew that she had to get away from him and clear her head.

"What about tonight?" he persisted.

"Still busy." She smiled up at him but felt her lips begin to tremble. He eyed her curiously and she wanted to shrink away from him and melt into him all in the same motion. As if he understood her feelings, he pulled her a little more closely and asked his final invitation in a whisper, his breath fanning lightly across her face. "What about tomorrow?"

Her eyes reached for his and she found it impossible to lie. "I... I don't know."

"Come on," he persuaded. "I'm new in town. You can show me the sights."

"I thought you wanted to discuss business...."

"We will."

"I don't date anyone I work with." His eyes touched her forehead, her cheeks, her chin, her throat.

"Don't think of it as a date," he murmured enigmatically. "Consider it...an orientation meeting."

"But..."

"I won't take no for an answer. I'll pick you up at ten."

"No!"

Kane released her. "I'll see you in the morning," he stated as if it were already a fact.

She didn't answer. Couldn't. But she found the strength to tear herself away from the imprisonment of his stare and walk out of the office with as much pride as she could muster. She wasn't thinking clearly; her thoughts were tangled in a web of emotions. Her mind was as ragged as her breathing, and there was an impulse and yearning that she had never experienced in her lifetime.

Once outside the building she hurried to her car and only paused to take in full, mind-clearing breaths of fresh air. Her fingers trembled as she fumbled with her keys. She kept telling herself that her reactions were bordering on insanity. She had met a man, a very attractive and charismatic man, under tense circumstances. The feelings that had flooded through her were merely a release of that tension—that was all.

But the more she tried to convince herself that she was once again in command of her feelings, the more helpless and vulnerable she felt. Not since her marriage to Lee had she let any man come so close to her, and the powerful magnetism and raw energy that she felt when she met Kane frightened her. She couldn't, wouldn't, let her emotions get so out of hand. She had to avoid being alone with him, for she couldn't trust herself around him. In the past she had always scoffed at the kind of chemical attraction that had received so much public acceptance. Now she wasn't so sure.

She started the engine and roared out of the parking lot, all the while mumbling to herself that she was acting irrationally.

Kane sat at his desk long after Erin had made her hasty departure. He had waited by the window until he had seen her actually leave the building and drive away. Now that she was safely gone, he lifted the long manila envelope from his briefcase.

The ordinary printouts that had seemed so dull yesterday had taken on a new luster and significance today. The desk chair groaned as he settled into it and pulled out the neatly typed report marked O'TOOLE, ERIN. He reread the information on its pages, slowly turning the facts over in his mind.

One piece of information leaped out at him. It seemed that Miss O'Toole had for a while been Mrs. Lee Sinclair before reassuming her maiden name after her divorce. Kane frowned deeply and inexplicably to himself. Erin had been employed by the bank for over ten years. In the past eight, with the aid of Mitchell Cameron, she had been rapidly promoted until she had reached her present position as second in command of the legal department. Quite an accomplishment for a thirty-two-year-old woman.

Kane rubbed his chin thoughtfully as he continued to study the file on Erin. It seemed that she had purchased a building a couple of years ago—with the help of an employee loan granted, of course, by Cameron. And just recently she had again applied for more funds, to renovate the building.

Several items didn't add up in Kane's mind. Erin seemed forever in need of money, but she had loaned her ex-husband a tidy sum about a year ago. A copy of the canceled check made payable to Lee Sinclair had been included in her file; Jim Haney had done his research well. The fact that she seemed always in debt was a bad sign. Also, for such a young woman, she had been promoted rapidly—too rapidly. Bad sign number two. And, from Cameron's comments on her personnel evaluation reports, Mitchell Cameron had trusted her completely. Bad sign number three.

And what about today? She had called out Mitch's name when Kane had entered her office. Was she expecting him, or had she merely been sent by Cameron to continue his dirty work? She had obviously spoken to Cameron last night; she admitted it herself. Just how deep was she in with Cameron and how much did she know? The suspicious questions rattled around in Kane's head until he scowled to himself and threw the report on the desk.

It was difficult to imagine Erin O'Toole Sinclair as an embezzler. Although the evidence was stacking up against her, he couldn't forget her delicate features and surprisingly innocent eyes.

Thoughtfully he rubbed the weariness from the back of his neck. Somehow the satisfaction that he had expected to feel while tracking Cameron's accomplice was missing. He chided himself and accused himself of being a fool. He was beginning to soften where Erin was concerned, and he couldn't let that happen, especially since she was probably robbing him blind at this very moment.

He slanted another severe glance at the file. The name that seemed to leap from the page at him was Sinclair. His lips drew into a thin, hard line. It was ludicrous, but the piece of information that bothered him the most wasn't the incriminating evidence against Erin, but rather the fact that she had been married at one time. It was infuriating for him to imagine another man making love to the dark-haired woman with the wide eyes and provocatively defiant tilt to her chin, even if it had been years ago. He chuckled to himself humorlessly. What did he expect, anyway? That any woman that attracted him be a virgin?

It was the word that his own mind had used that jarred him back to reality. He was *attracted* to Erin, and he couldn't allow himself that luxury. He couldn't let her get under his skin, especially if she was indeed what he suspected her to be.

With a disgruntled shove Kane pushed the file back into the drawer and slammed it shut. Then, after shaking himself mentally, he locked his desk, somehow wishing he could throw away the key.

Chapter 3

It was late afternoon by the time Erin arrived home. She had spent the day window-shopping and walking through the heart of the city, mindlessly watching the crowds of shoppers and breathing the salty air from the Sound. She had avoided going home, content to wander among the tourists as she attempted to sort out her confused feelings. She didn't want to deal with anything or anyone until she had set her uneven emotions back in balance. But try as she would, she was unable to push Kane Webster out of her thoughts.

Erin was angry and resentful of the way Kane had so high-handedly dismissed Mitch.

She was offended by his insinuations that she had compromised her morals for career advancement by sleeping with Mitch. And, perhaps more than anything else, she was afraid of and uncertain about the feelings that he could stir in her with only a look or a touch of his fingertips. It was as if he were attracting her and repelling her at the same time. What was it about him that caused such warring emotions to battle in her weary mind? Something about him excited her, fascinated her, and she felt helpless as a moth compelled to an irresistible flame. It was a flame that would surely burn her with a molten passion until she was consumed by heat and fire.

Even the old Victorian apartment house didn't seem as comforting as usual. As Erin was about to mount the stairs to the loft, Mrs. Cavenaugh, oldest of the tenants, opened the door of her apartment and called to Erin before she could escape.

"Erin, honey," Mrs. Cavenaugh cajoled sweetly while leaning heavily on her cane. "It's already getting dreadfully cold in here. I thought you were going to do something about that insulation. The floor is just like ice, and it's starting to bother my arthritis again." The kindly, bespectacled old woman smiled at Erin.

"Yes, Mrs. Cavenaugh, I know," Erin sighed as she paused on the lowest step. "And I promise that I'll get some bids on the insulation this week. There…uh, have been a few changes at the office. I've been pretty busy and I guess I've been neglecting my duties around here. But that's no excuse. I'll take care of it."

Wise, faded blue eyes scanned Erin's face, and Mrs. Cavenaugh shook a slightly crooked finger at the younger woman. "I could tell that something was bothering you from the moment you dragged yourself through the door. It's not that ex-husband of yours again, is it?"

"Oh, no! This has nothing to do with Lee…"

"Humph! Always said that boy would come to no good."

Erin began to protest again, but Mrs. Cavenaugh would have none of it. "You know what you need, don't you? A cup of my chamomile tea. A good strong one." She gave Erin a knowing wink. "You're in luck—I have a pot brewing this very minute." A crafty look came over the wrinkled face, and she turned to lead Erin into her apartment.

"Oh, no, Mrs. Cavenaugh, I couldn't…"

"Nonsense!" Mrs. Cavenaugh sputtered. "Now, you come in here and tell me what's really bothering you!"

Erin stopped protesting to smile and follow the bent figure into her apartment. The poor dear woman wasn't really looking for Erin to complain about the cold floors at all, Erin realized. Mrs. Cavenaugh just wanted some company to brighten the long afternoon and evening. Erin decided the least she could do was enjoy a cup of tea with her elderly tenant, even if it was the foulest concoction ever to be poured from a silver teapot.

As Erin expected, the long, lace-covered coffee table was already set for two. A service of shining silver teapot and fragile porcelain cups adorned the table, and the air was scented with the strong aroma of chamomile.

Erin sat graciously in the floral side chair while, with slightly shaking hands, Mrs. Cavenaugh poured the pale ochre liquid into one of the cups. "Sugar?" she suggested, and without waiting for an answer, dropped two lumps into the light-colored brew.

Erin took the cup and sipped at the tea while Mrs. Cavenaugh settled herself into her favorite worn rocker. "So now, Erin, tell me about your problems at work." Light blue eyes sparkled with interest as Erin briefly sketched out her morning at the bank. Erin glossed over a few of the details, carefully omitting any references to the bevy of emotions that her new boss had aroused in her. But Mrs. Cavenaugh's knowing eyes saw more than Erin had hoped to divulge.

"So this new boss of yours…what's-his-name…" Mrs. Cavenaugh began.

"Mr. Webster." Erin supplied the missing words.

"Yes…what's he like?" Eyes, crinkled at the corners, stared earnestly at Erin over the rim of the tiny cup.

"Oh, I don't know," Erin said with a shrug, hoping that she appeared aloof. "He's…all business, I suppose. You know, the typical banker type."

"I wonder…" The old woman paused dramatically, but Erin refused to rise to the bait and defend her position. "You say that he let Mitchell Cameron go? Why?"

Erin frowned into her teacup. "I don't know," she replied earnestly. "But I intend to find out!"

Mrs. Cavenaugh's laughter crackled through the apartment. "And I don't doubt that you will." Why did Mrs. Cavenaugh seem so pleased? "Do you expect to corner Mr. Webster at work on Monday and get to the bottom of this?"

"I hadn't really thought about it. He wants me to meet him tomorrow—show him the city, let him know firsthand about the bank. But I don't think it would be a good idea. You know how I feel about my free time..."

"Oh, nonsense!" The sweet, wrinkled woman smiled and waved her hand, dismissing Erin's argument as if it were a bothersome insect. "Yes, I know all about your need for privacy, and I know why. But, Erin, it's been eight long years since that louse of a husband walked out on you, and you can't hide away forever. Why not have some fun with this Mr. Webster? How could it hurt?"

"I have no intention of 'having fun' with Kane!" Erin exclaimed, bristling. Mrs. Cavenaugh's eyes seemed to dance at Erin's familiar use of her employer's first name. "*If* I were to go, it would be strictly as a business meeting!"

"Call it whatever you will, it doesn't matter. But for goodness' sake, honey, *go!*" Mrs. Cavenaugh seemed to sense that Erin was wavering, and she added one final incentive. "How else do you plan to find out about Mitchell Cameron, unless you confront this Webster? I would think that you would prefer to do it while you were alone with the man." She seemed thoughtful for a minute, letting her teacup rest in her hand. "This isn't the kind of thing that you would want to start a scene over—now, is it? It just wouldn't do to let on to all of the employees. It's too scandalous, don't you think? What would it do to employee morale?"

Erin laughed at the thinly veiled attempts of the kind but conniving old woman to persuade her. "Why is it that I feel manipulated?"

Mrs. Cavenaugh spread her palms upward in a helpless motion, suggesting that she didn't have the faintest idea what Erin was implying, but a devilish twinkle remained in her eyes.

"Look, Mrs. Cavenaugh, I just may go with Kane tomorrow. But don't make anything more of it than what it is—a business meeting. I've seen that look in your eyes before, so don't go playing matchmaker for me," Erin warned with a pleasant smile as she set her empty cup on the table.

Mrs. Cavenaugh chose to ignore Erin's bit

of advice. "More?" she asked, holding the teapot in midair over Erin's cup.

"No, thank you. I'm sorry, but I really do have to get upstairs. But you're right," she added, placing her palm on the hard wood planks of the floor, shiny with patina. "I think there's a draft coming from the bay window." She walked over to the window in question and ran her fingers around the sill. The cold air made her frown. "I'll see to it that somehow we warm this place up before winter really sets in." Erin rose and dusted her hands off against her jeans. "Thanks for the tea."

"Don't mention it," the elderly woman responded with a wave of her hand. "You know you're welcome here any time." She was smiling smugly to herself, seeming quite pleased.

Erin let herself out of the quaint little apartment and headed up the stairs. She glanced at her watch and realized that it was too late in the day to get anyone out to weatherize Mrs. Cavenaugh's apartment this weekend. She jingled the keys in the lock and gave a hefty shove to her own sticky front door. There were so many things that needed to be done to the apartment house and so little time and money to do them with.

With a sigh she took off her jacket and

headed for the kitchen. As she made herself a quick sandwich she thought about Mrs. Cavenaugh. She was right, of course. The only logical way that she would find out the circumstances surrounding Mitch's dismissal would be to confront Kane directly, especially since Mitch was so mysterious and cynical about the situation. However misguided Mrs. Cavenaugh's motives were, Erin had to admit that the little old woman made sense. And, no matter what, she couldn't run away from private discussions with her boss forever, could she? Any emotions that had started to entangle her would just have to be straightened out and dealt with in a professional manner.

The pastrami sandwich that she created tasted like mustard-covered cardboard, and after a few nibbles she put it back into the refrigerator. Mrs. Cavenaugh's biting words came into her mind. "It's been eight long years since that louse of a husband walked out on you. You can't go on hiding forever!"

Is that what I'm doing, Erin wondered as she flopped down on the soft cushions on the couch. *Am I hiding? From what—or whom?* Ever since her personal life had been thrown open to the public, and she had become the object of speculative gossip, Erin had vowed to keep her privacy securely guarded. Lee's open affair with Olivia had scarred Erin so badly that even today, eight years afterward, she refused dates with co-workers in an almost paranoid way. With the exception of a few close friends no one at the office had any ideas about her love life.

Some love life! She had to laugh at herself at the thought. Except for a couple of men who had interested her only slightly, she had hardly dated since the divorce. It was easier, and she preferred to keep her feelings under tight rein, thus avoiding any further conjecture about her personal life.

Eight years ago Lee had seen to it that Erin was the topic of conversation in the bank cafeteria. Whether he had intended that she discover his affair with Olivia, Erin couldn't guess. But it hadn't taken long to find out about his clandestine meetings with one of the most seductively beautiful women in the bank. When she had discovered the affair, Erin had crumbled. But Lee had seemed to blossom and feed upon her humiliation. Even during the first confrontation he hadn't been upset or contrite but rather smugly proud. Erin and Lee had separated, and Lee's fascination with Olivia continued to thrive. He was forever throwing the affair in Erin's face as if, somehow, she was to blame for the failure of their marriage. For a while she had tortured herself with the same thoughts.

But as Lee's attraction for uncomfortable confrontations with Erin increased, Erin realized that he drew a malicious satisfaction from taunting her. He saw to it that he and Olivia were everywhere that Erin went. During working hours he would come into the bank and meet Olivia for coffee. At office parties he would escort the sultry Olivia, never missing a chance to display his affection for her with a gentle kiss or a whispered endearment—always within eye and earshot of his former wife. At the time Erin told herself that it shouldn't bother her, and during the day she kept up a seemingly unconcerned and professional appearance. But at night, after long lonely hours working toward a law degree, she would find herself alone in the bed that she had once shared with Lee and she would cry bitter tears of frustration.

That was years ago, and somehow the pain had lessened. Now, looking back on the past, Erin wondered if she had ever really loved Lee. She had cared about him, yes, and her pride had been severely bruised by his betrayal. But she doubted that she had ever loved him, and certainly not with the passion that she knew he had found with Olivia.

After the liaison with Olivia had cooled, Lee had come back, hoping to rekindle the ashes of their broken marriage. Erin had waited for that day, falsely thinking that she would feel a vengeful satisfaction from slamming the door in his face. But when he had actually arrived on the doorstep, he looked tired and ragged. He was unshaven and had large purple circles under his eyes. His clothes were disheveled, and even his perfect blond hair had seemed to lack its usual luster. It had taken all of her strength to close the door on him in his embarrassed and confused state. She had turned him away, and instead of feeling the grim satisfaction of sweet revenge, she could only feel empty, dry and sad for her exhusband. After locking the door, she had run into the bathroom and been sick for the rest of the afternoon, retching until her stomach had emptied and her body shook from the ordeal.

Erin stretched out on the couch and shook her head, trying to dislodge those vivid and melancholy memories of the past. She ran her fingers through the thick tangle of her black hair. The long evening stretched ahead of her as she clicked on the television to clear her head. The selection of sitcoms and variety shows was dismal, so she picked up a mystery novel that was guaranteed to interest her and curled up again on the antique sofa. But the spy thriller that should have held her attention, didn't. She found her thoughts traveling backward in time to her marriage only to jump forward again to this afternoon and to Kane Webster. With a disgusted sigh she tossed the book onto the coffee table and stared into the dusk. She let her mind wander at will until late in the night.

The doorbell chimed precisely at ten o'clock the next morning. Erin paused for a moment as her defenses wavered at the thought of facing Kane alone. Impatiently the doorbell sounded again, and she forcibly steeled herself before opening it.

"I thought that just maybe you had run out on me," Kane joked. He seemed affable, yet there was still that underlying hardness about him, a doubt that she had felt yesterday.

"I wouldn't think of it," she quipped back lightly, but felt her stomach tighten as she realized just how many times last night she had thought of avoiding meeting him.

"Good. Now, how about a cup of coffee?" he asked as he walked into the apartment and rubbed the chill out of his hands.

"Are you offering me one, or asking for one?"

Hearing the sarcastic tone of her voice, he cocked his head in her direction. "Are you angry with me already?"

Erin hadn't realized until then that she *was* angry with him for setting her life off balance. "No…of course not. I didn't mean to snap at you," she apologized.

"Then you won't mind if I use your phone?" he inquired. "I promised to call my daughter this morning, but I didn't want to disturb her earlier."

"The phone is in the bedroom," she replied, and smiled at him for the first time that morning.

He excused himself and threw his jacket over the hall tree before he set off in the direction that she had indicated. Not wanting to intrude, she went into the kitchen and began brewing the coffee. The apartment was small, and it was impossible for her not to overhear part of his conversation, although she purposefully turned up the volume of the radio. The last thing she wanted to know about was

Kane's personal life. She had to try to keep things on a business level with him. Unfortunately even the classical music couldn't drown out Kane's voice as it rose in volume and unsuppressed anger.

"Krista! Don't even suggest such a thing! I'll be back in two weeks, and then we'll move you up here..." There was a long pause, and then Kane's voice softened. "I know how you feel, honey, honestly I do. But Dr. Richards thinks..." Another long pause. The conversation was extremely one-sided. "Look, Krista, I know that Aunt Sharon would like to have you stay until Christmas.... But the doctor and I think it would be best to get you into school here as soon as possible." Silence. "We'll talk about it later. Goodbye, honey."

It was several minutes before Kane came out of the bedroom, and in that time the lines around his eyes had seemed to deepen. Although he managed a smile, Erin could see that it was forced. He was preoccupied and tense. Through the soft folds of the fabric of his lightweight sport shirt, Erin could see the contours of his muscles, and they were tight. He walked into the living room and stared out of the window without seeing.

There was something in the droop of his

shoulders that made her want to reach out and place a comforting hand against his cheek. He was having problems with his adolescent daughter—that much was evident—and Erin wanted to soothe away some of the mental pain he was experiencing. But she hesitated and remained in the kitchen, dawdling over coffee that was already brewed. It was safer somehow, watching him from a distance, wishing that any pain that he might be feeling would disappear.

When at last he turned back to face her, some of the strain had left his face. He ran his gaze over the apartment, appearing to study its contents. At that moment Erin sensed that her life was laid bare to him. The dusty rose couch, her weathered volumes of Shakespeare, an array of slightly disheveled plants, the antique rocker—everything was explored by Kane's cold gray eyes. It was as if, from the objects in the room, he could understand her and penetrate her soul. A part of her wanted to be examined by his eyes and touched by his mind, but another, more suspicious side of her objected to his appraisal.

Thoughtfully he picked up the discarded paperback mystery novel from the coffee table along with a worn volume of poetry by

Keats. He opened the poetry book slowly and settled himself uncomfortably on the couch, with his long legs cramped under the coffee table. "You read this?" he asked, half to himself.

Erin poured the coffee but remained in the kitchen, still unsure of how to handle the conflicting emotions that surfaced each time she was alone with him. To answer his question she explained, "I read a variety of things, depending upon my mood."

"So I see," he agreed, eyeing the paperback spy thriller.

Suddenly she knew that she had made a mistake by seeing him in the intimacy of her own home. She felt too vulnerable, too transparent, too visible. Kane was alone with her, looking into the secret corners of her life, and unexpectedly she felt threatened. She had overheard part of his disagreement with his daughter, and she felt a desire to comfort him, and yet a need to turn her back on him and his problems. She couldn't let his life get tangled with her own; hers was too complicated and too precarious. She had to work with him as an employee; she couldn't let her emotions carry her away. She braced herself as she carried the two steaming mugs of coffee into the living room. "Kane," she began, placing a cup near him, "I don't think that it would be a good idea to go out today"

"You want to stay in?" he asked, deliberately misinterpreting her. "That would be fine with me.... Thanks." He reached for the cup and took an experimental sip while still watching her.

"No... I don't want to stay here. What I mean is I don't think that you and I should see each other..."

"Why not?"

"Because, for one thing, I make it a practice not to date anyone I work with."

He smiled to himself. "Then obviously, you're not as insecure about your job as you pretended to be yesterday. Wasn't it just yesterday morning that you accused me of plotting to fire you, along with all the other employees of the bank?"

"You're avoiding the issue," she challenged, a feeling of exasperation beginning to wash over her. "I'm not up to playing word games this morning!"

"Then let's be honest with each other, shall we? Why is it that you won't go out with me?" he asked, his silvery eyes capturing hers.

How could she tell him what she herself

really didn't understand? Was it possible to explain that she felt a desire to be with him and an urge to run from him?

"Are you afraid of me?" His voice broke into her thoughts.

"No!"

"Well?"

"I just don't think it's a good idea to mix business with pleasure."

"Then," he seemed to agree, "let me assure you that you'll have a very unpleasant afternoon!" He placed his cup down and smiled at her in a perfectly sickening and victorious manner.

"Be serious...."

"I am! So far, you haven't given me any viable excuse for not spending a quiet afternoon together."

"But I thought..."

"It doesn't matter what you thought." Kane reached for her hand across the table, stifling her protests. "I just want a chance to get to know you better. Is that such a crime?" His angled face was earnest and open. Any doubts she had conceived earlier were quickly cast aside with the touch of his hand on her palm and the peaceful serenity of his gaze.

"No..."

"Good! Then let's go, shall we?"

She pulled her hand away from his and reached for her jacket. He pulled his legs from their bent position under the table, stood up and let his eyes roam over the apartment. His perusal was slow, steady and deliberate. Erin felt herself once again becoming more uncomfortable as the silent minutes passed.

"Do you like living here?" Kane finally asked, all of his attention drawn to the features of her face.

"Why do you ask?"

"I guess because this apartment house isn't exactly what I expected." He lifted his shoulders and shrugged into his jacket.

"Just what did you expect?" Erin was intrigued by the conversation. Perhaps if she could draw him out, he would explain his feelings about her and wash away those last traces of doubt that nagged at Erin's mind. She could sense that there was something he wasn't telling her. It was as if he was purposely being wary with her.

"Oh, I don't know," he began in answer to her question. "But this place—it seems a little out of character," he remarked, looking at the faded Persian rug and running his fin-

A Twist of Fate

gers over the antique craftsmanship of the lead-glass windows.

"Out of character?"

"You're a career woman, right?" he asked, and Erin nodded her head in agreement, all the while wondering what he was leading up to and somehow not wanting to know. "This apartment—for that matter, the entire building—just doesn't fit with my interpretation of today's liberated woman…"

"Why not?"

"Truthfully," he chuckled, "because it looks like the set for one of those black-and-white slice-of-life movies of the forties."

Erin arched an inquisitive black eyebrow. "And you expected smoked glass, chrome fixtures and black vinyl upholstery?"

"Something like that."

"Sorry to disappoint you," she quipped, leaning against the door.

"You haven't disappointed me—not at all." His eyes found hers for an instant, and then his gaze swept the loft. "I knew when I met you that there was a darker, more private side of you. A side that you prefer to keep hidden away. Am I right?" His hands came up to the door, pressing on the wood and creating an imprisoning barrier near her head.

Erin met his questioning gaze with defiance. He was too close to the truth, too close to her. She drew in a deep, trembling breath. "You're right. I am a very private person, and I like it that way. What I don't like is anyone coming into my home and attempting to psychoanalyze me!"

A smile tugged at the corners of his mouth, but his eyes revealed only arctic cold. His breath whispered across her face. "Is that what I'm doing?"

"I hope not," she breathed, trying to still her racing heartbeat. Surely he could hear it—he was so near.

His finger reached out and stroked her cheek and his eyes covered her face and throat. "Maybe it would be a better idea to stay here today," he suggested silkily, but abruptly changed his mind. "On second thought it might be too dangerous to stay here...come on. I don't like being late."

"Late? For what?"

"You'll see..." There was just a hint of intimacy in his tone.

Erin pulled her jacket tightly around her shoulders, as if she were experiencing a sudden chill. "What have you got planned for today? Where are we going?" she demanded.

"You really don't want to know!" He moved one of his hands and helped her with the light calfskin jacket. His fingers brushed against her arm and lingered. Or did they? She pulled abruptly away from him and cinched the belt securely over her waist.

"Of course I want to know! Where are you taking me?"

"Just come along. And don't try to kid me. I haven't known you very long, but believe me, I know you well enough to realize that you like surprises and mystery in your life."

"I'd just like to know what makes you such an expert on me," she muttered and reached for the door angrily. She was angry because he was correct in his assumption about her, but she hated to admit it. Before she could open the door, he grabbed her forearm and whirled her around to face him.

His eyes reached into the depths of hers. "You can't hide from me, Erin," he whispered. "I won't let you." She could feel herself trembling at his touch. Her lips parted, but the denial that was forming in her mind died.

He lowered his head slowly, and his lips melted into hers in a kiss that was soft, beckoning and full of promise. She found herself yearning to respond to the warmth and tenderness of the embrace, but she forced herself to pull away. If he had any questions about her reaction to him, he didn't ask them. Instead he pulled her tightly against him and led her down the steep steps of the apartment building.

There were many thoughts that crossed her mind, and just as many questions that didn't have answers. She ignored the flood of emotions that carried her out of the house and into the sleek black sports car. Kane helped her into the car and then slid into the driver's seat. He started the engine and the sporty machine roared to life. Neither Erin nor Kane spoke, and the silence was as heavy as the gray Seattle fog, but Erin discovered an inner warmth that she didn't know existed.

Chapter 4

Kane drove steadily toward the heart of the city, carefully maneuvering the sporty little car down the steep inclines of the hills in order to save the muffler on the roller-coasterlike grade. Through the fog the gray waters of Elliott Bay lapped lazily against the waterfront. As they crested a final hill Erin was able to see the wharf and the bustle of activity along the crowded and colorful piers.

After parking the car, Erin and Kane strolled on the boardwalk that flanked the water's edge. Kane's hands were pushed deep into his pockets and his gaze slid over the water. Salt spray brushed against Erin's cheeks in a chilling embrace. Seagulls marauded the shore, calling out their lonesome cries. White, gleaming ferryboats plowed their way through the water, leaving only a frothy wake on the gray-blue waters as they disappeared into the fog.

Kane led Erin into a tiny bistro on the wharf. The warmth of the cozy restaurant was a welcome relief from the chill of the seawater and fog. They were seated at an intimate table near the window where they could watch the activities along the piers from the shelter of the bistro.

As the waiter brought the fresh seafood omelettes, Kane studied his empty coffee cup before looking into Erin's eyes.

"I suppose that you overheard my conversation with Krista." It was more of a statement than a question.

"Part of it."

"Why didn't you ask me about her?"

Erin met his gaze unwaveringly and noticed the rigid line of his jaw. Was he always so tense when he thought about his child, she wondered to herself. Aloud she responded, "I didn't want to pry."

Kane took a deep breath and looked out over the waters. He seemed to be wrestling with a weighty decision. Finally he turned his head back toward Erin. "Krista's disabled."

A startled look threatened to possess Erin's features, but she managed to make her voice steady. "I'm sorry," she whispered.

"So am I," he groaned and threw his napkin on his empty plate.

"Do you want to talk about it?"

"Do you want to listen?" His face was a mask of indifference, as if he suddenly regretted his outward display of emotion. *No,* she wanted to scream. *I don't want to know anything more about you. I'm attracted to you and I'm afraid of the attraction. I can't learn anything more about you that might bind me more tightly to you. I have to push away from you... I have to.*

"Of course I'll listen," she murmured, quieting the voice of suspicion that nagged at her.

"Krista is eleven. She was ten when the accident occurred." A dark, faraway look crossed his features. As he continued, his voice was flat, betraying no emotion. It was almost as if the words were part of a well-rehearsed speech, devoid of feeling or life. "She was riding in the car with her mother, my ex-wife. They were going to some 'retreat' or 'support group' meeting for the weekend. I really don't know much about it except it was the latest self-improvement seminar to be offered. Jana, my ex-wife, was forever following the latest self-improvement craze. It was one encounter group after another. Maybe I'm in part to blame for that, too."

Kane shook his head, as if clearing out unpleasant memories. Erin waited in silence as he continued.

"Anyway, it doesn't matter what new kick she was on. It just so happened that she had called and told me where she was going. I was angry. I didn't think that Krista needed to be exposed to all of that pseudopsychiatric garbage, and I told her so. We got into a helluva fight and she hung up on me. Two hours later I got a phone call from the police telling me that Jana was dead and Krista was in the hospital. To make a long story short, Krista's been in and out of the hospital ever since. She's still unable to walk unassisted."

"She's paralyzed?" Erin asked cautiously.

"Not exactly." Kane's eyes clouded for a minute. "It seems that she was lucky—nothing was actually broken in the accident. Jana was thrown out of the car and killed instantly, but Krista remained in the car, and other than a few cuts and bruises and a sprained left wrist, the doctors can find nothing physically wrong with her."

"But..."

"I know." Kane nodded his head. "It seems as if the cause of her paralysis is mental."

"I don't understand." Erin's brows knit in concern. What was Kane actually saying?

"I don't either. But what I can gather from the doctors is that she blames herself, or perhaps me, for the accident."

"No! That's not fair!"

Kane shrugged his shoulders. "Why not? Maybe if Jana and I hadn't fought, she would be alive today. Maybe the argument was the catalyst for her reckless driving."

"You can't blame yourself," Erin argued.

"Then who can I blame?"

"No one. It was just an unfortunate accident..."

"Try explaining that to a ten-year-old girl who has just lost her mother."

"Oh, Kane," Erin sighed, and reached for his hand.

Her hand was warm and comforting, and for a moment Kane forgot that he suspected Erin O'Toole of thievery. What was it about her that had made him open up to her and tell her the story of Krista's paralysis? Why was it so necessary that she know about him, that she care?

The waiter came to remove the dishes and bring the check. Kane helped Erin out of her chair and smiled disarmingly down on her. "I'm sorry," he apologized. "I didn't meant to bore you with my problems."

"You didn't bore me," Erin admitted.

"Well, let's push all those black thoughts aside for the day, shall we?" he asked, and took her hand powerfully in his. "I'm sure that when Krista gets up here and settles in, she'll be fine." Convincing as his words were, he didn't seem to believe them himself.

It was nearly afternoon, and they hurried down the boardwalk to catch the Blake Island ferry to visit Tillicum Village. Once on the island, they were entertained by the folklore and art objects of the native inhabitants. Erin was fascinated by the blending of the modern and ancient cultures. The fog had lifted and the day was cool, but pleasant.

They spent the day hiking over the island and watching the everyday rituals of life in a tribal village. Late in the evening Erin and Kane, along with the other tourists, were guests of the tribe and feasted on baked salmon cooked in hot coals, as they had been for centuries. As twilight descended, the torches were lit, and Kane wrapped his arms possessively around Erin's waist. They sat on the hand-carved stone steps of the amphitheater and watched the colorful display of folk culture as enacted by the inhabitants of the island. In the flickering light of the stars and the torches, Kane's features looked stronger, more masculine. The scent of his cologne wafted over Erin, and involuntarily she pressed closer to him.

Darkness covered the island as the entertainment faded. Erin and Kane made their way back to the waiting ferry. The warm lights inside the vessel winked at them, but Kane led Erin onto the deck. The wind had become stronger, sending a salty spray into their faces as they stood on the deck of the boat and watched the sparkling lights of Seattle call to them across the narrow stretch of water.

Kane held Erin tightly, the power and warmth of his body molding to hers. During the day all of her defenses had melted. Ever since he had opened up to her and explained about his daughter, she had felt a kinship and warmth toward him. And the doubts that she had experienced were withering.

He stood behind her with the strength of his arms wrapped securely over her waist. They were silent as they watched the distance and felt the giant boat move through the black water. The engine of the large vessel whirred noisily and rhythmically and the darkened waters churned white as the ferry headed inland.

A light drizzle had begun, but Erin didn't move, afraid to break the spell of the evening. Although the September nip in the air was cool, Erin was warm, pressed firmly against the heat of Kane's body. It was as if they had made an unspoken pact that neither wanted to violate by speaking.

The drizzle increased into raindrops, and even the hardiest of the tourists shuffled into the interior of the ferry. Erin and Kane remained outside alone, content to feel the salty breeze against their faces and the heated promise of each other's body. Kane nuzzled the back of her neck, letting the wind whip her hair over his face. She could feel her skin become alive with his touch, her blood begin to warm with his caress. Unconsciously she leaned closer to him.

He murmured her name, seeming to give it a special and intimate quality as it caught on the wind. She pivoted to face him and he cupped her chin in his hand before pressing the moist tenderness of his lips firmly over hers. She parted her lips involuntarily, letting his tongue trace a silken path over her mouth tentatively before slowly and sensuously exploring the moist recess and enticing her to do the same. He wrapped himself more closely around her as his tongue stroked and danced with hers.

The rain came down in silvery droplets, sliding over Kane's face and past Erin's cheek to her throat and finally to hide below the collar of her blouse. Kane's kiss deepened and his hand moved gently but persistently against her back. His lips roved over her face and neck, kissing and licking the drops of rain from her eyes, cheeks and throat. An urgent moan escaped from his lips, and he finally pulled his face away from hers. His eyes slid over her body, seeming to probe every inch of her being. They had darkened to misty gray, and a pulsating passion was blazing in their dark depths.

A raindrop passed over Erin's neck, and Kane stooped to kiss it away, his lips brushing over the hollow of her throat. She shuddered, more from his delicate kiss than from the cool night air. Her knees buckled and he pulled her to him, but a blast from the ferry's horn announced that they were docking. All too soon the jewellike lights of the city had blossomed into streetlamps, and the intimate water journey was over.

They walked back to the car in silence, each absorbed in private thoughts. Erin wondered how she could possibly work for a man she needed so passionately as a woman. And what about his daughter, who blamed him for his wife's death? And Mitch—could she bring up the subject of Mitch's dismissal with Kane, or would it be the wedge that would come between them? For, as unlikely as it seemed, Erin was unwittingly beginning to look upon herself and Kane as a man and woman with a deep understanding of each other. *But that's crazy,* the realistic side of her mind argued. *You don't even know the man.*

And Kane wondered about Erin. Could this enigmatic and beautiful woman really be a viable suspect in the embezzling scheme? She seemed so…innocent, if that was the right word. It was so easy to talk with her; he had already confided in her concerning Krista. That was probably a mistake, he thought now. But for the moment he didn't want to believe anything about Erin other than what he felt. She was bewitching and he meant to find out all he could about her—tomorrow. Tonight he just didn't give a damn whether she was embezzling or not.

The black sports car whipped through the quiet streets, sending sprays of water as its tires slashed pools of standing water. The windshield wipers moved in tempo, pushing the raindrops off the glass. Night closed in on Erin as the black interior of the car seemed to melt into the darkness of the evening.

Erin's senses were heightened. In the warmth of the enclosed sports car, she could smell the tangy scent of Kane's cologne and the masculine essence of his rain-drenched body. For the entire short ride Erin was aware of the man next to her. As he shifted gears, she could see the long hard lines of his fingers and the athletic slant of his legs straining against the fabric of his pants. She had trouble concentrating on anything other than his potent masculinity.

As they approached the apartment house, he killed the engine and sat motionless, his hands still gripping the steering wheel. He glanced toward the windows of Erin's third-floor apartment.

Erin cleared her throat. "Would you like to come in? For a drink—or a cup of coffee?"

He rotated to face her, and even in the darkness she imagined flames of smoldering passion burning in his eyes. "I'd like it very much."

He opened the door for her and they walked up the long staircase noiselessly. Although they didn't touch, Erin felt a bond between them bridging the inches of open air that separated their bodies. She licked her arid lips as she reached into her purse for her keys. Many emotions had come and gone since he had hurried her out of the apartment this morning. God, was it only twelve hours ago? Erin had hesitated only slightly when she thought about asking him up to her apartment. She knew how precarious it was for her to be alone with him, but she couldn't resist extending the invitation and the evening. Mrs. Cavenaugh had been right; she had hidden herself away from the world of men for much too long.

Her fingers shook as she tried to unlock the door, and Kane took the keys from her hand. He escorted her through the doorway and into the small apartment. Erin went through the motions of taking off her jacket, but her mind was on Kane and the intimacy of the apartment. There was no place to hide. "Could—I offer you a drink?"

He took off his jacket and let it fall casually across the arm of the couch. "Sure."

Erin moved into the kitchen and opened the liquor cabinet, but her thoughts didn't leave Kane. Although he was in the living room, the air was charged with electricity and anticipation. It was difficult to think, to move. Why had she asked him up to her loft, and why had he accepted?

She managed to put together some Irish coffee, and the cups were steaming as she carried them into the living room. Kane was standing at the window, looking into the night as if he could penetrate the darkness. His shirt was moist and clung to his body, and the ripple of his muscles was evident through the fabric.

When she entered the room, he turned to face her. His face was ragged, torn with emotion, and she knew that he was as tense as she. "Anything wrong?" she asked.

"Nothing," he whispered, but the besieged look on his face didn't disappear. "Thanks," he said with a tight-lipped smile and sampled the hot drink.

"There is something wrong," she challenged. "I can feel it. It's something about me, isn't it?"

"You're imagining things," he retorted, and took a long swallow of his drink.

"No... I'm not. It all started yesterday, at the office."

His gray eyes bored into her, daring her to continue. "I don't know what you mean."

"I think that you do. You were angry that I was at the office—don't deny it. And all of those ridiculous questions about Mitch. It has something to do with him, doesn't it?"

"Why don't you tell me," he suggested huskily. "What do you know about Mitchell Cameron?"

"Nothing—except that you fired him, and I don't know why!"

He set his cup down on the table and strode quietly over to where she was standing. His voice was barely audible, but he pinned her with his gaze. "You can't even hazard a guess?" he coaxed.

"No!"

"Why don't you try?" His fingers reached upward and found the nape of her neck. He lifted her hair from her shoulders and clasped both of his hands gently around her neck, massaging her shoulders through the light rain-washed fabric of her blouse.

"I have no idea. I only know that the legal department wasn't profitable..." His gray eyes snapped.

"Is that it? Would you let him go because of one bad year?"

"What do you think?"

"I don't know. I don't know how you work..."

"Sure you do," he suggested smoothly, and Erin felt that she had known him all of her life.

"Aren't you going to finish your drink?" she asked, not able to concentrate on anything other than the warm enticement of his hands. His thumbs traced lazy patterns of seduction along her throat, gently persuading her mind to think of nothing other than his overpowering maleness.

His eyes looked over at the half-full cup of Irish coffee. "Is that my cue to leave?"

Erin braced herself, trying to ignore the dizzying sensations that seemed to build up from within her and explode at his touch. "It's...it's getting late."

"And you'd like to go to bed?" he cajoled, his dark eyes alive.

"I...you...we have to work in the morning,"

she stammered, her senses reeling from his closeness.

"That we do," he agreed.

Erin's pulse was beginning to dance wildly as Kane's hands coaxed her to newer heights of sensuality. She could feel his breath, smell his clean masculine scent, and she knew that he was going to kiss her.

His arms moved to her waist and coiled possessively around her as his mouth brushed velvet-soft kisses down her cheek and throat. Her head fell backward, and he rained kisses up and down the length of her exposed neck. Erin's chest grew tight, and her breath began to whisper in short, shaky breaths.

His hands toyed at the hem of her blouse, at first tentatively, and finally with determination as he tugged the blouse out of the waistband of her slacks. His fingers explored the soft, supple muscles of her back, warming her skin to a rosy glow. Her knees began to give way, and he caught her, pushing his lips over hers in silent union. She moaned, and at the invitation of her parted lips, his tongue found hers, flicking and dancing with moist sparks of unfettered passion.

Moving steadily upward, his hands inched up her spine in a delicious spiraling motion.

Her skin heated and caught fire. All her nerve endings ignited in hot boiling passion. His fingertips slowly and sensuously moved forward until he was kneading the tight muscles of her abdomen.

Her breasts ached against the confinement of her bra, and when at last his fingertips played with the lacy garment, she sighed. He pushed her gently and persuasively to the floor, and she felt the cool floorboards press against her fevered flesh. Slowly he let his hands slide to the buttons of her blouse, slipping each button easily through the buttonholes. As the blouse parted he unleashed her breasts from the lacy bra. "God, but you're beautiful," he moaned, looking directly at the full white curves of her soft breasts.

She felt her fingers working at the buttons of his shirt. When at last it was opened, and the expanse of golden bronze skin was visible, she moaned with pure animal pleasure. "So are you," she said huskily, watching his firm muscles flex under her admiring gaze.

His thumbs idled over her nipples as he fondled her breasts. Masterfully, he enticed her nipples to erection, and a smile of triumph lighted his eyes as he noticed them harden. He looked once into her eyes, the smoky gray of his gaze blending into the lilac-blue passion of hers.

It was as if she were drugged; all she could concentrate on was taking and giving pleasure. Her female body was overshadowing her mind. As Kane loved her, explored her, exulted in her, she, too, took satisfaction from touching and enticing him. Body was controlling mind in the sweet dreamlike mist of lovemaking.

They rolled together on the floor, and he rained kisses upon her face, her neck, her breasts. His tongue licked paths of fire over her body and kindled an aching need in her innermost core.

Endearingly his mouth descended on her breasts, and he suckled as if a babe, kneading the sensitive tissue with his hands as his lips lured love from her nipples. His body was upon hers and she felt the bittersweet pain of his weight over her. The cold floorboards touched her back, and his warm, naked torso inflamed her soul, causing boiling currents of lava to course through her veins.

"Oh, Erin," he called against her, and her pounding heart was triggered to a more passionate rhythm. He tore himself away from her and saw the disappointment in her eyes.

"I want to go to bed with you," he breathed, "and I want to make love to you."

"Are…are you asking me?" she gasped, drawing much needed air into her lungs.

"I've been asking you all night." He levered himself over her and leaned on one elbow while one hand still massaged her breasts.

"I want to…" she murmured, closing her eyes and trying to think rationally. Would the ache subside? Would she really be able to make love to him? Would she be able to stop?

"But…" he prodded, his breath ghosting over her hair.

"But…" She breathed heavily. "But… I'm afraid."

"Of what? Me?"

"No…"

"Then it must be that you're afraid of your husband," he guessed.

"Lee? How did you know about him?"

"A small surname discrepancy in your personnel file."

"Oh," she murmured, pulling her blouse over her breasts. Suddenly she felt conspicuously naked.

"He is the problem, isn't he," Kane asked gently, but there was a cold and calculating edge to his voice.

"No... Lee has nothing to do with us," she managed, but her mercurial temperature had cooled.

"You're still in love with him, aren't you?" His eyes regarded her gently, and he pulled her closer to his body and rocked her.

"No...you're wrong. You've got it all wrong. I'm not in love with Lee. Sometimes I wonder if I ever really was." His eyes followed hers to look out the window. "Oh, I thought I loved him, once, but some of the things that he did...that he said..." She still couldn't talk about it without getting a catch in her throat.

"Erin, honey. It's been a long time, and still he affects you. Are you sure that you're not still emotionally involved with him?"

Tears began to flow from her eyes, and he brushed them away. She tried to look away from him, but he forced her head in his direction, softly cupping her chin in his fingers. His movements were gentle, but his thoughts were grim. Lee Sinclair, whoever the hell he was, had scarred Erin, and Kane meant to know all about him.

"Have you seen him recently?"

"No...he moved to Spokane about a year ago." For some reason Erin couldn't tell Kane about the phone calls and the fact that Lee was back in Seattle.

Kane continued to rock her in silence, only the thin line of his lips belying his calm and comforting actions. Slowly Erin composed herself. She wondered how she had ever let things get so out of hand. She felt an embarrassed burn on her cheeks as she realized that she was sitting half-naked on the floor of her apartment with her new boss, weeping like a teenager, nearly jumping into bed with him. It was frightening and confusing, completely out of character.

"I'm sorry," she sniffed, managing a feeble smile. "I really don't know why I fell apart."

"It's all right. Here." He pulled the afghan from the couch and wrapped her in its rainbow-colored tiered folds. "Are you sure that you're okay?" She nodded, and he rose from the floor, pulling her with him. "Why don't you go in and get in bed? I'll bring you some tea."

"No! Oh, no... I'm fine, honestly." She was embarrassed by her emotional outburst, and the last thing she wanted was that her boss should wait on her. She hiked the awkward blanket over her shoulders, but it seemed determined to slide to the floor.

"You're sure?" he asked, cocking a suspicious eyebrow in her direction and buttoning his shirt.

"I'm sure." Her voice was still husky, but the firm quality and tone that he recognized as control were back in her words.

She could tell that he was reluctant to leave, but after a final kiss to her forehead, and his hastily scribbled hotel phone number, he left her alone.

After he closed the door, she listened to the sound of his shoes clicking down the steps. Silently she counted them. Finally she heard the front door open and close with a thud. A sporty engine roared to life and faded into the night. Erin felt more alone than she had in years.

Chapter 5

The morning newspaper was spread before her as Erin sat down to a light breakfast of toast and jam. Her eyes wandered aimlessly over the headlines on the front page, but her mind refused to budge from the intimate moments she had shared with Kane. What had seemed a natural and beautiful lovemaking experience in the darkness had somehow lost its enchantment in the morning light. It wasn't that she regretted getting to know Kane, not at all. But he was her boss, and she couldn't let her body control her mind where he was concerned. Professionally it just wasn't sound judgment to get emotionally involved with an employer. And, although she could still conjure up the enigmatic image of his tanned masculine body and mirthless gray eyes, she wouldn't let it control her.

She applied a healthy spoonful of raspberry jam to her toast as she turned to the financial section. As her eyes met the black-and-white photograph of Mitchell Cameron, she let the knife fall to the table. The picture was several years old, and Mitch was smiling with his pleasant self-assured grin, but the caption in black boldface print captured her attention. FINANCIAL LAWYER ALLEGED THIEF—and in smaller print— Mitchell Cameron Accused of Embezzling Bank Funds.

"Oh, no!" Erin gasped, and her eyes read and reread the newspaper article several times. "There must be some mistake," she murmured to herself. "There has to be!" According to the article Mitch had been manipulating bank funds for the better part of two years. When the bank was sold, an audit found him out, and the new president, Kane Webster, had fired Mitch. The police were summoned and Mitch would be arraigned for indictment within the week.

Erin raced to the telephone and dialed

Mitch's number. A busy signal beeped flatly in her ear. Either Mitch had taken the receiver off the hook, or he was already being plied by inquisitive friends and reporters.

As quickly as possible she scooped up the paper, grabbed her purse and slipped on her coat. She took the steps two at a time and nearly ran over Mrs. Cavenaugh on her way out the door. On the run, she apologized to the startled old woman and hurried out to the car. She turned on the ignition, the little car sparked to life and Erin proceeded on a mad dash to the bank, hampered only by the early-morning rush-hour traffic.

When she got to the bank, it was already crawling with employees. Although it was still early, it seemed that everyone had arrived with time to spare on this first day of new bank ownership. Erin pushed herself into the crowded elevator and wedged herself between two women.

"Have you seen the paper today?" a middle-aged woman with a faddish, curly hairstyle asked her friend.

"Not yet—I usually wait until coffee break. There's just not enough time in the morning, what with getting the kids off to school, you know," the shorter woman in a pink raincoat replied.

The elevator started its upward motion. "Then you haven't heard about Mitchell Cameron?" the curly-haired woman asked.

"Cameron? The head of the legal department?"

"That's right. Seems that the new president— that Mr. Webster—had him fired."

"No!"

"That's right," the taller woman said with a firm shake of her head. Her voice lowered, and she looked over her shoulder as she continued. "They suspect that Mr. Cameron was involved in some embezzling scheme…"

"The head of the legal department? Are you sure?"

Erin pretended not to hear the conversation. The elevator stopped on the seventeenth floor and the two women continued their conversation as they disembarked. Erin closed her eyes for a minute. By this time the entire bank staff had heard about Mitch. Could it possibly be true? She fervently hoped that Kane was wrong about Mitch.

The elevator stopped with a jolt, and Erin walked into the legal department. She was early, and only a few of the more aggressive young employees had made it to their desks. There were a few new faces in the crowd, probably some of Kane's imported trouble-shooters from California, Erin guessed as she passed by the reception area and picked up her telephone messages. The most compelling of the notes was a handwritten memo from Kane indicating that he wanted to see her in his office immediately.

After taking off her coat, she armed herself with the newspaper and marched into his office. An eerie, nostalgic feeling gripped her when she discovered that the familiar brass nameplate of Mitchell Cameron had been torn from the door. Only two fine drill holes remained in the wood panels to remind Erin that just last week Mitch had occupied this office.

Kane was sitting behind the desk when she entered. He motioned her to be seated in one of the side chairs as he finished scribbling some notes on a legal pad. But instead, she remained standing with her arms folded against her chest. The rolled newspaper was clamped firmly under her left arm.

"Have you seen the paper?" she asked him, echoing the conversation she had overhead in the elevator.

"Yes," he replied, looking up from his work.

"And you read the article on Mitch?" she accused.

"I've read several, starting last evening," he replied evenly. His eyes searched her face and he studied her intensely.

"Is it true?" she asked, her incredulity registering on her face. "Did Mitch really embezzle? How do you know—and why did you let the press find out about it? Do you know what you've done? You've ruined his career. He worked for this bank for over twenty years, and in one clean sweep you destroyed him!"

Her voice had risen with her emotion. She flung the paper onto his desk and turned her head away, biting on her fingernail and trying to piece together her shattered poise. Kane rose from the desk and crossed the room to close the door. He came back beside her and placed his hands on her shoulders. Gently he rubbed the tension out of her neck and shoulders.

"Don't," she implored. "Don't touch me—just give me answers, preferably straight ones!"

His fingers stopped their comforting motion but remained against the back of her neck. Her hair was pinned into a businesslike knot, twisted behind one ear, and Kane rested his hands on her exposed neck. Her head was bent, and she pressed a hand to her forehead as she waited for his explanation.

His voice was low and soft as he began to speak. "You've met my associate, Jim Haney?" His fingers felt the barest of movements as she nodded. "During the conversion, while Jim was still working here in Seattle, he…discovered that funds were being funneled out of some of the larger trust accounts. It took Jim quite a while, but finally he tracked down the culprit."

"Mitch?" she asked in a voice that was barely audible.

"Yes."

"But…how can you be sure?" She pivoted her head upward to find his face, and there was an unhidden pain in the depths of her eyes.

"Erin. We caught him red-handed. There's no doubt." The words were spoken softly, but there was an almost cruel hardness in his features.

Tears threatened to spill from her eyes, but she forced them backward and vainly attempted to keep her voice from shaking. "I… I just can't believe it." She averted her face from his intent study.

Kane propped her chin between his fingers and let his thumb rub it caressingly while tracing the line of her jaw. "You were very close to him?" he asked gently.

Erin shook her head faintly and bit her lip. "He's been a good friend to me." Her eyes were shining with unshed tears when she looked up at Kane's face once more. "He... he helped me through a very difficult time in my life..." she explained, and gave in to the urge to lean against him. His arm wrapped securely around her, and for a moment Erin forgot everything other than Kane's comforting presence. This couldn't be the same cold-hearted man who had fired Mitch, could it? Had Mitch really stooped to thievery?

"The difficult time," he whispered. "The divorce?"

She nodded mutely against the smooth fabric of his jacket.

A knock resounded on the thick mahogany door, and before Kane could respond, the door swung open. Olivia Parsons, with all of her self-assurance and poise in place, breezed into the room with only a brief apology.

"Excuse me, Mr. Webster... Erin." She included Erin out of courtesy. Her cool green eyes swept over the intimate scene before her, and although they reflected a glimmer of interest, her professional aplomb never wavered. Erin moved away from Kane with as much grace as was possible, but she was sure that Olivia hadn't missed the tender embrace between employer and employee. "I didn't mean to disturb you, but your secretary indicated that you needed these financial statements before the board meeting this afternoon." The tall brunette with the svelte figure and sleek Halston original dress handed Kane the stack of papers that she was carrying. The confident smile that she was wearing never left her face.

"You must be Miss Parsons," Kane surmised, his eyes traveling appreciatively over the neatly typed pages.

"Please call me Olivia," she responded. She gave Erin a fleeting head-to-toe appraisal, as if seeing her for the first time. Turning back to Kane, she continued. "I really didn't know that you were busy," she apologized again, and Erin felt a tide of crimson creep steadily up her neck.

"No problem," Kane assured Olivia, and escorted her out of the room. "Thank you for taking the time to bring the reports by."

"Anytime," Olivia suggested in a voice so throaty that Erin barely heard it.

Once Olivia had made her exit, Kane closed the door and deliberately turned to face Erin. His back was pressed firmly against the polished wood grain of the door, as if he were using his own body as a barricade against another intrusion. His body had stiffened, and all of the familiar fondness had escaped from his features. His face had become a mask devoid of emotion, and his words were no longer tender or caring. They were brittle in the air.

"I don't think that my office is the place to continue this discussion," he said tersely.

"I think it's a perfect place to discuss Mitch—right in the middle of his office!"

"Is that how you still think of it, as Mitch's office? If so, you had better change your mind. Mitchell Cameron is gone. He was an embezzler—a thief—and he's no longer with Consolidated Finances. I hope that fact doesn't hamper your work." He strode across the room to the desk. "We can discuss this later...tonight if you like. But right now I'm very busy." He sat at the desk and started reading the reports that he had received from Olivia.

Erin watched him with disbelieving eyes.

How could he change so rapidly? It was as if he were a kind, considerate gentleman one moment and a heartless bastard the next. He looked up at her and flashed a perfectly condescending smile at her, but she knew it was an act. She had been with him enough to recognize the cool distance in his gray eyes.

"You're the one who called me in here," she reminded him, and waved the green personal memo in the air. "Just what was it that you wanted to discuss?"

The petrified smile fell from his face and a darker, more volatile expression took over. "I wanted to ask you to dinner tonight."

"You've got to be kidding! First you call me in here. Then you nearly throw me out. And now you expect me to go out with you?" Sarcasm dripped from her words. "Not a chance!"

"Why not?"

Erin sighed wearily, tired of the argument. "For the same reasons that I spelled out to you yesterday."

There was a pool of darkness in his eyes. "You're afraid of me, aren't you?" he suggested, and then continued. "Or is it yourself who scares you?"

"It has nothing to do with fear, and you

should know it! It's just that I don't think it would be good for either of us, profession-ally that is, to be the subject of office gossip or speculation."

"Don't you think that you're putting the cart before the horse?"

"I don't know what you mean," she sighed.

"In order for there to be any gossip, there's got to be a glimmer of truth. Someone has to start the rumors, and since I'm not one to 'kiss and tell,' I've got to assume that you are. Otherwise, there would be no cause for con-cern, would there?"

"You don't understand," she accused with a vehemence that interested Kane. "Gossip…it can be vicious—ugly! It can ruin your life!"

"Only if you let it—the same as anything else. Now, why don't you be honest with me—no, make that honest with yourself—and tell me what's really bothering you. I can't believe that a little innocent speculation about what you do after-hours is all that traumatic. For God's sake, Erin, you're a thirty-two-year-old divorcée, not a whimpering virgin! What kind of lily-white reputation are you trying to create?"

Her eyes narrowed and she planted her hands firmly against her hips. "The point is that I like to keep my personal life just that—private! And even though you and I won't go around telling anyone that we're seeing each other, believe me, the word will get out."

"And everyone will just naturally assume that because we're dating we're sleeping together, right?" he surmised, elaborating on her logic. He threw the neatly stacked reports down into an unruly pile on his desk and covered the floor space that separated them in long, swift strides. He didn't touch her, but he was close enough that she could feel the delicious warmth of his breath as it fanned against her hair. She stood her ground, not moving an inch, but every nerve ending in her body was rigidly aware of him and his nearness. "And even if some of the people around here think that we sleep together—" his fingers touched the silken skin of her cheek softly "—what's so bad about that? What do you care what other people think?"

Erin's lips thinned into a white line. She tried to control her temper and ignore the warm feelings that Kane was commanding from her. She pushed herself away from him in order to think clearly and avoid the compelling magnetism that seemed to surround him. "I've worked very hard to get where I am with this bank, and I don't need the frustration of knowing that co-workers think that I sleep with the boss to promote my career."

"Would you mind it if they thought you slept with the boss because you wanted to and not for career reasons?"

"You can't possibly understand!" she whispered, and turned on her heel to leave.

As she pushed open the door to make her exit, she heard Kane's parting words. "You, Miss O'Toole, are paranoid! And I'll pick you up at seven-thirty!"

Kane's voice boomed through the open door. Several of the secretaries looked up from their typewriters to stare openly at Erin. She tried to ignore their curiosity and continued toward her office. She could feel their speculative glances boring holes into her back, but she managed to return to the security of her office with a modicum of poise.

Outwardly she controlled her ragged Irish temper, but once in the sanctity of her own office, she could feel the fumes of anger rising steadily within her. No doubt half of the legal department had already sized up her situation with the new boss, and it wasn't even ten o'clock yet! She tried to concentrate on her work, and she told herself not to be childish, but she couldn't help but feel that Kane had betrayed her trust by announcing that he planned to see her after work. To make matters worse, he had brushed off the subject of Mitch's dismissal with an arrogant wave of his hand and very little explanation.

During the remainder of the day Erin saw little of Kane. All of his contact with her came via his secretary in the form of interdepartmental memorandums. They had no personal contact. She had seen him only in passing, and he had smiled at her with the same polite but less than enthusiastic smile that he rained upon all of his employees. He showed her no special attention, which was exactly what she had wanted. And yet, a small and very feminine part of her yearned for the vaguest sign of emotion from him. Affection, endearment, friendship—anything that demonstrated that he cared for her in a more intimate way.

For most of the afternoon she attempted to bury herself in her work to avoid any further confrontations with Kane. It also helped her ignore the whispers about Mitch and the speculations about the embezzlement.

It was long after five o'clock when she rose and tucked away the paperwork that was still spread unfinished on her desk. Although she had worked diligently, she had accomplished very little because of her preoccupation with Kane. He had asked her out early that morning, and she had refused, but her mind had wandered relentlessly back to the invitation. *What would it hurt?* her persuasive mind taunted.

But what good would it do, her more rational nature inquired. Yes, Kane was an interesting man, and yes, she would like to spend some time alone with him, and perhaps she would, if circumstances were different. But as things stood, she couldn't reconcile herself to live a double life of daytime employee and nighttime lover. No matter how she would try to convince herself otherwise, she was attracted to Kane as she never had been to any other man. Given an alternative set of circumstances, she knew that she could fall deeply in love with him. But, as fate would have it, she couldn't allow herself the pleasure of falling in love with a man for whom she worked.

It had taken her all day to come to the decision that she would have to explain her position to Kane once and for all. She threw her coat over her arm and clicked off the lights to her office. Most of the staff had left the building, but she knew that Kane was still working. She could hear his voice through the door. Rather than disturb him, she continued past his office toward the elevator.

Before the elevator doors parted, the door to Kane's office opened. Erin quickly resolved to herself that this would be as good a time as any to have it out with him. She turned to face him and discovered that he wasn't alone. Olivia Parsons was with him, looking as if she was hanging on his every word. Rather than intrude, Erin whirled and faced the elevator. Just as the doors were opening, Erin heard Kane call out to her.

"Erin, wait!" Kane hurried to Erin's side. "I'm glad I caught up with you. Do you need a ride home?"

"I've got my car," Erin replied, a little tartly. Why did Olivia always seem to be a part of the conversation? She looked cautiously at Olivia, but the calm expression on the brunette's face didn't appear to hold the slightest hint of interest.

"Then I'll see you at seven-thirty," Kane rejoined.

Erin looked from Kane to Olivia and back to Kane. "I…don't think so…not tonight." Olivia's eyebrows raised just a fraction of an inch. The gesture was almost unnoticeable, but Erin caught the movement and the silent gleam of fascination in Olivia's perfect green eyes.

"Going out?" Olivia asked casually. "I don't blame you. Who wants to cook after a full day at the office?"

Erin couldn't resist the temptation of disagreeing with Olivia. "Oh, I don't know. I've always enjoyed cooking."

Olivia's face registered disbelief, but it was Kane who answered. "Good!" he interjected. "I haven't had a home-cooked meal in ages. We'll eat at your place."

Erin was about to reject Kane's suggestion, but Olivia stilled Erin's tongue. "That's terrible!" she sang out sweetly to Kane. "I tell you what. Why don't you come over to my house for a special dinner? We'll have fresh seafood from Puget Sound..."

"Thanks, Olivia. I appreciate the hospitality." Kane seemed to agree, and Erin could feel her heart beginning to shred. Kane shot Erin a questioning look and continued, "But I've got other plans." His response was gentle but firm.

"Some other time…" Olivia persisted, only slightly dejected.

"Some other time," Kane agreed evasively.

There was a slight pause in the conversation, and finally Olivia broke the silence. "I guess I'd better be running along. I'll see you in the morning." Although the farewell was meant for both Erin and Kane, Olivia's warm green eyes looked directly into the cool gray depths of Kane's gaze. Erin could almost see the invitation in those emerald pools.

Olivia slipped into the elevator, and it started its descent before Erin began. "Look, Kane. I've made a decision. You can't come over tonight…and I can't go out with you. It's as simple as that!"

She pressed the elevator call button and waited for Kane's reaction. She expected that he would be violent, but when he spoke it was with quiet deliberation.

"You…would deny me a home-cooked meal?" he asked, and there was a mischievous smile in his eyes.

"Of course not, but you've got to understand…"

"It's settled then. I'll bring the wine." He slipped his hand beneath her elbow and guided her into the elevator. As the doors shut he wrapped his arms tightly around her and kissed her feverishly on the lips. All of the warmth and intimacy that had been denied during the day was surfacing again in his passionate embrace.

Before Erin could respond, the elevator stopped on the fifth floor, and Kane released her to smile at two of his new employees. Erin was sure that even in the slightly dimmed elevator light, the two young women could see her swollen lips and the trace of passion still lingering in Kane's eyes. When she stepped out of the building she hurried to her car, and Kane didn't follow. How was she going to deal with him and the web of emotions that was entangling her more tightly each day?

It was crazy and she knew it, but she felt that she was beginning to fall in love with Kane Webster. The thought made her shudder as she reached for the headlights and the windshield wipers. *You're a damn fool, Erin O'Toole,* she chided herself. She couldn't be, wouldn't be, in love with her boss. It was an impossible and ridiculous situation, but nonetheless, it existed.

She was still arguing with herself as she stopped the car in her familiar spot in front of the apartment house. She bent her head against the wind and slight drizzle of the evening. A welcome light came from Mrs. Cavenaugh's window and Erin stopped at the doorway to the little old lady's apartment. She waited several minutes before Mrs. Cavenaugh's voice called through the door.

"Who's there?"

"It's me, Mrs. Cavenaugh… Erin," she responded, and immediately heard the click of locks as Mrs. Cavenaugh opened the door. The old woman peeked timidly through the crack in the door before removing the final chain and opening the door widely.

"Come in…come in," Mrs. Cavenaugh welcomed her.

"I can't… I'm having company tonight."

"Oh?" Mrs. Cavenaugh didn't even have the decency to hide her interest. "Mr. Webster?"

Erin eyed the half-bent old woman with loving suspicion. "How did you know?" she asked.

"Lucky guess," the old woman murmured, her blue eyes dancing with pleasure. "Don't you have just a minute to tell me all about it?"

"No, I'm sorry, truly I am." Erin's face was earnest, and Mrs. Cavenaugh didn't doubt her sincerity. "I just dropped by to tell you that I got hold of someone to install the insulation. They'll be here by the end of the week."

"Good!"

"Look, I've really got to run."

"I understand," was the kindly reply. "Oh, by the way, Erin, did you know that Mr. Jefferies is planning to move out by the end of the month?"

"Oh, no," Erin sighed, and then quickly hid her disappointment. "I knew that he had been thinking of moving in with his daughter and her husband, but I didn't think that he had made up his mind."

"Seems they made it up for him," Mrs. Cavenaugh asserted. "I'm sure he left his notice in your mailbox."

"Oh, thanks for reminding me." Erin crossed the hallway and opened her mailbox. Among the various bills was Mr. Jefferies's notice of vacancy. The last thing she needed right now was one more empty apartment. She needed the rental income just to keep up the mortgage, let alone the repairs and upkeep. But she couldn't show her worries to Mrs. Cavenaugh. She called out to the friendly elderly woman as she mounted the stairs, "I'll let you know exactly when the repairmen will be here."

"Thanks, honey," Mrs. Cavenaugh responded before closing the door to her apartment. Erin raced up the remaining stairs, anxious to get into the familiar and secure surroundings of her own apartment.

Kane pulled the small black sports car to the curb and snapped off the motor. He sat in the darkness for a minute, staring at the apartment house that Erin called home. He was angry and he was tense, but he tried to control his emotions so that Erin wouldn't become suspicious.

Erin was already home. The lights in her apartment glowed in the night, and the Volkswagen Rabbit was sitting where she had parked it in front of the house. Kane's eyes moved from the car back to the building. Even in the unearthly glow of the streetlamp he could see the signs of age and disrepair in the large old home. Was this apartment house the cause of Erin's financial woes? Could she possibly be moving funds out of the bank for the upkeep on the costly old house?

He had thought he would feel a deep satisfaction in catching Cameron's accomplice in crime, but as he came closer to the truth, the satisfaction had soured in his stomach to a feeling of sickening disgust. He knew now that Erin was lying to him, and somehow he had to find a way to prove his theories about her, as much as he despised the idea.

He took in a long breath as he thought about Lee Sinclair. Erin's ex-husband was supposedly in Spokane, but with a little checking, Kane had discovered that Lee had moved back to Seattle over six weeks ago—about the same time that Erin had applied for her employee loan. Could she still be involved with him, and was he the drain on her money? Perhaps he was the catalyst in the partnership with Cameron.

Kane's hands tightened on the steering wheel until his knuckles whitened. He could only hope that he was wrong and that someone else was the embezzler. God, how he hoped so. There were still a few more possibilities, but unfortunately, right now the evidence was stacking up very heavily against Erin O'Toole.

Angrily Kane pushed his disturbing thoughts aside and got out of the car. He was furious at himself, at Erin and particularly at Lee Sinclair, whoever the hell he was.

Erin had just placed the pan of lasagna in the oven when the doorbell rang. Before she could cross the room, the door swung open and thudded against the wall. Kane strode into the room and closed the door just as angrily as he had opened it. Erin had begun to smile, but when her eyes met his, her face froze. His gray eyes were guarded, a stormy fog clouding their depths. His casual clothes, the same ones he had been wearing earlier, were disheveled and his tie was loosened rather haphazardly. "Don't you ever lock your door?" he muttered.

"Of course I do…but I was in a hurry…"

"That's no excuse!" he rifled back at her.

Erin was confused by his only slightly suppressed anger, and she felt her temper rise to meet his. "Look, Kane, thanks for your concern, but it's really not your problem."

"It is my problem, when it concerns your safety."

"I'm all right. I just forgot to latch the door. That's not such a crime."

A more contrite look softened his features. "I suppose you're right," he sighed, raking strong fingers through his coarse brown hair. "I didn't mean to jump down your throat." He walked over to her and brushed a light kiss across her forehead. "But I do wish that you would be more careful."

"I'll try," she agreed in order to ease the tension that was building between them. She could see that he was beginning to relax, but the lines near the edge of his eyes looked deeper than they had this morning. She tried to tell herself that it was probably just the first day at the bank that had taken its toll on him, or possibly that he was concerned about Krista. But she couldn't help feeling that there was a larger problem storming through his mind—a problem that concerned her.

"Would you like a drink?" Erin suggested.

"Oh." He slapped a palm against his forehead. "I forgot the wine—something came up at the bank. Forgive me?"

He was teasing, Erin knew, but she could sense an inner turbulence below his light attempt at humor. "Consider yourself forgiven," she agreed, "but my liquor cabinet isn't all that great."

Kane walked over to the cupboard that she indicated and searched through the bottles. "Saying that is being kind. It's downright pathetic."

"I don't see that you have much room to complain, since you were the one who forgot the wine in the first place," she reminded him, trying to suppress a smile.

"Touché, Miss O'Toole. Now let's see what we have in here." His voice was muffled as he pushed aside partially filled bottles of liquor and finally pulled out an unopened bottle of brandy. With a triumphant flourish, he held out the bottle for Erin's inspection. "Look at this. Maybe the evening won't be a total loss after all!"

"A loss? You practically insisted on inviting yourself over to a home-cooked dinner, and already you're insinuating that the evening will be wasted?" She could feel him looking at her, but she didn't turn around and started slicing the greens for a salad. She was only kidding, of course, but he deserved a shot after barging in that way.

In a moment his arms were encircling her waist and his breath moved her hair as he whispered in her ear. His voice was low and full of promise as he spoke. "I don't think that any time would ever be wasted if I could share it with you."

She let the knife slip to the counter. His touch was warming her abdomen, and the feel of his hot breath against her neck made her heart race. She tried to keep her head and recapture the light mood of the minute before. "That sounds like a line if I ever heard one."

"A line? Oh, Erin, don't you think I'm a little too old for lines? Don't you know what you mean to me?" There was a torture in his words as if he was admitting something that he himself didn't want to hear.

His hands persuaded her body to rotate and face him, and when her eyes found his, she saw that his gaze had darkened with a smoky passion. Smoldering embers lit his eyes as he bent his head slowly downward to capture her trembling lips with his. The warm, seductive pressure of his mouth roving passionately over hers made her dizzy. She tried to blink and restore some sanity to her emotions, but she couldn't. It was as if her entire body began and ended where her lips met his. Her knees began to give way and melt beneath her. And as he tasted her, an aching need began to consume her.

Her response was complete. Her blood warmed in a swirling moist heat. She began to return his kiss, hesitantly at first. But as he kindled the fires of desire within her body, she responded in kind. Her kisses became anxious pleas for a more intense lovemaking. Boldly her fingers crept up his chest until her arms encircled his neck. She felt the thick muscular cords near his spine and unconsciously began to massage away the tension that seemed to devour him tonight.

Kane groaned with pleasure, his voice an echo of hers as she gasped for air. His tongue met hers and danced hungrily in a torrid fever, first flicking light touches to hers and finally molding it with a moist and fevered need. "Erin," he breathed, letting her name whisper against her. "I need you...tonight."

Erin's mind continued to remind her that she should stop him now, while she still had the chance, but she found herself resisting common sense and embracing temptation. Never had she felt so ignited, so completely female.

His lips scorched a trail of featherlight kisses from her eyes to her throat and on to her tender ear. His delicious breath tingled her inner ear, sending shock waves of passion resounding through her mind. She let her head fall away from him, hoping to somehow make her neck and earlobe more available to him. His thumb traced the hollow of her throat, gently at first, but with increased pressure in tight little circles...around and around, until she thought that she wouldn't be able to breathe.

Erin sighed briefly and resigned herself to

the fact that her mind wanted him as much as her body did. "Oh, Kane," she murmured, "I need you, too." She succumbed body and soul to her desires and arched her hips against his. His breath ruffled her hair and he smiled down at her before lifting her off her feet and carrying her into the bedroom.

"I know that you need me, Erin. I thought that you would never realize that we were meant to be together."

"Together?" she breathed.

"As man and woman. I knew it from the first time I saw you, sitting amid that ridiculous pile of books in your office."

Together as man and woman, she thought, *but for how long? For an hour, a day, a week?* Her mind raced forward, but her body wouldn't let go, not tonight. She felt him pressed hotly against her, smelled his warm clean scent and saw a stormy passion in his face that she had to capture. She needed him every bit as much as he needed her, and perhaps much, much more.

Erin let herself follow the path of her emotions. The magic of his kiss had aroused her to the point of no return, and she was heedless of anything save his sensitive touch. She couldn't deny herself any of the pleasures that he could spark in her. Since that first moment in her dimly lit office, she, too, had been aware of him first and foremost as a man. His sensuality couldn't be ignored, not for a second. His dark eyes, well-muscled body and virile self-assurance had enticed and beckoned to the center of her femininity, and she was tempted beyond reason to respond.

Erin's body seemed to warm from the inside out, melting in fevered washes of heat and desire. Any reservations that might still have lingered in her mind were slowly and unconsciously stripped away from her as he rained liquid kisses over her skin.

The bedroom was bathed in moonlight. Kane laid Erin on the bed, and she felt the cool satin of the comforter through the sheer silk of her blouse. She was still dressed, although as he stood over her, she felt naked. Naked to the pain of needing him. Naked in the knowledge that she loved him. And naked in the recognition that her love was unreturned. His heavy-lidded eyes were unreadable, but Erin was very certain that although there was a smoke of passion in his gaze there was no flame of love.

Regardless of that fact, she couldn't and wouldn't deny the urges of her body. She loved him, despite his lack of love for her. The bed sagged beneath Kane's weight, and Erin felt herself tremble. His finger traced the length of her arm, but his eyes never left hers. He was watching her, almost studying her, seeming content to let his gaze caress her.

"Tell me no if you want me to stop," he commanded in a hoarse voice. His lips brushed tentatively over hers.

Her response was a grateful moan. Their lips met in a hot embrace, and she let her arms wind around his neck in a display of total abandon. She wanted all of him with a burning need that she had never before felt.

He let his hands stroke her face and throat in moth-soft caresses, until at last they reached her collar and finally the buttons of her blouse. He opened the blouse slowly, letting the fine silky fabric part of its own accord. And then gently he raised her shoulders to let the blouse slip to the floor. His eyes watched her torso as her breasts rose and fell with each of her gasping breaths.

"Erin... God, but you're beautiful," he sighed, fingering the lacy bra that was still a seductive barrier between his flesh and hers. His fingers teased and finally unclasped the skimpy piece of lingerie, until at last her aching breasts were unrestrained.

A groan escaped from his lips as he slowly massaged each dark-nippled breast to arousal. When he could feel the hardness of her breasts, he cuddled them softly and buried his head between the two feminine peaks. Erin arched against him, unable to control the hot urges that were firing her. She reached for his shirt, and as quickly as possible, removed it from his body, until her anxious fingers found the thick soft mat of fur that covered his chest and the male nipples beneath it.

As he enticed her, so did she him. She let her fingers touch and caress the firm muscles that flared rigidly over his body. Her hands traveled up his spine, vertebra by vertebra, feeling the hardness of his back through the moisture of his sweat.

The room was dark; only the soft glow from the partially opened door mingled with the moon glow to add a shimmering pallor to the night. But Erin could see Kane as clearly as if it were a bright summer day. All of her senses were alive to him. His touch fired her, his scent encouraged her and his salt-sweet taste lingered on her lips and tongue.

His hands traveled to her skirt and pantyhose, quickly discarding a portion of the clothing that separated them. He cast off his pants as rapidly, never for a moment leaving Erin alone. Always one part of him was pressed warmly and possessively over her.

Her blood was boiling through her veins, spiraling upward from the deep mercurial well that was vibrating from the essence of her femininity. His lips traveled over her breasts, teasing and tasting each one while his hands slowly and rhythmically rubbed soft patterns against her abdomen, dipping deliciously below the elastic of her panties, and then letting the fabric snap tantalizingly against her skin.

Kane toyed with her last article of clothing until she thought she would go mad with the urgency of her need for him. When the agonizing last flimsy barrier was finally freed from her body, she groaned in pure animal pleasure and desire. He let his lips graze the muscles of her abdomen to circle her navel. His tongue warmed her flesh and she pulled him more closely to her.

All thoughts of anything but the mastery of his lovemaking were torn from her mind, pushed aside as quickly as her clothing. She was conscious of only one thing: the bruising, pulsating desire that dominated her mind and body. Time had ceased. Doubts had fled. All that she cared about was Kane: the skillful play of his fingers on her thighs and buttocks, the searing brand of his kiss over her breasts and abdomen, the enticing lure of his strong body.

She could feel the granitelike touch of his naked leg against hers, the soft hair tickling her cleanly shaven skin. She could also tell that he was holding back his physical needs to give her the utmost pleasure. In the half light of the moon she could see his arousal and feel the warm length of him brushing against her.

Just as she felt that she would surely melt with need of him, he came to her, fusing the fine muscles of his body with hers in a hot, rhythmic blend of passion. She felt him push her over the delicate edge of desire to fulfillment, and in the warm wash of exploded passion, he came with her in a burning torchlike shudder of surrender.

Erin felt a sigh flow from her lips as she held him tightly and securely, holding on to him as if her life depended on him. It had been many, many years since she had made love to a man, and never had she felt the wonder or the magic that Kane had aroused and satisfied in her tonight. Although she felt an incredible bliss, her torn emotions got the better of her, and she began to feel the hot sear of tears burn at the back of her eyes.

Embarrassed at herself, she tried to move away from Kane and blink back the unwanted tears. But as she slid against the satin comforter, his arms locked over her, imprisoning her.

"Where do you think you're going?" he whispered silkily, his voice still holding the satisfaction of afterglow.

Erin's voice caught in her throat and she couldn't force herself to answer him.

"Erin?" Kane's voice was more aware than it had been. "Is something wrong?"

She shook her head negatively, but when she did, she felt his strong fingers reach up and stroke her face. His hands stopped their movement as his fingertips encountered the first tear that had slid unrequested down her cheek. "Oh, no," he murmured.

"It's not…what you think," she managed to sigh.

"Did I hurt you?" His voice was uneven in the night.

"No…no… Kane…"

"Then why? I don't understand." His words were raw with concern.

"Neither do I," she admitted as the tears began to flow freely past the web of her lashes and down her cheeks. She shook her head in self-deprecation, letting the ebony curtain of her hair fall loosely around her face. How could she do such a thing to him, she asked herself silently. And how, when she was so deliriously happy, could she feel so confused and torn?

"Erin." His voice had lowered an octave, and he brushed her hair away from her face so as to kiss the tears from her cheeks. "Is something wrong?" He held her gently to him, letting her skin press tightly to his, while he covered them both with the comforter. In the quiet room, he rocked her in the cradle of his arms.

"No…nothing…nothing's wrong…" Her voice wavered.

"What is it? You're not ashamed of making love to me, are you?"

"No…no…never." She felt his breath feathering the back of her head as he sighed with relief. "It's nothing I can explain," she continued. "The last few weeks have been hard…." Could she tell him about the badly needed repairs to the building, the confusion she felt about Mitch or the taxing telephone calls from Lee? "...I guess I've been tired." She wanted to explain how she felt, but there were so many conflicting and unsettling emotions warring within her that she didn't want to think about them. Not tonight. She just needed to feel the peaceful security of Kane's arms around her.

Kane clutched her more urgently to him in a protective embrace. He could feel the beating of her heart, a warm pulse fluttering lightly under his fingertips and vibrating against the velvet smoothness of her breasts. He wanted her to speak—to confess. He needed to assure her that he could make everything right. He would find a way to help her out of the mess that Mitchell Cameron had created.

Kane's voice rumbled against his chest, and she could feel the deep manly tones pulsing against her naked back. "I want you to know that if you do have a problem—any problem whatsoever—you can come to me." His last words sounded like a confession. "I'm on your side."

"Oh, Kane," she breathed, wanting to confide her innermost thoughts and share everything with him, yet unable to bare her soul any more than she already had. "There's really nothing to tell. I'm...just a little keyed up. That's all...." She could feel herself smiling at him through her tears.

Outside a cloud crossed the moon, giving a misty aura to the light that passed into the bedroom. She turned to face Kane, and his eyes looked all the more omniscient in the unnatural moon glow.

"I hope you realize that if you ever need a friend, you can count on me," Kane murmured, before lowering his head to hers and kissing away the final tears that stained her cheeks.

As his lips found hers, she tasted the salt of her own tears, mingled seductively with the uniquely male taste of Kane. She parted her lips, and in a moment the kisses deepened to rekindle the fires of passion that possessed them.

With a gentleness that belied the tension that pushed against him, Kane caressed Erin and together they discovered the secrets of inflamed desire and glorious love. Erin fell dreamlessly to sleep in the warm strength of Kane's arms. But Kane didn't sleep. Too many uneasy thoughts about Erin strained against his mind. He looked at her asleep and brushed an unruly wisp of raven hair off the perfect alabaster sheen of her face. Sleeping in the moonlight, she seemed so childlike, innocent and vulnerable.

But his mind continued in its ugly pursuit of the truth. Why had she lied to him? And why did he care so much?

Chapter 6

Erin felt comfortably warm and drowsy as she stretched lengthwise in the bed and tucked the silken comforter more cozily around her neck. She sighed softly to herself in pleasure as she slowly awakened. All the tension that had been gathering in her body over the last six months had somehow ebbed gently away from her. She smiled to herself contentedly before realizing that she felt so dreamily happy because she had made love to Kane Webster—her new boss!

Her dark lashes flew open as the reality of the situation dawned upon her. The bedroom was dark and the bed was empty. Kane must have left her and disappeared into the night as she slept. A feeling akin to desperation cascaded over her, and the bed, once warm and comforting, seemed cruelly cold and empty. She wondered silently to herself how she could have been so foolishly naive to expect him to stay with her. She was achingly aware that she loved him, and although she didn't want to care for him so deeply, she accepted the naked truth of her love. But she wasn't so foolish as to expect that he could possibly reciprocate her feelings of the heart.

Erin mentally chided herself for her thoughts of love. For all she knew, Kane might consider her just another easy conquest. The infuriating phrase "one night stand" crept into her mind. For all her bold talk of not mixing business with pleasure, she had invited Kane all too easily into her heart and into her bed.

You're an idiot, she swore at herself as she decided to get dressed. She reached for her teal blue skirt that was still lying in the discarded heap of wrinkled clothing at the side of the bed. After pulling her pantyhose on furiously, she began to step into the skirt.

"Don't get dressed on my account," Kane's voice whispered across the darkness to her.

Her disappointed heart leaped at the sound of his voice, and she whirled toward the doorway to find Kane leaning casually against the doorjamb, his gaze wandering recklessly over her body. Involuntarily she crossed her free arm over her breasts, while with the other she tugged vainly at the skirt.

"I… I thought that you'd gone," Erin murmured, and feeling somewhat embarrassed by her partial nudity, she hastily grabbed the sheet from the bed and pulled it togalike around her body. Kane watched her swathe herself with the white sheet, and in his mind he likened her to a Greek goddess.

"Now, why would I want to leave?" he drawled huskily as his eyes traveled lazily over her one exposed slim leg and up to her eyes. Her fingers tightened around the sheet and yet she felt naked.

"I don't know," she admitted, "but when I woke up, you were gone and I didn't hear any noise. I thought that you must have…" Her words died as she interpreted the expression in his clear gray eyes.

He stood still in the doorway watching her. One well-muscled shoulder rested against the doorjamb. The light from the living room was behind him, and his silhouette in the darkness seemed to intensify the broad strength of his shoulders and the powerful play of muscles on his chest. His shirt was still unbuttoned as if he were just in the process of getting dressed when he heard her awaken. Erin found it hard to concentrate on anything but his tanned skin and the invitation of his open shirt. Unconsciously she gripped the sheet a little more tightly.

"I'm not going to leave you," he replied seriously, and then wondered at the promise he heard echoing in his words. He could see Erin's face in the cloud-shadowed moon glow—a delicate, regal oval placed in relief by the tangled mass of black hair that cascaded down to rest against the marble texture of her bare shoulder. The hollow of her throat beckoned him, but he resisted reaching for her. She was beautiful, almost an inspiration, and Kane had difficulty reining in his emotions. Her lilac eyes shimmered in the half light, and Kane was sorely tempted to go back to the bed and crush her passionately against him. How could he ache so much for one woman, he asked himself. And how could any woman who appeared so innocent and vulnerable be mixed up with something as gut-wrenchingly dishonest as embezzling?

The onerous thoughts that battled in his mind must have been evident on his face because Erin's expression changed from innocence to wariness. God, why did he want her so badly?

Kane cleared his throat, and in an attempt to break the heady silence that was entrapping him, tried to lighten the suddenly tense moment. He cocked one dark eyebrow in mock suspicion and effectively changed the subject.

"So you thought that I had left you, did you? Wishful thinking on your part, wasn't it?"

"Wishful thinking? What do you mean?"

"You've been trying to weasel out of fixing dinner for me all day, but it won't work. I'm here and I'm famished!"

"The lasagna! Oh, no! I forgot all about it!" Erin wailed. She started to hike her skirt upward over her hips, while still grasping the sheet.

Kane stood, unmoving and bemused, in the doorway. His silvery eyes never left her body. Erin sucked in a deep breath. Although she was uncomfortable about dressing in front of him, intuitively she knew it would be useless to try and dissuade him from watching her. She gave him an irritated glare that only seemed to amuse him further as she tried to squirm into the tight blue skirt and attempted to keep the sheet positioned modestly. Her efforts were in vain, and a deep chuckle erupted in his throat as he unabashedly studied her dismal efforts at privacy. Finally, when she slipped the skirt up to her waist and tried to tug at the zipper, it got caught in the sheet and Erin gave up. After the passionate intimacy of only an hour before, Erin realized that her modesty must appear slightly neurotic. With a burning flush of scarlet on her cheeks, she untangled the sheet from the zipper and let the sheet fall to the floor.

"Damn!" she swore under her breath when the skirt was in place at last. She raised her deep round eyes to him and met his gaze unwaveringly. Her breasts, two white soft mounds, were unshielded, and she moved slowly as she finished dressing. "You're not making this easy, you know," she accused, her eyes never leaving his. He met her challenging gaze with an amused twinkle in his eyes. "The least you could do," she continued, "is take the dinner out of the oven so it doesn't burn!"

A condescending smile touched the corners of his lips. "You expect me to help with the cooking?"

"Why not? You obviously intend to help with the eating," she bantered back at him, and attempted to hurry through the doorway. Just as she tried to pass him, he placed a strong arm across her path. The action effectively barred her passage and barricaded her into the bedroom.

"Not so fast," he murmured seductively. Erin felt her throat tighten.

"But the meal—the lasagna. It's probably cremated!"

"It'll keep," he breathed, his eyes holding hers. His head dipped downward, and before she could utter any further protest, he kissed her softly. His lips lingered over hers for only an instant before he dropped the imprisoning arm and pulled his head away from hers. "I just wanted to thank you."

"For what?" she asked breathlessly.

"For just being you." His words warmed her, and she felt more than a little lightheaded and dizzy, but the steady pressure of his warm hand against the small of her back forced her into the living area of the apartment. She couldn't help but smile as she noticed that he had set the table for two and pulled the slightly overcooked casserole from the oven. Candles graced the intimate table.

The wine was poured. The meal was already served.

"You did this?" she asked, surveying the table that he had set with enviable care. "And I slept through it?" Amazement was evident in her voice.

"Surprising, isn't it?"

"That's putting it mildly." She shook her head in concentrated thought. "I'm normally a light sleeper," she murmured as she walked into the kitchen.

"That's because you haven't been keeping the right company."

"And just what is that supposed to mean?" she inquired cautiously as she put the finishing touches on the meal and placed the salad on the table next to the lasagna and warm bread.

"Just that you'd probably sleep more soundly with me."

Her eyes jumped to his face as she took the chair opposite his at the table. She took a deep breath and decided that it was time to set him straight about her. Perhaps he had gotten the wrong impression and thought that she was somewhat promiscuous.

She began slowly and deliberately. "Kane,

I want you to understand something about me," she requested.

"Such as?"

"Contrary to what you might think…" She struggled with her next words as they caught in her throat. "I don't normally… I mean…" She shook her dark curls in frustration. "What I'm trying to say is that I don't make a habit of sleeping with a man whom I barely know." She watched for his reaction.

"Oh?" His voice was interested, and he pushed his plate aside to give her his full attention. She saw no criticism in his misty eyes, only concern.

"I hope that I haven't given you the wrong impression about me…."

"You mean because you slept with me?"

Two dark scarlet points of color brightened her cheeks, but she bravely continued. "That's exactly what I mean." Her words were hushed, and for a moment she was forced to look away from him. When she brought her eyes back to his, she held his gaze steadily and her voice became coolly even. "I don't really understand why I think that you have to know this, but for the sake of my own somewhat Victorian morals, I want you to realize that I don't have casual affairs. In fact, other than my ex-husband, there has been no one. Until you."

"I know that," he assured her in a voice as grave as the night.

She fingered her wineglass and took a long swallow of the rosé. She studied the pale pink liquid and swirled it in the long-stemmed glass before continuing the conversation. "Then why did you ask me all of those insulting questions about Mitch?"

At the mention of Mitchell Cameron's name, a scowl darkened Kane's features. Once again his face was guarded and his eyes became two silver shields. "I didn't know you then," was the terse reply.

"And in just three days you know me well enough to evaluate my love life?" she returned, and heard the sarcasm in her voice.

"I probably know a lot more about you than you think."

Her lilac eyes fastened on his, and a rush of indignation that she couldn't conceal colored her words. "You haven't been checking up on me, have you?"

"No more than I have any other employee of the bank." It was a lie and he knew it, but he couldn't let her think any differently at this point. He hated himself for the lie, but he was trapped by the web of suspicions that plagued him and by the storm of emotions that captured him every time he looked into her eyes.

"Then why all the insinuations about Mitch? Can't you believe that a woman can make it on her own without sleeping with the boss?"

He arched an expressive dark eyebrow, and she felt immediately contrite. The question that was unspoken hung between them on a charged electric current. Unashamedly Erin answered it. "You know that I didn't make love to you because of my job."

"Then tell me, why *did* you sleep with me?" he coaxed.

"For the same reason that *you* slept with *me*," she responded, lifting her chin proudly. "Because I wanted to." His tight frown seemed to relax, and he took a sip of his wine as he surveyed her over the rim of the wineglass. His gray eyes concentrated on her. She seemed so honest. It was impossible to think that her beautiful face would lie. Why hadn't she been truthful about her ex-husband? Erin O'Toole was an enigma, a ravishing, seductive enigma.

Erin struggled with her meal. Why did she feel such an uncontrollable urge to explain everything to Kane? And why did she feel the need for caution? As she put aside her fork, she spread her hands outward on the table, her fingers reaching up in a supplicating gesture. "Mitch was my boss, and he was and is a very dear friend. No matter what he's done, nothing will change that. But there was never anything more between us than personal friendship and professional respect for each other. Can't you believe me?"

"Of course I do—now," Kane replied. "But you can't blame me for my suspicions. Until I met you in the bank last Saturday, I didn't know anything about you other than what was in your personnel file. I knew that you had been promoted rapidly—perhaps too quickly—and I wanted to know why. You have to understand that no matter how close you are to Mitch, he is a thief!" Kane's cold gray eyes grew dark. "It's my responsibility to the bank, the stockholders, the savings customers, everyone, to know everything I can about each employee. It would be ridiculous to think that I would rely on Mitchell Cameron's judgment."

Kane's words hit Erin like a splash of cold water. She was stunned, and her voice was brittle as she asked the question that was uppermost in her mind. "Are you trying to tell me that you don't think I'm qualified for my position, that the only reason you could see that I would get the job was because I might have slept with Mitch?" she challenged, stricken at the thought.

His voice was strangely devoid of emotion. "I'm saying that it's difficult for me to believe that a thirty-two-year-old woman is second in command of the legal department of a major Seattle bank...."

"And if I were a man?" she fired back at him, her eyes deepening to the color of a midnight storm.

"Sex has nothing to do with this!"

"Sex has everything to do with this," she argued, slapping her palm against the table and rattling the silverware. "You seem to overlook the fact that I spent the last six years of my life in night school, for the most part doing postgraduate work in corporate law! If it weren't for the fact that you bought First Puget Bank, I would probably be a practicing attorney today!"

It was Kane's turn to be angry and his words sliced through the air. "I don't see how I could have possibly hindered your legal career! What does my ownership of the bank have to do with it?"

Erin swallowed with difficulty and licked her arid lips. She tried to think calmly and took a long swallow of wine to quench her parched throat. Getting angry wouldn't solve anything, she told herself, and giving in to her sometimes volatile temper would only hinder the situation. Carefully she explained her position. "There are several reasons that I haven't been able to take the bar exam."

"And somehow they are all my fault," he surmised.

"I'm not blaming you," she insisted, and began toying with her napkin. "First Puget was paying my way through school. Any class I took that pertained to my job was paid for by the bank. Other classes I paid for myself. That is—until the bank sale."

"You mean, until Consolidated Finances bought out First Puget?"

She nodded.

"Lack of money prevented you from taking the exam?" His jawline hardened and a tiny muscle began to work in his jaw as he clenched his teeth together. One more reason Erin needed money, as he saw it. Just how desperate was she?

"Money isn't the only problem," she sighed, wishing there were some way to avoid this particular discussion. "You see, in the past six months, there have been several departmental changes...and Mitch wasn't around a good deal of the time. I had to spend a lot of my free time at the bank, working."

"And you didn't have time to study for the examination?" Was there a slight undercurrent of sarcasm to his question?

"It's not as simple as going out and getting a driver's license, you know!" she snapped back at him, her strained temper unleashed at last. Viciously she speared a portion of the lasagna and forced the bite into her mouth.

For a few seconds neither she nor Kane spoke, and they finished the remainder of the meal in silent battle. When she hazarded a surreptitious glance in his direction, she felt her anger flow out of her. Perhaps it was the deep concentration of his knit brows, or the play of light on his gold-streaked chestnut hair. Or maybe it was the seductive way his mouth curved, or his bronzed chest as it peeked out from beneath his shirt. Whatever the reason, she felt her temper cool as she watched him. Her heart was torn and she ached to understand the man whom she loved so urgently.

Why, she wondered, did she feel that he was holding something back from her? Why did there always seem to be a dark, unasked question in his eyes? Was he like she was, insecure about a commitment to a fellow employee? Was it possible that he had a girlfriend, or perhaps a fiancée, waiting for him in California? Or was it a brooding concern for his daughter that made him seem so remote at times? How could she love a man so desperately and still feel that he wasn't being completely honest with her?

She finished her meal, excused herself and began brewing some coffee in the kitchen. Despite the uncomfortable conversation, Kane ate hungrily and Erin was pleased. What was it about preparing a meal for the man she loved that made her feel so satisfied? Some age-old maternal instinct, she supposed and smiled to herself. She had experienced the same satisfied sensation with Lee in the first few months of her marriage. It hadn't lasted long, she reminded herself!

At a time like this why would she remember her ex-husband and the few good times that they had shared? She tried to dispel her mood of melancholy remembrance by pouring the coffee and carrying it into the living room.

Kane had risen from the table and was standing at the window, staring out across the darkened Puget Sound. From his position, he could see the jeweled lights of Seattle winking on the quiet black waters. A deep blanket of fog was beginning to roll into the Sound.

"Even at night this is a spectacular view of the city," he thought aloud, accepting the coffee that Erin offered. She, too, looked into the misty night.

"That's one of the reasons that I had to have this place," she agreed, and then laughed. "Along with a very long list of other things."

"Such as?"

"The charm of this old house. Everything about it speaks of a different time, a more romantic period in history." She ran a caressing finger across the cool wood of the windowsill. "The craftsmanship is exquisitely ornate, and I doubt that it could be duplicated today. This house was built with love. Look at the woodwork, the carved stairs, the beveled windows, everything! Even the builder who separated it into apartments and added all the modern conveniences took enough care to keep the flavor and the grandeur of the house in mind. I fell in love with it the minute I saw it," she admitted, and was surprised at how easily she had opened up to Kane about her feelings for the old mansion.

"Didn't anyone warn you about the expensive upkeep of such an old building?" he asked cautiously as he sat down on the couch. She took a seat next to him and shook her head thoughtfully.

"Everyone I knew tried to talk me out of it. Even my parents, who live on the East Coast, flew out here to try and dissuade me. They all told me that I was throwing money away. How does the expression go? 'Good money after bad'? They swore that the upkeep of the place would ruin me financially." She shrugged her slim shoulders and looked out the window again. "But the more people tried to talk me out of it, the more I absolutely had to have it!"

"Watch out," he cautioned with a smile. "Your rebellious side is beginning to show."

"Is it?" she asked, turning her attention back to him. She had considered herself many things, but never rebellious.

"That dark, private side of you that I told

you about yesterday. It's surfacing," he suggested.

Once again the conversation was becoming too intimate for Erin. She was beginning to feel claustrophobic, as if he were closing in on her. Something made her draw away; she tried to change the subject. "In any event I bought this place and haven't lived to regret it yet."

"And were all those people who gave you advice correct?"

"What do you mean?"

He took a long, experimental sip of his coffee and studied her intently. "I mean, has this house become a financial burden to you?"

Erin swallowed before answering. Just how much did she want him to know about her, and how much did he already guess? "It hasn't been easy," she admitted reluctantly.

"Tenant problems?"

She shook her head negatively. "Not really. Most of the people who rent here have been with me for years, and they are very nice people who take pride in their homes. Once in a while I have a vacancy problem, but the primary difficulty with this place is the repairs. You see, I'm not exactly handy with a hammer or a saw."

"I wouldn't worry too much about that," he teased and lightly touched her shoulder. "You have talents in other fields." His whispered words were tender and comforting, and she felt that she had known him all her life. His fingers touched her hair. He felt himself drawn to the ebony sheen of her curls. They were as black and inviting as the night itself. He caught himself and struggled to maintain his objectivity where Erin was concerned, but found it difficult to put his feelings for her in their proper perspective. She had lied to him and he knew it. Whether she admitted it or not, Lee Sinclair was back in Seattle. Kane felt that he had to press Erin tonight, before he became all the more entangled in her mysterious womanly charms. He couldn't let himself forget that it was imperative that he understand what devious thoughts were being spun in that regal head of hers.

"What about your ex-husband?" Kane prodded.

"Lee?" she asked, perplexed. "What does Lee have to do with anything?" Nervously she pushed an errant strand of hair back in place. Why did Kane continue to bring up the subject of a man whom Erin would rather forget?

"What did he have to say about this place and your purchasing it?"

"He couldn't say much. We were divorced at the time," she responded with a finality that she hoped would effectively close the subject. But still he persisted.

"Tell me about the divorce," he coaxed.

"Why?"

A smile toyed with the corners of his mouth. "Because I want to know all about you..." he suggested silkily.

"I don't like to talk about Lee."

"Why?"

"Are you interrogating me again?" she asked, promptly regretting the acidity in her words. She got up from the couch and shrugged her shoulders. "It bothers me...to talk about Lee."

"Did he hurt you so badly?" he asked, his voice gentle.

Her eyes glazed over with the shame that she had borne. How could she explain the embarrassment of Lee's affair and the messy divorce? "Yes," she whispered, "I suppose that he did hurt me, but only because I let him."

"By loving him too much?" he asked severely.

"No, by being so young and naive. At the

time I thought that all marriages were made in heaven, and I didn't think that I would fail, or that he would *use* me...." She found that she was trembling. The cup of coffee shook in her fingers, and she was forced to set it on the bookcase in order to hide her reaction from Kane.

"There was another woman?" he guessed, and Erin, with her back to him, let her shoulders droop as she nodded.

"My pride was wounded very deeply." She pulled her lips into a thin line of self-deprecation and squared her sagging shoulders. "I just never thought that I would end up as a divorce court statistic!"

"You didn't want the marriage to end?"

She turned and faced him. "You don't understand. I didn't want to fail, but I *had* to get out of the marriage to Lee. I couldn't bear the hypocrisy!"

Quickly Kane moved off the couch and reached for her. He pressed her quietly against the strength of his chest. Although she was still shaking, she could hear the steady beat of his heart, and his silent support helped calm her.

"Erin," Kane breathed, sharing in the agony that had embittered her.

"It's all right," she murmured against him. "I don't know why it still bothers me... at times. The pain has been gone for a long while."

She felt his arm tighten around her, and his voice was barely a whisper when he asked the question. "Do you ever see him?" Kane asked with an urgency she couldn't understand.

"I haven't seen him for over a year, since he moved to Spokane." The pressure of his hands against her back increased and she felt compelled to continue. "But he has moved back to Seattle, and he has called me."

His grip slackened, but the deep lines of concern that etched his forehead remained. "He wants to see you again?" Kane asked, and his eyes narrowed a fraction.

"I don't want to see him," she sighed. "So I haven't."

"Is he being overly persistent?" There was a thread of steel in Kane's voice.

"Yes...no...no, not really..." She rubbed her temple in confusion. "Couldn't we talk about something else? I really don't like to be reminded of that period in my life. What about you?" she asked, her lilac eyes searching his. "What was your marriage like?"

Kane released her and scowled. His lips

formed a thin line that was neither a smile or frown. "I suppose that's a fair question, since you bared your soul to me."

He strode purposely back to the couch and raked his fingers through the thick waves of his hair, before picking up his lukewarm coffee and staring into the black liquid.

"My marriage to Jana was a mistake from the beginning," he admitted with a frown. "I guess I probably knew it at the time, but I was much younger then, and it took me quite a few years to finally admit to myself that we had made an error that was destroying us."

He looked vacantly out the window into the fog before continuing. His dark brows pulled together in concentration and carefully Erin came closer to him and perched on the arm of the sofa as he began to speak.

"In the beginning I was attracted to her because she was an incredibly beautiful and famous woman. You know, the glamorous model. I was just getting started in my business at the time, and I was flattered that she would even give me the time of day. I convinced myself that I loved her, when actually there was never any love between us. I was young enough to think that beneath all the glitter was a beautiful person hidden in that gorgeous body. A typical male mistake. And of course I was wrong.

"We had a whirlwind romance, I guess you might say. Lusty affair would be more exact. In any event just as I was beginning to suspect that we were too different ever to get along, it was too late—she was pregnant. I talked her out of the abortion and into marriage."

His lips thinned and he shook his head derisively. "I guess that I was a damned fool to think that a baby would change things between us, that our differences would work themselves out. And as it turned out, Jana and I had very different impressions about family life. She resented having to give up her figure and her career for the sake of her pregnancy, and she resented being a mother and a housewife. After five years of battling with her I agreed to the divorce that she wanted so desperately. As I said before, the marriage was a mistake from the beginning, and I knew it. But no matter what, it was worth every minute of the arguments—because of Krista."

He cleared his throat as he thought about his daughter and a sadness stole across his features. Erin felt an urge to brush away the signs of strain that seemed to age his face.

The line of his jaw tensed as he spoke. "The biggest error in judgment I made was that at the time I didn't fight for custody. I subscribed to the same myth as the rest of the world: a young girl needs to be with her mother, regardless of the weaknesses or the frame of mind of the woman." A tortured look came into his steely eyes. "And then, to compound the mistake, I threw myself into my work, trying to erase the memories that had become painful. My attitude—it wasn't fair to Krista. To put it bluntly, I neglected my child. Not because I wanted to, but because I wanted to hide from the memories." He closed his eyes for a moment and rubbed the back of his neck to ease the tension that had knotted at the base of his head as he thought about the divorce and his child. He seemed tired and weary; Erin felt the burn of tears threatening to spill from her eyes.

His voice was a muted whisper when he continued. "I saw Krista occasionally of course, but not nearly as much as I wanted to or should have…it was just too difficult, too much of a struggle." A dark eyebrow cocked sardonically. "A selfish attitude, wouldn't you say?" he asked her rhetorically. His next sentence was one of self-condemnation. "I was a bastard of a father!"

He hesitated only slightly, and that was to wave his arm emphatically, stilling the protest that was forming in Erin's throat.

"Within a year Jana was trying to rebuild her career. It was difficult for her because she was six years older and slightly out of shape. Modeling, for the most part, is for the very young woman with an almost boyishly slim figure. No one in the New York or Los Angeles agencies was interested in Jana. As far as they were concerned, Jana was yesterday's news.

"Then this Hollywood actress obsession took hold of her, and unfortunately she failed, dismally trying to remember her lines as the cameras rolled." He rubbed his chin thoughtfully. "It was at about that point that she began making the self-help and group therapy rounds. She went through periods of fad diets, deep depression, sensitivity groups—you name it and she was into it. I suggested that she go to a respected local psychiatrist, but she ignored my advice as usual and preferred to stick with the most faddish encounter group of the day.

"That's when I decided to do something

about Krista. As poor a father as I had been, even I knew that all Jana's neuroses couldn't be good for an impressionable nine-year-old girl. Damn!" He swore at himself and bit his lower lip in annoyed remembrance. "I should have seen it earlier. Maybe I could have prevented all of Krista's problems. Perhaps if I had been paying a little more attention to my kid rather than my business interests, Jana would be alive today and Krista would be walking like a normal and healthy eleven-year-old!"

"You can't blame yourself," Erin objected. "You tried to help."

Steely gray eyes flashed fire at her. "'Too little, too late,' as the saying goes."

Erin had trouble keeping her silence. She saw the emotions that were ripping him apart as he thought about his past. His fist clenched tightly before he thrust it into the pocket of his pants.

"There's really not all that much more to tell," Kane admitted in a softer, more controlled voice. "I was concerned, and I suggested that Krista come and live with me, at least for a while, until Jana could—how did she phrase it—get her head together. But she wouldn't have anything to do with it. Krista was a burden to her, and both she and I knew it, yet she wouldn't allow my own daughter to come and live with me! Sometimes I felt that Jana was using Krista as a weapon against me." An almost evil look stole over his lips. "And it worked! Not only did it bother me, but Krista became steadily more introverted. She always had been a somewhat shy, quiet child, but it seemed that she was withdrawing too deeply into herself, becoming sullen." There was a long pause while Kane drew in a steadying breath. "And then, of course, there was the accident. Up until that time, at least I could talk to Krista." His eyes darkened with a quiet rage at the circumstances that had led to the isolation from his only child. "But since the accident and her paralysis, I have trouble communicating with her about anything. It's as if she's punishing me for what happened to Jana…." He shifted his weight uncomfortably on the couch before murmuring, in a barely audible voice, his own self-condemnation. "I suppose that I deserve it!"

"No!" Erin challenged.

"For God's sake, Erin. Krista watched her mother die!"

"Oh, Kane, don't go on blaming yourself

for something that no one could prevent," she begged.

"Easier said than done," he muttered.

Telling the story had been an ordeal that Kane hadn't prepared himself for. He was nervous and amazed at his own confessions to Erin. It was never his intention to divulge so much of himself to her. He didn't want her to be able to see into his mind, and yet he had just given her the chance.

Kane had told himself that he needed to get to know Erin to find out more about the embezzling scheme at the bank, but the pleading look of innocence in her eyes, the soft, petulant curve of her lips, and her clear-sighted, intelligent mind all trapped him into admitting things that he had hidden from the rest of the world. Why was it so damn easy to talk to her, to confide his most introspective thoughts to her?

Erin was obviously moved by his story; he could see that in the caring look of pain she directed toward him and the unshed tears in her eyes. God, he reminded himself, he had to get away from her while he still could.

He cleared his throat and put his empty coffee cup on the table. Avoiding her eyes, he reached for his jacket and slipped the sport coat over his shoulders. "I guess that we had better call it a night," he declared with a touch of tenderness in his voice. He fought the urge to draw her into his arms and kiss away the tears she was trying courageously to hide.

"You're leaving?" Was it a surprise or disappointment that made her touch her lips provocatively?

"I think it would be best."

"Why?"

"I thought you were the one who wanted to keep our relationship strictly business…."

"It's too late for that now," she whispered, and her wide violet eyes touched his.

"Convince me," he coaxed huskily, and mentally cursed himself for his own weakness.

"What would it take to convince you?" she teased, still blinking back the tears that pooled in her eyes.

"Use your imagination…."

A slow seductive smile lit her eyes. "You're wicked," she accused. "You know that, don't you?" She crossed the living room and let her fingers slide inside his jacket to press warmly against the light cotton fabric of his shirt. Powerful muscles tensed under the sensitive touch of her fingertips.

A slow groan of agonized pleasure escaped from his throat before he lowered his head to hers and captured her lips with his. "Oh, Erin," he whispered as he swept her off her feet and carried her toward the bedroom, "why is it that I can't resist you?"

Chapter 7

The bed creaked and shifted in the darkness.

"What are you doing?" Groggily she asked the question. Erin's eyes fluttered open as she felt Kane stir and move out of bed.

"I have to get up—I have work to do today," Kane replied and rubbed her tousled head fondly. In the inky blackness of the pre-dawn hours, he could see her. Even after a passionate night of lovemaking, she looked serenely enchanting against the stark white-ness of the bedsheets.

She groaned and rolled over. "But, oh, God, it's only—" Erin reached for the alarm clock and pulled the luminescent dial within inches of her face and sleepy eyes "—four-thirty in the morning." There was another agonized groan as she pushed the clock back on the nightstand. "No one in his right mind gets up at this time of day," she moaned, and stuffed her face back into the downy softness of her pillow.

The bed sagged under Kane's weight and he pressed a warm kiss against her forehead. "Do you want me to stay until dawn?" he asked quietly. "What about your tenants, not to mention our fellow bankers? You were the one who didn't want our relationship open for public viewing," he reminded her. "Besides all of that nonsense, I need a shower, shave and a change of clothing."

Even to Erin's cobweb-filled mind, Kane's reasoning seemed logical and clear. She propped up her head with her hand and tugged at the quilt close to the base of her throat. An autumn chill stung the morning air.

It took a little time, but slowly she began to awaken, and with interested eyes, she watched him get dressed. It was strange how comfortable she felt just being with him, how natural and right it all seemed. But he was correct. The fewer people who knew of their relationship, the better.

Kane left just as dawn was stretching its golden rays through her bedroom window. She listened as his car roared off down the hill and faded in the distance. It was a faraway, lonely sound that retreated into the misty morning air.

It was impossible to fall back into the heavy slumber that had come to her in Kane's arms. And so, with one final assessing and dubious glance at the clock, she got up, showered and dressed for the day.

Surprisingly, with only a few hours' sleep, Erin felt wonderfully refreshed after the hot needlelike spray of the shower pulsated against her skin. She toweled herself dry, applied a thin sheen of makeup, twisted the ebony strands of her hair into her businesslike chignon and stepped into her favorite burgundy suedelike suit. As she tied the broad white bow of her silk blouse she glanced in the mirror, and the woman in the reflection smiled back in genuine fondness. Erin felt good about herself this morning.

Fingers of fog still held the city, but the bright morning sun sent prisms of colorful light streaming heavenward in what promised to be a gorgeous fall day.

Unwittingly Erin smiled as she pushed her

way through the large plate-glass doors of the bank building. The dismal feeling of trepidation that had been with her during the transition of ownership of the bank seemed to have disappeared. Even as she brushed by Kane's office, she felt only a tinge of regret for Mitch. She still had a fondness in her heart for her ex-employer, but she realized that there was nothing that she or anyone else could do to help him. He had never returned any of her calls, although she had left several messages on the mechanical answering device that Mitch had installed. She had tried her best. Now, surely, if he needed to get in touch with her, he would.

As she passed by the outer reception area, she reached, by habit, for her messages stacked neatly on the main reception desk. She smiled inwardly as she read the bold scrawl that she recognized immediately as Kane's handwriting. It was concise and stated only "Tonight, eight o'clock." Erin couldn't restrain the blush that slowly climbed up her neck nor the look of satisfaction that touched the corners of her eyes. She wondered how transparent she must appear.

The secretary who had compiled the messages for her was a professional woman of about sixty, who neither commented nor indicated in any manner that she had read or interpreted the intimate message in Ms. O'Toole's slot. Relief washed over Erin as she read the look of total disinterest in the gray-haired woman's smile and the professional "Good morning" that was her usual greeting. Nothing appeared out of the ordinary. Even before Erin began to move toward her office, the secretary resumed the quick staccato rhythm of her lithe fingers on the keyboard of the typewriter.

It was midafternoon before Erin actually saw Kane again. He was conferring in the hallway with a man whom Erin recognized as a vice-president of the loan department. For a quick instant Erin's mind traveled to the employee loan that she had requested and wondered fleetingly if it was the topic of conversation. From Kane's reaction she doubted that he was discussing her need for funds.

As she passed the two bankers Kane gave Erin a perfunctory nod of his head to indicate that he had seen her, but there was nothing the least bit intimate in his gesture. It was an act of courtesy to acknowledge an associate. For a moment Erin's temper began to rise, and she felt angry until she understood the reasons for his discretion and feigned lack of interest in her. It was what she had requested, insisted upon—that their relationship remain secret, clandestine—and he was adhering to her request to the letter.

As she closed the door to her office she found herself still thinking of Kane and the tenuous relationship that existed between them. How could something so wonderful as falling in love with Kane seem so wrong? Why did she feel two conflicting urges warring within her mind? One feminine part of her wanted to share the happiness she had found with him with the world. The other more cautious and rational side of her nature urged her to silence. After all he was still her boss, the man who signed her paychecks, and it would be easy for anyone to misconstrue her feelings and relationship with him. She had been the target of curious and malicious gossip before, and she had vowed never to let herself be put in such an emotional and compromising position again. She knew how devastated she had been eight years ago, and she steeled herself against any intrusions into her private life. She hadn't wanted to fall in love with Kane; it had just happened. Perhaps, together, they could avoid the speculation and gossip. Surely it couldn't be that difficult to keep things on a professional level at the office, could it?

Erin lulled herself into a sense of serenity. It was a brilliant autumn afternoon, and other than the slight snub from Kane, the day had gone well. It wasn't until late afternoon that her tranquil mood was destroyed.

Contrary to what she had expected, Erin had accomplished more work this day than she had in weeks. Kane Webster had seemed to more than amply fill Mitchell Cameron's shoes, and all the disturbing telephone calls and interruptions that Erin had become used to had vanished. For the first time in over six months she could devote all her attention to the piles of probate work that had accumulated in her "Incoming" basket.

Erin was actually giving herself a mental commendation as she surveyed the clean desktop and slipped into the burgundy jacket before leaving the building. Just as she reached into the open desk drawer for her purse, there was a sharp rap on the door, and Olivia Parsons, not waiting for an invitation, glided into the room.

At the sultry brunette's entrance, Erin felt a cold tingle of apprehension at the back of her neck. Olivia was holding a clipboard pressed firmly to her breasts and jangled something metallic in the air.

"New keys!" Olivia announced, and dropped a ring of keys with a jingle onto the desktop. The green shimmer of Olivia's street-length designer dress matched the emerald essence of her eyes. "I'll need all your old keys," she stated flatly, and waited, somewhat impatiently, with her long fingers resting against her hip. The action emphasized the long, seductive curve of her leg.

"My keys? Why?"

"Standard procedure, after something like this embezzling thing with Mitch. Who can guess just how many sets of keys he's had made for any door in this building?"

"Of course," Erin agreed, and found herself relaxing a little as she realized that Olivia was just doing her job. Erin understood the liability of the bank. Even if Mitch had turned in his set of keys, he could have a dozen copies hidden away. The bank couldn't take the chance that he might sneak back into the building or the vaults.

"Here they are," Erin stated, producing the keys from the side pocket of her purse. She handed them to Olivia and the dark-haired girl frowned as she counted them. "Where's the other one?" Olivia asked, a puzzled expression crowding her neatly arched brows.

"I don't have any others. Just the key to the front door, the probate file cabinet, and Mitch's office—unless you want my desk key."

"No," Olivia answered, checking the corresponding numbers on the keys against her chart. "What about the key to the securities cart?" she asked, her green eyes reassessing Erin.

"I haven't had the key to that cart in years," Erin said, thinking aloud. Absently she rubbed her temple. "It had to have been over seven years ago." Again a chilly feeling of apprehension swept over her and her stomach began to knot.

"But the ledger here indicates that you should have a key to that cart," Olivia maintained. Laying the white formal sheet of paper on Erin's desk, she pointed to a line showing that Erin did, in fact, receive the key in question within the last year.

"It's a mistake…" Erin sighed. "I never had that key!"

"But aren't those your initials next to Mitch's signature?" Olivia pressed.

"Yes…it looks like I signed out for the key. But I didn't. There must be some mistake…." Her voice trailed off. She knew that she had never had that key. The whole situation was absurd. And a little frightening. Anyone with that key could withdraw negotiable stocks and bonds from the cart if given the right opportunity. A perfect plan for embezzlement. The thought sickened her.

Olivia studied the report for a few seconds more and then, with an elegant wave of her hand, dismissed the subject. "I guess it really doesn't matter since all of the new locks have already been installed. Just sign here for the new keys and I'll see that this securities key matter is cleared up." Erin scribbled her initials next to Olivia's, relinquished the old set of keys to the leggy brunette and snapped the new ring of keys into her purse.

Just as she was about to leave Olivia paused at the door. She thought for a moment before turning to face Erin once again. Her voice was low as she asked, "What do you think about Mitch?" Her normally lively green eyes had deadened. "Isn't it awful…."

Erin slowly shook her head and rubbed her chin nervously. "I don't like to think about it—or even talk about it. It's something that

I don't understand at all," she confessed, and hoped that the conversation with Olivia had ended. Something about the brunette always made Erin uneasy. But Olivia wouldn't let the subject die.

"I know what you mean." Olivia seemed to agree. "I would never have guessed—not in a million years." She paused once again, her gaze flicking up the length of Erin's figure as if something else were on her mind. A flame of life leaped into her eyes. "It must be especially hard for you," Olivia intimated.

"It's been hard for all of us," Erin agreed cautiously.

"Yes, but with you it's a little different, wouldn't you say?"

"I don't know what you're getting at."

"Oh, sure you do," Olivia replied as she brushed back an errant wave of thick copper hair. "You don't have to play naive with me. I know how close you were to Mitch."

Erin's patience, which had been thinning ever since the lanky girl had entered her office, snapped. She pulled the strap of her purse over her shoulder and said with a coolly professional voice that suggested the subject was closed, "Mitch is a good friend of mine—nothing more!"

"Oh?" The question seemed innocent enough, but the curl of Olivia's petulant lips suggested disbelief. "The same way that Kane Webster is your good friend?" The color drained from Erin's face, confirming Olivia's vicious accusation. "Well, honey," she continued with an exaggerated wink, "no one can accuse you of not knowing which side of the bread the butter's on!" After her final invective, and with a self-satisfied smile, Olivia slipped out of the office.

Erin stood in stunned silence in the aftermath of Olivia's remarks. Although she was alone, she felt a storm of scarlet embarrassment climb up her neck. It was happening again! Already! The gossip had started, and who better to start it than Olivia. Erin swallowed hard, and sagged against the desk. Why had she been so foolish—she should have seen it coming. All the gossip, the knowing glances, the snickering laughter behind her back, all over again!

She let her forehead rest on the palm of her hand as she slowly tried to recompose herself. It had been a good day, she reasoned, and she shouldn't let Olivia ruin it. But that was the trouble, Olivia had ruined it. Why, after all the years that had passed since the divorce from Lee, did any little biting comment from Olivia still wound her? Eight years had passed since Olivia's tempestuous affair with Lee. Although at the time, Erin had blamed the slim brunette for the breakup of her marriage with Lee, she knew now that she had been grossly unfair. If Lee hadn't taken up with Olivia, another pretty face would have caught his wandering eye and lured him away from the bounds of the marriage. Lee was only too willing. It was just unfortunate that Lee had been reckless enough to choose to have an affair with someone whom Erin saw on a daily basis. It seemed to compound the pain.

The problem with the marriage had not really been Olivia, but rather the differences between Erin and Lee. Although Erin recognized that now, she still found it hard to accept Olivia for what she seemed to be: a very knowledgeable and efficient assistant officer of the bank. Although the problems of the past were long dead, Olivia's presence at the bank and her vicious tongue continued to plague Erin. She never felt that she could completely trust Olivia.

Was she being unfair? Erin asked herself as she once again gathered her purse over her shoulder, straightened her skirt and headed out the door. Perhaps Olivia's attempt to communicate with Erin about Mitch was only natural. Both Olivia and Erin had cared very much for Mitch, and each had worked for him for nearly a decade. Perhaps Olivia felt the need to lash out because of Erin's cool attitude toward her. It was just possible that Erin was holding too much of a grudge against the sultry woman who wore the designer dresses and tailored suits with such seductive bearing. Erin sighed heavily to herself. Maybe she had never given Olivia a chance.

But the knot in Erin's stomach continued to tighten. She just intuitively didn't trust Olivia. It wasn't so much what Olivia said that managed to get under Erin's sensitive thin skin, but the way the words came out. Double entendres, sly winks, suggestive innuendos— all at Erin's expense.

As Erin found her way downstairs and out to the parking lot, she tried to dismiss the anxious feeling that had seized her with Olivia's interruption. But as she unthinkingly put the key into the ignition switch of the car, she hesitated and watched, nearly hypnotized, as the other keys jangled and swung near the steering column. How had her name gotten on the list of people who had keys to the securities cart? Try as she would to remember otherwise, she knew that she had never, in the last few months, signed out for that key! And yet the presence of her own initials negated her perception. Would someone within the bank use her good name for his own purposes? Could someone have forged her initials? Mitch, perhaps? Would Mitchell Cameron stoop so low? With a disgusted grunt to herself and a firm shake of her head, she started the car and dismissed her traitorous thoughts. Where had her loyalty gone? Mitchell Cameron had been kind to her, a friend when she needed one most. She wouldn't turn her back on him now— nor would she imagine that he would use her name for his own advantage. But then, how could she explain about the key? Could it be, as Olivia said, just a mistake? Probably. And yet...

There were still slight traces of fog along the waterfront and in the downtown area of Seattle, but as Erin's yellow VW climbed the hill that supported the apartment house, the mist thinned and by the time she was home the evening was cool but clear. Only a trace of fog could be seen in the wisps that clung to the dark waters of the distant Sound.

It was nearly seven, and Erin wanted to dash up the stairs to get ready for Kane, but propriety stopped her. She set her purse and briefcase on the lowest step of the staircase and knocked softly on Mrs. Cavenaugh's door.

A curious blue eye peeked at her through the peephole. Then quickly the door opened, and the slightly bent figure of Milly Cavenaugh greeted Erin with a warm smile.

"Good evening, Erin. I didn't expect to see you tonight," Mrs. Cavenaugh said cheerily, and winked broadly at her young landlady.

Erin's face creased with anxiety. "Why not? Didn't the repairmen show up?"

"Did they ever…" Mrs. Cavenaugh replied with a disapproving purse of her lips. Disgust darkened her eyes and she shook her head as she remembered. "They were here… an entire battalion of them…tracking in mud and heaven-knows-what-else into the house!" Erin's eyes followed the sweep of Mrs. Cavenaugh's hand as it included the front porch, entry hall and stairway. The oaken planks of the hallway were, indeed, imprinted with scrambled tracks of mud-laden, booted feet.

"Did they finish the job?" Erin asked, dragging her eyes away from the mess on the floor and back to her elderly tenant.

"Partially, I think. It seems that it's going to take more work than the original estimate showed," Mrs. Cavenaugh announced, thinking carefully.

"More work? Why?" Dollar signs flashed in Erin's mind.

"Something about dry rot in the floorboards, I think," Mrs. Cavenaugh explained with a shrug of her bent shoulders. "I'm sorry, dear, I really didn't pay too much attention— I was too busy trying to get them to wipe the dirt off their boots."

Erin felt her heart sink. Dry rot? What was that exactly? Something to do with the condition of the subfloor and support beams, she thought. It sounded like it would cost money—lots of it.

"Is something wrong, Erin?" Mrs. Cavenaugh asked, assessing the worried look that had appeared on Erin's face. "Would you like to come in and sit for a moment? I could brew a pot of tea…."

Forcing herself to smile, Erin shook her head. "Nothing's wrong, Mrs. Cavenaugh.

I was just a little surprised to find out about the dry rot."

"Oh, it's probably nothing to be concerned about anyway," the elderly lady thought aloud, dismissing the subject with an expansive wave of her hand. Her pale blue eyes took in the concerned look on Erin's features before asking the question that had been entering her head ever since she had seen Erin through the peephole.

"How did things go at work today?"

Erin was still concentrating on the bad news of the dry rot, wondering how extensive the damage was and just how many hundreds or thousands of dollars it would take to correct the problem. Mrs. Cavenaugh's question startled her.

"Pardon me?"

"Work. The new boss. How're you two getting along?" Thinly veiled interest sparked in her kindly blue eyes.

Erin pulled out of her reverie at the mention of Kane. "Everything's going just fine, I guess. Mr. Webster seems to be quite capable."

"And Mr. Cameron?" the old lady coaxed inquisitively.

Once again concern clouded Erin's violet

eyes. "I don't know," she replied honestly. "I haven't been able to reach him."

Mrs. Cavenaugh played with the strand of pearls at her neck and clucked her tongue. She wagged her head in disbelief. "I read about it in the papers. Embezzlement—it's a nasty business."

"I just wish that I could talk to him," Erin sighed, and leaned heavily against the banister of the staircase. "It's all so hard for me to accept."

"But your Mr. Webster..."

"He's *not my* Mr. Webster," Erin interrupted, her cheeks coloring in indignation. Mrs. Cavenaugh's blue eyes sparkled more brightly.

"Whatever," she replied with a dismissive shrug. "What does he think?"

"Oh, he's convinced that Mitch is guilty," Erin murmured, her slim fingers running along the clean cool lines of the wooden railing. Talking about Mitch and the embezzlement drained Erin, and she realized that she shouldn't be discussing bank business with her neighbor. She straightened her shoulders and changed the subject to a less personal issue. "Have you seen Mr. Jefferies?" she asked Mrs. Cavenaugh, and motioned toward the apartment on the other side of the staircase. "He hasn't changed his mind about vacating his apartment, has he?"

"As a matter of fact, I saw him this morning when I was getting my mail," the gray-haired woman replied importantly. "No, his daughter insists that George will be better off closer to his family." With a catty wink the wrinkled woman continued, "He is getting on in years, you know."

Erin suppressed the smile that tugged at the corners of her mouth. She knew for a fact that Mr. Jefferies was a good ten years younger than Mrs. Cavenaugh, although the sprightly little old lady would be loathe to admit it.

Erin lifted her shoulders in a dismissive gesture. "Oh, well, you win some and you lose some. I guess I'd better put an advertisement in the *Times* and put the Vacancy sign back up. It seems that I just took it down!"

"Has anyone ever told you that you worry too much?" Mrs. Cavenaugh asked, shaking a knowing and gnarled finger in Erin's surprised face.

Erin laughed in spite of herself. "Everybody and anybody. Or so it seems."

"Well, they're right! And what does all that worry get you? Nothing but stomach ulcers and trouble! Now, you take my advice, and—what is it they say these days—you loosen up!"

Erin grinned and impulsively gave the little old woman a bear hug. "You're right," she murmured, and patted the elderly woman's frail shoulder.

"Of course I am! You should do yourself a favor and listen to me more often," Mrs. Cavenaugh rejoined with a proud lift of her chin. "And...if you're as smart as I think you are, you'll put your hooks into that Webster fellow in a big hurry!"

"Mrs. Cavenaugh! Have you been spying on me?" Erin inquired with mock dismay.

The older woman shook her gray head savagely. "Just looking out for your best interests, honey. That's all!" Then, with a dismissive shrug of her thin shoulders, she added, "Call it spying, if you will. But somebody's got to take care of you. I saw the way that ex-husband of yours treated you—and I want to make sure that you don't get hurt again..."

Erin tried to protest, but the severity of Mrs. Cavenaugh's wizened blue eyes held her tongue.

"Now...this Webster fellow, I've seen the way he looks at you."

"And?"

"Unless I miss my guess, which isn't very often, I'd say he's fallen head over heels for you!"

"You can't be serious!"

But the knowing and pleased look on Mrs. Cavenaugh's weathered face added silent conviction to the little old lady's words.

"I… I had better be running along," Erin said a little breathlessly as she thought about Mrs. Cavenaugh's words. Could she possibly be right? Erin picked up her purse and her briefcase and called over her shoulder, "Don't worry about the mess in the hallway, Mrs. Cavenaugh. I'll have the janitor clean it in the morning…."

"Oh, Erin," the lady at the bottom of the stairs beckoned.

"Yes." Erin turned to look back down at her, and she could tell that the woman was struggling with some sort of decision.

"I thought that maybe you'd want to know—Lee was here today, asking about you."

"What?"

"He left you a note, I think." Her blue eyes beseeched Erin. "Everything's okay, isn't it?"

Erin hesitated only slightly. "Of course,"

she managed, but she heard the hollow sound of her own words. As she mounted the final stairs to her apartment, she heard Mrs. Cavenaugh's door close and the sharp sound of a bolt being turned in the lock. All of the airy feeling that had cascaded over her from Mrs. Cavenaugh's suspicions about Kane's feelings for her had vanished at the mention of Lee. As she thought about it Erin wondered how the little old lady had even seen Kane, but there was something in Mrs. Cavenaugh's pale blue eyes that bothered Erin. The dear little woman really believed that Kane was falling in love with her. But how would Mrs. Cavenaugh even suspect?

Erin shook her head and pulled the pins from her hair as she closed the door to her loft. If only she could believe that Kane could love her or at least learn to love her. Erin's vivid imagination began to run wild.

But just as her heart began to race in anticipation of Kane's love, her rational mind cooled her response. What about the wariness she had sensed in the steely depths of Kane's gray eyes? Why did she always feel that he was studying her—trying to read her mind? Why did she feel that he didn't completely trust her? Her blood cooled and a shudder raced up her spine. The situation was impossible.

It was then that she noticed the white envelope that had been shoved under her door. The note from Lee.

Chapter 8

It had been nearly two weeks since Erin had found the note thrust intrusively into her apartment. The message was a simple request, "Please call," and a number that she recognized as a suburban Seattle telephone listing. She had tried to call Lee once, but was relieved when no one answered. Several other times she had been tempted to try and reach him once more, but before she had found the nerve to dial the number, she had changed her mind and left well enough alone. If he really needed her, she reasoned, he would get in touch with her again. A few times she had wadded up the note in an effort to throw it away, but she hadn't. This morning the note was once again before her as she leaned against the kitchen counter, studiously stirring a bit of honey into her tea. It sat menacingly on the counter, inviting her to make a call that she knew would only bring her more heartache. Was she a coward? Why did she let him linger near her to remind her of the past and the pain.

She took an experimental sip of the warm amber liquid. As the hot tea slid down her throat, Erin thought about the past two weeks of her life. The days had gone fairly well. On the surface it seemed as if everything in the office was running efficiently, just as a well-oiled banking machine should. For the first time in months Erin had cleaned out her pending probate file along with a series of other nagging paperwork problems that had been building on the corner of her desk for several weeks. Her fear over gossip or rumors spreading concerning her relationship with Kane had been unfounded, other than the one unfortunate and vicious incident with Olivia. Kane proved himself to be a capable and fair employer, and outwardly Erin appeared to enjoy working for him. It had even been possible for her to work professionally with Kane by forcing her personal feelings for him into the background and never letting her emotions color her objectivity or judgment. It had been excruciatingly difficult at times not to reach out and touch him or smooth the worried look from his brow. But she had managed to look the part of a disinterested employee. At least she hoped so.

It was the nights that disturbed her, she realized now as she moved restlessly from the kitchen, taking the teacup and the crumpled note from Lee with her. Then, after carefully setting the teacup on the coffee table, she spread out the crushed piece of paper and smoothed its creases against the arm of the sofa. The seven digits of Lee's home phone leaped out at her, and in a moment of sudden decisiveness, she shredded the note into tiny pieces and tossed them disgustedly away in the wastebasket, something she should have done two weeks ago!

Erin sunk into the soft rose-colored cushions of the couch and continued to reflect on the changes in her life. When she was alone with Kane, she felt a freedom and a rapture that were hard to describe, an enthusiasm and exhilaration that she thought had been lost with her teens. Just the light touch of his hand on her shoulder or his throaty whispered voice could send her spiraling into an emotional bliss that was both wonderful and frightening. Never had she given her heart so willingly or so easily. She knew that a part of Kane wanted to love her; she could feel it as they made love. But for some unknown reason, he wouldn't let himself enjoy the pleasure of loving her. At first she had thought that the failure of his marriage had hardened him against a commitment to the future, but lately she had sensed that it was a more personal problem that made him withdraw. A problem somehow directly relating to her.

She shook her tangled curls and looked into the teacup as if she might find the answer to her dilemma in its amber-colored depths. Why the restlessness? Why did she feel like an aerialist carefully balancing her life on a flimsy tightrope and knowing that sometime, although she couldn't be quite sure exactly when, the tense, frail wire would snap and send her catapulting downward into an empty black emotional abyss? The conflicting roles of daytime employee and nighttime lover were constantly at war in her mind.

Erin sighed deeply and ran her fingernails in deep grooves along the overstuffed arm of the antique sofa. There were times when she was alone with Kane that the stone wall of wariness in his eyes would weaken, and she would feel an exquisite happiness, the blush of love. But on other occasions, when she lay alone in her bed, listening as he drove off into the night, she discovered a sense of desperation and loneliness that caused feverish nightmares to disturb her sleep.

Why the torment? Where was the relationship leading them? Why couldn't she come to grips with and accept the affair for what it was—a pleasant, sensuous experience? Why did she insist on coloring her feelings with love?

A key turned in the lock. Kane had returned. Erin could feel herself beginning to coil in tension. Nervously she waited for him to enter—just as he had every night for the past two weeks. But tonight would be different, she vowed to herself. Tonight she would insist upon answers. Why was there always a darkness in his eyes?

Kane entered the room and shut the door behind him. The stern look on his face only made Erin's heart hammer more wildly. He was dressed casually in jeans and a tan pullover sweater. His chestnut hair was slightly messy as if he had forgotten about it over the last few hours. It was obvious that he had hurriedly stopped by his hotel before coming to see her. Unusual. The pattern of their life together had been established over the last two weeks, but this Friday night was obviously different to Kane as well as Erin. Even under the intensity of his gaze she reminded herself that she had to know, tonight, what it was that held him away from her.

"Pack your bags," Kane commanded without even a smile as a greeting. She jumped at his abrupt command, and for a moment his arctic gray eyes collided with hers. She felt a chill of dread pass over her body. His mouth was a tight, grim line that was neither a smile nor a frown. The grooves across his forehead seemed deeper tonight, as if he, too, had been wrestling with a troublesome and weighty decision.

"Do what?" she asked incredulously. Surprise and indignation registered in the startled expression that crossed her face. She was still sitting on the couch with her legs curled up and tucked underneath her. She almost dropped her teacup at his abrasive command.

Kane ignored her question. Preoccupied, he paced distractedly in front of the couch, his fists balled deeply in the pockets of his jeans. As he passed in front of her, Erin couldn't help but notice that his jeans, slung low in the waist, strained against his thighs and buttocks with each of his long strides. As he paced she was reminded of a caged animal, and she could almost visualize his tightly controlled muscles rippling beneath the fabric of his clothing. Forcefully she pulled her attention away from his virile male anatomy and tried to read the expression on his face.

"Didn't you hear me?" he growled, and stopped his absent pacing. "I asked you to go and pack."

"No, you didn't," she corrected, her eyes locking with his. "You *ordered* me to pack without so much as a greeting or explanation!"

Anger snapped in his eyes, but his reply was strangely soothing. The rage that was burning quietly within him was controlled. "You're right," he expelled in a long breath, "and I'm sorry. I… I'm a little distracted this evening," he offered as an apology.

"I noticed!" she retorted, and then seeing the worried creases that pulled his thick dark brows together in concern, she amended her hot retort. "I guess it's my turn to apologize," she admitted wearily. "I didn't mean to snap. I've been a little distracted myself."

"Oh?"

"Nothing to be concerned about," she averred with a wan smile, and wondered why she didn't have the strength of character to lay her cards on the table and confront him with her unanswered questions about their relationship and the future. Instead she chose to sidestep the issue. "Now." She smiled feebly, luminous lilac eyes looking pleadingly up at him. "What's been bothering you?"

"Oh, God, Erin," he moaned and let his forehead drop to his hand in a gesture of total defeat. He raked long tense fingers through the wheat-colored highlights of his burnished hair. How could he explain that he was only a hairbreadth away from confirming his suspicions about her? Could she imagine how close he was coming to finding all of the pieces of the puzzle that would tie her into the embezzling scandal? Although everything was still circumstantial, it was stacking together so neatly that it was actually beginning to scare Kane. Although no more money had been taken from the bank, the most damning piece of evidence that he had found so far—a discrepancy in the securities cart key registration—proved as well as anything that Erin had been lying to him. How long did she expect the charade to work? How could he help her and get her out of this mess? What could he do? It would all be so much easier if he just didn't give a damn!

"Kane," Erin said unsteadily, still sitting, looking both childlike and wise at the same moment. Oh, God, he thought, was she going to confess? Could he bear it? His muscles tensed, and he could feel the pressure as his jaws tightened together in a viselike grip. "Is there anything I can do?" she offered in a whisper.

Erin had noticed Kane stiffen at the sound of her voice, and she was aware that the wall between them was rigidly back in place, but she felt a strangling need to climb the invisible barrier and reach out to him. Why was he suffering so?

"There's nothing you can do," he stated flatly. "There's nothing anyone can do."

She twisted her fingers together. "Is it Krista?" she asked with a shaky breath.

His gray eyes smoldered with indecision. "That's part of it," he conceded, and hated himself for his duplicity. Dropping his body down on the couch next to her, he let his head fall backward as if it were too heavy to support. He sat staring ahead, with only inches separating him from her. Her senses were alive to him, her nerve endings stretched taut. Erin could feel the heat of his body, smell the inviting scent of his aftershave, see the darkening shadow of his beard. But he still didn't touch her. His hands rubbed thoughtfully against his knees, and he looked straight ahead through the window into the late-afternoon sky. "I talked with Krista again today," he said in a voice that seemed remote.

"And?" Erin prodded, not knowing why she should be concerned with Kane's reclusive daughter.

"She doesn't want to move to Seattle," he sighed, and drummed his fingers against his thigh. "Absolutely refuses!"

He turned his head to look in her direction and their eyes met in a chilly embrace. "I'm going to California next week to get her and move her up to Seattle with me."

"And you're worried about her and the adjustment," Erin guessed.

"Wouldn't you be?"

"That goes without saying. Is…there anything I can do to make it easier on you?"

"Would you come to California with me?"

"To get Krista?" At Kane's cursory nod, Erin expelled a long breath and shook her head firmly and negatively. "I don't think that would be a very good idea. She's going to have to adjust to a whole new city. I think you should be alone with her. She doesn't need the intrusion of a virtual stranger."

She could see in his eyes that she had convinced him and she continued, "But if there's anything else that I can do...."

"There is something," he suggested, and for a moment the tension seemed to vanish.

"What?"

"Pack your bags for the weekend" was the brief reply, but the passion that had been lurking in his eyes came alive. His silvery eyes embraced hers, and he reached for her hand. His thumb drew slow, lazy circles on the inside of her wrist, and heat began to climb up her body. "Oh, Erin," he breathed, and his lips found hers in a feverish kiss that seemed to pulsate with need and urgency. When he dragged his mouth away from the supple curve of her lips, he looked savagely into her eyes, asking questions that she couldn't understand. Then a softness stole over his features as he took a handful of her hair in his palm and pressed her head against the protection of his chest. In a ragged breath he asked, "Do you know how hard it's been for me, forcing myself to keep my hands off you at the office?" He growled deep in his throat. "There were times when I thought I would actually go insane, having you so close and not being able to touch you...."

Her arms circled his waist, and she kissed the swell of his cheek. "I know..."

"No, I don't think that you can imagine what it's like—seeing you every day and not being able to touch what is mine."

"Yours? Possessive, aren't you?" she quipped sarcastically.

"Absolutely!" His grip on her tightened, and when she tilted her face to meet his, the warmth of his lips captured hers in a passion that spread fire through her veins. With great difficulty she pulled her head away from his.

"What did you say about packing my bags?" she inquired, trying to ignore the warm intimacy of his breath as it tickled her face.

"You and I are getting away for the weekend," he stated, and with apparent effort he released her from his tenacious embrace. "Hurry up," he ordered. "We don't have all day. I want to get moving before we run out of daylight!"

"Kane!" Erin said with mild irritation. "What are you talking about? Where are we going? Why do I need to pack?"

His smile twisted grimly and Erin saw the weariness and cynicism deep in his crystal gray eyes. "You and I are leaving this city, the bank—" his eyes swept the homey apartment "—this house, everything! We're going to get lost in the wild for a couple of days!"

"The wild?"

"That's right!" Half dragging her into the bedroom, he opened the closet, against her protests, and found her suitcase. "I'm tired of sneaking out of your bed in the middle of the night like some…gigolo!" He ignored Erin's gasp of indignation and began opening her bureau drawers. She caught his reflection in the mirror and saw that a hard, tense mask had come over his angular features. He looked up, his gray eyes held hers and he said with disgust, "And I'm tired of not being able to touch you in the light of day!" His hands were pressed firmly on the dresser top, and he pinioned her with his gaze, cold and distant, in the looking glass. Tense fingers slowly rubbed the wooden surface of the dresser. "Damn it, woman!" His fist pounded against the cool wood. "I'm sick of hiding, and I won't do it anymore! So, beginning to-night, we are not going to keep this affair in the dark, as if we're ashamed of it! You and your paranoia over rumors can go to blazes!" He spit the words out as if they were a bad taste in his mouth. His anger was burning in the darkness of his gaze.

"Kane," Erin implored. "Why are you so upset? What…"

"Look, Erin. We've played the game your way for nearly two weeks, and it's tearing me apart!" His entire body tensed for a second before he took in a long steadying breath and controlled the note of rage that had entered his speech. In a softer voice he continued, "Let's have an entire weekend alone together—what do you say?"

"I don't understand…"

"Let's go somewhere where we can walk in the sunlight together—where we can be seen kissing…."

"Is this what's been bothering you?" she asked, as she put a staying hand on his sleeve.

"Oh, Erin," he sighed, holding her at arm's length and letting his eyes search her face. "There are so many things that are bothering me," he admitted, and a tortured look twisted his features.

"Can we talk about them?" she asked quietly.

"That's exactly what I have in mind. But I thought a change of scenery might do us both some good."

"You know that I can't leave at the drop of a hat."

"Why not?"

"My tenants… I've got an advertisement in the paper to rent the apartment downstairs."

"The apartment on the first floor, across the hall from Milly?" he asked.

"That's the one—how did you get on a first-name basis with Mrs. Cavenaugh?" Erin asked, a suspicious black eyebrow arching heavenward.

"That little old lady has excellent taste," he laughed. "She likes me."

"And she told you about the vacant apartment?" Erin guessed.

"That's right," he agreed with a smile that any Cheshire cat would envy.

"Then you understand why I have to stay here…"

"Don't worry about the apartment," he said dismissively. "I'll rent it until I find a more permanent residence. Does it have two bedrooms?"

"Of course, but—"

"Then it will be perfect!" he exclaimed.

"Perfect? For what?"

"Krista and myself."

"I don't know…"

His eyes grew dark. "It's the perfect solution to our problem."

Her breath caught in her throat. "I didn't know that we had a problem," she returned, and began to place her undergarments in the open suitcase on the bed. Was he actually going to tell her what had been bothering him, why he had been so wary of her?

He came up behind her and let his arms encircle her waist. His words fanned her hair and the sensitive skin at the back of her neck. He captured the black silk and entwined it in his fingers. Burying his face in her hair, he groaned. "The problem is that I want to be near you…always!" The confession was a tortured, unwonted admission.

"What are you saying?" she asked, and a tightness constricted her breath.

"I want to live with you!"

Her voice was unsteady. "And what about Krista? What would she think about her fa-

ther and his business associate living together? What kind of example would we set?
No, Kane…" She shook her head sadly. "It
wouldn't work!"

"Lots of people…"

"I'm not 'lots of people,'" she interrupted.

"So I noticed," he agreed, and his hands
slowly kneaded the softness of her abdomen.
Warm curling sensations grew to life within
her. Slowly he stopped his seductive movements. "I'm sorry," he whispered. "I'm pushing you too quickly. Let's forget the entire
suggestion—for the time being. But, please
come and spend the weekend with me…"

Pulling herself away from him, she planted
a fist firmly against her hip and forced back
a smile that flirted with her lips. "I'll come
with you—on one condition!"

Kane crossed his arms over his chest
and leaned against the dresser. The sweater
strained across his shoulders. "Okay. I'm
game. What's the condition?"

"That for once you tell me where you plan
on taking me!"

"Spoilsport!"

"Kane!"

"Where's that girl who loves mystery and

old movies?" he inquired, a twinkle coming to his eyes.

"You're not going to tell me, are you?"

"Not unless you think of some wildly erotic torture that will force me into submission."

"Dreamer," she shot back at him, before turning to pack.

The small motorboat churned through the cold gray waters of Puget Sound and out toward the Pacific Ocean. When Erin had stepped into the tiny vessel, she had guessed that Kane was taking her to San Juan Island, but he had preferred to keep the destination and his secret to himself. Now, as the frigid salt spray tickled her nose and clung to her hair, she was grateful that she had had the foresight to bring her down jacket with her. She drew the warm collar closer to her neck in an effort to keep the moisture-laden air off her skin.

By the time they reached Orcas Island the sun had set, and only a long orange glow remained along the horizon. Night was closing in, and the lights of Deer Harbor winked like silvery diamonds against the black island as the launch continued on its journey around the small piece of land.

Erin rubbed her hands together, and then pushed them deep into her pockets in an effort to warm herself. At that moment the rhythmic rumble of the small craft's engine slowed, and Kane maneuvered the boat inland. It was difficult to see clearly in the evening light, but Erin made out a small cove with a relatively private beach and a ramshackle cabin.

Kane cut the engine and jumped out onto the private dock. He secured the craft and helped Erin out of the boat. Her eyes swept the beach until she spotted the cabin. A slow smile spread over her features.

"Well, what do you think?" Kane asked, his arm draped possessively over her slim shoulders.

"I think this all looks suspiciously like a set from one of those 1940s, black-and-white, slice-of-life movies," she commented as her eyes studied the small cozy cabin and its state of apparent neglect.

"I knew you'd like it," Kane replied with a self-satisfied smile. "Come on. Let's take a look inside…"

The cabin was, if nothing else, rustic. A broad, sagging front porch protected the front door. The cabin was constructed of cedar, and to Erin's discriminating eye, had never been painted. It bore the weathered look of exposed gray wood blanched by the salt of the sea. At one end of the porch a worn rope hammock swung in the breeze coming off the ocean. The front door groaned as it was opened, and the interior of the cabin had a musty, unused odor. There was no electricity, but running water was pumped into the kitchen. A woodstove in the kitchen and a massive stone fireplace at one end of the living area provided the only sources of heat in the building. Erin surveyed the cabin with a skeptical eye. She had never been much of a believer in "roughing it" when modern conveniences were the available alternative.

Kane unpacked the boat and started searching for firewood, while Erin lit the rose-colored kerosene lamps and removed the dustcovers from the furniture. To air out the interior, she opened all the windows, heedless of the chill in the air, and felt the tickle of salt air burn in her lungs.

The cabin was rather barren, and what little furniture there was appeared threadbare. But she had to admit that once she had swept the dust from the floor, and the fire was lit, the warm scent of burning wood mingled with the fresh fragrance of the salt sea air, and the cabin seemed bearable, if not cheerfully inviting. Fortunately Kane had the foresight to stop off at a delicatessen in Seattle before picking up Erin, and he had purchased sandwiches and a bottle of wine. Erin rummaged in the old-fashioned kitchen and was able to find an unopened package of paper cups along with a tarnished but necessary corkscrew for the wine.

Pleased with her discoveries, she retraced her footsteps back into the living area. Brandishing the corkscrew dramatically in the air, she captured Kane's attention. *"Voilà!"* she announced theatrically, and placed the cups on the floor next to the couch.

Because of the chill of the evening sea breeze, Kane was closing the final window in an effort to retain the heat from the fireplace when Erin reentered the room. He snapped the window latch closed and turned to face Erin, who wondered aloud, "How in the world did you ever find this place?"

"It's not exactly moonlight and roses, is it?" he asked, crossing the room to the fireplace. He squatted near the golden flames and warmed his palms against the heat that the fire offered.

"Who needs moonlight and roses?" she asked rhetorically, and shrugged.

"Don't you?" Gray eyes searched her face as if she were a puzzle to him.

"I'm a little too much of a realist to think that the world revolves around silver moonlight, cut flowers and soft music," she admitted dryly.

"Are you?" A smile of disbelief tugged at the corners of his mouth.

"Does it matter?" she asked, and unwrapped the sandwiches. "Anyway, you're avoiding my question—how did you come to find this private little hideaway?"

After dusting his hands on his jeans, Kane sat down next to her on the floor, allowing the slightly weathered couch to support his head and shoulders. His long legs stretched in front of him, and nearly reached the warm red coals of the fire. Erin silently offered him a sandwich, which he gratefully accepted, and between bites he explained.

"As you already know, I'm looking for a permanent residence for Krista and myself in Seattle. I read the classified ads every day, hoping to find something suitable." He paused to open the wine and poured the cool clear liquid into the paper cups. The light from the fire reflected and danced against the deep green bottle and in his clear gray eyes.

"Anyway—" he shrugged, as if it wasn't all that important "—I came across an ad for this place. I've always had a fascination for the sea and the wilderness, not to mention rustic old cabins. And I thought it would be good for Krista. This place sounded perfect."

Erin nearly choked on the wine that she had been sipping. She eyed the interior of the cabin speculatively. "You're not telling me that you bought this place sight unseen?" she gasped, unable to shake the astounded look from her face. It hardly seemed "perfect" for anyone, much less an eleven-year-old girl bound to a wheelchair! Erin surveyed the living quarters more closely. The old cabin needed a lot of work. The cleaning alone would take several days, and the varnish on the pine walls was cracking and beginning to peel. There was no hot water, the floors needed to be refinished, and the furniture— all of it needed to be replaced or repaired. The list of jobs seemed endless to her practiced eye.

Kane watched Erin with obvious amusement. The deep-timbred tones of his laughter drew her attention back to him. "No," he laughed, "I haven't bought this place. In fact, this weekend is just a trial run. A widow owns the place, but she hasn't been up here since her husband died a couple of years ago. She knows that I'm interested in buying it, but she agreed to rent it to me for the weekend—to look around for myself."

"You're really serious about buying it?" Erin gasped. "It doesn't even have electricity!"

"Part of its charm, wouldn't you say?" He grinned at her obvious dismay.

"It's your money," she conceded with a dismissive shrug, and took another sip of her wine. The bright embers from the fire and the heady effect of the wine lured her into a serene sense of complacency. She watched Kane over the rim of her cup, and noticed the mood swing that seemed to come over him.

At her offhand comment about money, Kane stiffened. "That it is," he agreed almost inaudibly. He set the remains of his uneaten dinner aside, and stared into the orange and black coals of the fire. His mood had indeed shifted, and Erin, even in her peaceful state, could sense that the tension was coiling within him again.

The fire crackled and popped as it burned

the pitch-darkened wood. The movements of the flames reflected in menacing shadows over the angular structure of Kane's masculine face. His question surprised Erin.

"Did you know that Mitchell Cameron's arraignment hearing is scheduled for late this week?" he asked in an accusatory voice. Gray eyes slid sideways, trying to catch her reaction. His pose was relaxed, his hands crossed comfortably over his chest, but Erin could sense the strain due to the twist in the conversation, and saw the tense rigidity of the muscles in his face.

"I read about it in the paper," she replied unevenly. Carefully, with nervous hands, she set aside the rest of her suddenly unappetizing sandwich and took another drink from her cup. The cool wine felt smooth against the rough texture of her throat. Mitchell Cameron had become a taboo subject between Erin and Kane, a topic that was never brought out into the open. It was as if, by silent agreement, neither person would chance the subject of Mitch. For reasons Erin didn't understand, the subject of Mitch was a potential powder keg. Why then, tonight, would Kane turn the conversation in Mitch's direction?

Kane's voice broke into her fragmented

thoughts. "There's a chance that I'll be out of town at the time of the hearing."

"But don't you have to testify?"

"I've already signed a sworn deposition," was the clipped reply. "I'm sure it will satisfy the court."

"Oh, Kane." Erin sighed, suddenly feeling very tired and unnerved. "Are you sure that you want to prosecute Mitch?" she asked, her hand reaching out to touch his shoulder.

He withdrew as quickly as if he had been seared by her touch. Twisting his head to meet her startled gaze, he drew his lips into a thin and menacingly grim line. "Is that what this is all about?" he demanded, and grabbed her wrist harshly.

"What—I don't understand!"

"Is that what you want, for me to drop the charges against your ex-employer? Is that why you've been so willing?" Steely eyes swept over her body and charged her with a crime she couldn't understand.

"Why, you...bastard!" she gasped, suddenly understanding at least a part of his vicious accusation. Involuntarily she drew her free hand backward in an effort to slap him. But she stopped in midswing as the same tortured look that she had seen so often in the past softened the severity of his dark gaze.

He dropped her wrist and closed his eyes for a second. "I'm sorry," he whispered huskily.

"You should be!"

"All right!" He reached a hesitant hand to her cheek and caressed its regal lines with exploring and sensitive fingers. "I have no choice," he assured her. "I have to prosecute Cameron. The board of directors would insist upon it, the bonding insurance company...."

"But if you did have a choice?" Liquid violet eyes melted into his, and he drew his caressing hand away from her face.

"Nothing would change! I would still prosecute!" He stood up and put some distance between her body and his. He found it difficult to think when he looked at her or touched her. She was too close to him and to the truth. Perhaps, even now, she knew that he suspected her of involvement in the embezzlement. He had to be cautious with her—or did he? Damn it! Never in his life had he let a woman come between him and his purpose in life. Never had a woman been so intimately involved in his private thoughts. Dear God, why did it have to be this woman who attracted him so achingly? His thoughts weighed heavily on him, and he leaned against the broad mantel of the fireplace and let his head rest against the worn wood. He needed time to think, time alone, to put his life in perspective. It was a mistake bringing her to this isolated haven; he should have realized that before he insisted that she accompany him. How could he have been such a fool? Where was his common sense? His voice, a throaty whisper, crept across the thick silence that separated them.

"Can't you understand, Erin?" he pleaded. "Mitchell Cameron is a crook, and he has to pay."

"But surely, as president of the bank, with your influence..."

His gray eyes held hers frozen. "Oh, God, Erin. My influence has nothing to do with my *responsibility*!"

"Why is the subject of Mitch always so difficult?"

"You tell me!"

"I don't know!" she admitted honestly.

The silence was an electric current that seemed to bind them together and yet sever whatever peace they had shared. Kane eyed Erin with a haunted wariness that seemed to tire him, and Erin watched him with eyes naked in love and confusion. What was he trying to say?

He leaned against the mantel and rubbed the base of his head with his palm. He closed his eyes and gritted his teeth, as if he were trying to rid his body of tension. Slowly he seemed to relax; his tight muscles lengthened. With the effort his weight sagged wearily against the fireplace. "I think," he managed to say, "that you and I should drop the subject of Mitchell Cameron until after the arraignment hearing."

Erin let out a steadying breath. "Do you really suppose that I can just ignore the fact that Mitch's fate depends on your decision?"

"Correction," he cautioned sharply. "His fate depends upon his decision, one that was made quite some time ago. Not mine! I had nothing to do with it except unfortunately to catch a thief."

"I don't know that I can just erase it from my mind—as if we've never had this conversation."

"Just for the weekend?" he suggested, and bent near to her. He took both of her hands in his and forced her to look deeply into his eyes. "I'm sorry for the outburst. The past two weeks have been a strain on both of us," he said in an effort at apology. "But let's just spend this time together and get to know each other a little better." Deep lines of intense thought creased his forehead. "I—well, I need some time with you. Alone. Apart from Mitchell Cameron and the rest of the world." His voice was a reluctant plea, and before she could answer him, he buried his head between her breasts and held her close to him. "Oh, Erin," he whispered, his hot breath tantalizing her skin and arousing her breasts to an aching tautness. "Why do you tempt me so?"

Ignoring the doubts and warnings that still crowded her mind, she felt herself surrender to him, and her hands wound themselves in the thick strands of his burnished hair. Feeling her reaction, he slowly pulled his head away from the softness of her body and looked longingly into her eyes. Her breath came in short gasps, and she felt the warmth of desire curling upward in her body. A nearly wicked grin stole over his face as his fingers played with the buttons of her blouse. She made no move to stop him, and when the blouse finally parted, his gaze sought and found the swollen ripeness of her breasts.

She longed to be touched by him, to feel the heat of his body capture her soul and the essence of her being. Red and orange flames were reflected in the burning passion of his gaze.

"Do you know, do you have any idea, just how much I need you?" he asked, before covering her lips with his and seeking the open invitation of her warm, moist mouth. She couldn't get enough of him. The delicious scent and tantalizing taste of his body, in kisses flavored by the wine, lingered upon her lips and teased her senses into a yearning ache that she couldn't control. His lips explored the length of her body, all of her, gently nuzzling the hollow of her shoulder, rimming her ear, searching out the soft flat contour of her abdomen. "Dear God, how I want you," he admitted.

"Then love me, Kane, love me," she pleaded.

"I will, Erin," he vowed, and moved over her, gently probing the most intimate part of her. Even in her drugged sense of well-being, she realized that he was speaking only of physical love, not the eternal love that she had requested. But for the moment it was enough.

Chapter 9

The two days that they spent together on the island were carefree and warm. After a light cover of morning fog, the late-autumn sun would warm the sand, and for the most part the days were crisply cool and invigoratingly clear.

Erin taught Kane how to dig for razor clams along the edge of the tide, and after a few hesitant tries, he became rather adept at kneeling in the wet sand and furiously shoveling after the escaping mollusks. Once, when a particularly large wave caught him off guard and sent him sprawling headlong into the bitter, cold surf, Erin laughed, only to find herself dragged down into the icy water by Kane.

"That will teach you not to make sport of me," he quipped, before kissing her soundly on her bluish lips. Another cold wave climbed over them, and they both hurried indoors to escape the frigid water and the cool air of autumn. They stripped off the wet, sandy clothes in front of the fire, while warming hot water to clean up the grit from the beach that had clung to their skin.

For most of the two short days, they spent their time beachcombing or taking the boat into nearby Deer Harbor for sightseeing and browsing in the various antiques stores. It was a wonderful time to be together, and by the end of the weekend, Erin found herself more in love with Kane than she ever imagined possible. She hated the thought of leaving the island and dreaded returning to the city, the job and the pressures that always seemed to build between them at home. She enjoyed the freedom that the island provided and loved being alone with Kane, loved touching him whenever she had the desire, and loved kissing him in the light of day, unafraid of what others might think. Disturbingly she wondered if it was such a fairy-tale existence that it could never be re-created, only remembered. All too soon it would end.

During the nights they spread a large sleeping bag on the floor in front of the fire, rather than chancing the well-worn and musty bed in the attached bedroom. They spent hours in front of the fire, talking, laughing and making love until dawn.

It was a glorious, heady experience. The entire weekend was too good to last.

When, finally, after what seemed a short afternoon, the sun began to set against the cold gray sea, Erin found Kane standing studiously on the porch. She had packed together all of her things, and she knew that it was well past the hour that Kane had planned to leave. And still he lingered. He half stood, half leaned against the railing and stared endlessly out toward the broad expanse of the ocean and into the beckoning twilight.

Quietly Erin watched him. She knew that he, too, was hesitant to leave the solitude of the romantic haven that this otherwise miserable excuse for a cabin had provided for them. She lowered her body into the rope hammock, which sagged and groaned against her weight. The noise distracted Kane, and he slowly turned to face her. His eyes were distant; his mind was light-years away. Lazily he leaned against the post that supported the roof of the porch and let his eyes slide caressingly over her body.

"I'm…ready to go," she stated. It was a poor attempt at conversation.

"Are you?" he drawled.

"Everything's packed. We really should get going."

"I know," he agreed reluctantly, and looked longingly once more at the ceaseless gray tide. He spoke softly, as if to himself. "It surprises me that I'm not itching to get back to the office. Usually I'm anxious and just can't wait to get back behind my desk. But tonight—I don't know—it all seems so pointless."

When he faced her once again, his gray eyes moved over her face, as if he were memorizing every contour of her creamy skin. He made a simple statement with measured slowness. "I'm going to buy this cabin. We'll come back together."

"I hope so," she breathed, and wondered why it was so important to her. Unconsciously she clung to the first promise that hinted of a future that they might somehow share together.

The week that followed was a dismal and lonely time for Erin. As Kane had promised, he refused to keep their affair quiet or in the dark. Although he didn't actually make an announcement of the fact, his cold indifference in the office had disappeared, and it was with difficulty that Erin had managed to keep up appearances during working hours. His eyes caressed her, and his affection was never hidden. Although inwardly Erin was pleased, she couldn't help but notice the reaction of the other employees of the bank, the expressively uplifted eyebrows whenever she was with Kane and the accusatory glances that were cast her way when she wasn't with him. She tried to ignore the gossip that was blazing through the bank, but she couldn't calm the churning of her stomach.

When Kane had to leave on Wednesday for California, Erin was slightly relieved that the pressure of keeping him at arm's length at the office would be relieved for a while.

It was on Friday morning when everything seemed to happen at once. Kane's absence, as expected, had created a little extra work for Erin as well as the rest of the staff, but what she hadn't anticipated was an outbreak of the flu, leaving the office very shorthanded. Nor had she expected that the bank's main computer would break down, slowing the month-end posting to a snail's pace. It was a hectic, frustrating day, and when the telephone rang for what seemed to be the twentieth time within the span of five minutes, Erin couldn't keep the tight strain of anxiety out of her normally composed voice.

"Miss O'Toole," she nearly shouted into the mouthpiece.

"Erin?" a familiar voice inquired.

"Mitch? Is that you? I've been trying to reach you for weeks," she exclaimed, and felt a pang of regret that she had answered the phone so harshly. "How are you?" she asked with genuine interest.

"I've been better," was the matter-of-fact reply.

"Oh, Mitch. I'm so sorry," she began, suddenly at a loss for words. What could she say to him? Any condolence sounded foolish.

"I know, Erin," he replied as if he really did understand that she still cared for him and considered him her friend.

There was an uncomfortable pause in the conversation, before Mitch cleared his throat indecisively and stated the reason for his call. "I was wondering if you would like to go to lunch with me today?" he inquired.

"Oh, Mitch, I'd love to, but I'm absolutely

swamped," Erin replied as she gazed at the stack of unanswered telephone messages that had been growing on the corner of her desk.

"Too busy for lunch with an old friend?" he joked, but the humor fell flat.

"Of course not. It's just that…well, Kane is out of town, and everyone here is down with the flu—including the computer."

There was a harsh laugh on the other end of the line. "Yeah, well, I get the message" was the curt retort. "Some other time…"

Indecision tore at Erin. She knew that today was the day of Mitch's arraignment hearing, and she also knew that if the judgment was turned against him, it was unlikely that she would see him again for an indefinite period of time. Kane wouldn't approve of a meeting with Mitch; Erin was sure of it, and yet he had no control over her friendship with Mitch. For once her reason was cast aside as she thought about the lonely man on the other end of the telephone line.

"Oh, Mitch," she said suddenly. "I'm sure I can meet with you today," she choked out. "I'll just have to make some room."

"Good!" Was there excessive relief in his voice? "How about Shorty's at one-thirty?"

"Perfect," she agreed lamely, and felt herself something of a traitor.

The few short hours until her agreed rendezvous with Mitch flew by, and with an uneasy feeling in the pit of her stomach, Erin set out on the short walk to a local pub known for its specialty: barbecued spareribs. Located in an older hotel in Pioneer Square, Shorty's had become a favorite with some of the employees of the bank, as much for its earthy San Francisco atmosphere as its flavorful food. Erin had been to the restaurant bar with Mitch several times in the past, but today, under the shroud of the allegations against him and the twisted set of circumstances surrounding them, she felt apprehensive about the lunch. *Don't be silly,* she chided herself. *This is the same old Gay Nineties restaurant, and he's the same old Mitch. Don't let any of this talk of embezzlement go to your head.* But still her stomach knotted, and without thinking, she pulled her pewter raincoat more closely around her throat and shook off a chill that ran up her spine.

She swung the heavy wooden door inward, and stepped into the dimly lit and secluded restaurant. The tangy odor of honey and tomato sauce assailed her nostrils, and she felt herself relax a little with the familiar aroma. It was forced, but she even managed a smile for the blond hostess who led Erin to a table where Mitch was already seated. She hadn't seen her ex-boss for over three weeks, and it was difficult to hide her surprise and embarrassment for the shell of a man that Mitch had become. Although more sober than the last time she had faced him, he carried with him a haunted look that destroyed the pleasantness of his face. His features, once bold, appeared gaunt, and his once-bright eyes had faded to a watery blue. A small, thin cigar was burning unattended in the ashtray.

At the sight of Erin, Mitch visibly brightened. His smile, though slightly strained at the corners, appeared genuine as he rose from the table while she was being seated. After she was comfortably settled in her chair, Mitch reached across the small table for her hand and clasped it warmly. "Erin," he shook his graying head in wonderment. "If possible, you're looking lovelier than ever!"

"Thank you," she murmured, and nervously pulled the napkin from the table in an effort to steady her hands. It wasn't like Mitch to gush, at least not the Mitch she remembered, and his bubbling enthusiasm seemed somehow phony and out of character. The uneasy feeling grew in the pit of her stomach. Perhaps it was the way he didn't quite meet her gaze, or the way he played with his cigar, but something about him made Erin definitely uncomfortable.

"So," he said with forced joviality, "how's it going at the old salt mine? Still as busy as ever?"

He had asked the question, but Erin had the distinct impression that he was totally uninterested in the topic that he had introduced.

"We're busy—all the time," she admitted, and when he didn't immediately respond, she continued chattering to break the uncomfortable silence that was building. "Kane— that is, Mr. Webster, has been out of town for a few days, and well, that just tends to make things all the more hectic for everyone else...." Why did she feel compelled to rattle on about the bank, and why did she feel so nervous around a friend whom she had once respected? She wiped her damp palms on the napkin in her lap.

The waiter deposited two platters of ribs on the table, and Erin turned her attention to the saucy food, hoping to dream up a polite way of excusing herself at the earliest possible moment. She knew now that it was a mistake to have met with Mitch; she wasn't ready to deal with him or any of the problems in his life. Loathing herself for her turn of feelings, she managed to continue to feign interest in her ribs, wondering why Mitchell Cameron had changed so much, and how she could manage an escape from the uncomfortable and intimate lunch.

It was then that Mitch brought up the subject of his courtroom hearing. "I suppose you know that the arraignment hearing is this afternoon?" he began slowly, and lit another cigar. His faded eyes waited to study her response.

"Oh, Mitch… I wish that all of this—problem—could be avoided," Erin claimed, and he could read the honesty in her eyes.

"Yes, well, it's a little too late for that now, isn't it?"

"I suppose so," she sighed, touching her napkin to her lips and pushing the uneaten ribs aside. Her appetite had diminished. "If there's anything I can do to help you, just let me know."

Blue eyes lighted. "There is something." His voice was bitter cold.

"Oh? What?"

Mitch shifted uncomfortably in his chair. "Nothing much." He shrugged his shoulders and reached inside of his jacket for a neatly folded piece of paper. "I was hoping that you could borrow a little information from the bank...."

"What?" she asked, perplexed, and ran a shaky hand through her sleekly restrained hair. "Information? What information?"

Mitch waved off her questions dismissively with the clean white envelope. "Well, it's really not all that important, except that I can't get my hands on the records, as I'm no longer employed with the bank." He puffed furiously on his cigar, cloaking his head in a thin veil of blue smoke as he offered her the envelope.

Reluctantly she reached for the paper, as her uneasy stomach began to churn. "This information—what do you need it for?"

"I know it's rather sudden," Mitch rattled on, "but I need documents that would help clear my name. Bank records, trust documents, computer printouts on the dividend accounts, stock certificate registrations... nothing all that important...."

"You're not serious!"

"Of course I'm serious. Everything I need is listed in there." He pointed dramatically to the envelope that Erin was holding. She dropped it onto the table.

"Mitch!" Erin's cool voice was tightly formal. "Are you suggesting that I confiscate private bank records and give them to you?"

"Not give... I just want to borrow the stuff, until I can get this embezzlement fiasco straightened out."

"But you know that I can't do that," Erin exclaimed. "For one thing it's against the law. All that information is confidential!"

"Erin!" Mitch interrupted her. "This is my life that we're talking about. I face more years in prison than you'd want to count!" His eyes beseeched her, but she didn't waver. She spread her hands against the linen-clad table, and looked him directly in the eyes.

"Mitch, you know I'd love to help you out, but you can't expect me to do anything illegal, for God's sake!"

He chewed on his cigar and rolled it from one side of his mouth to the other. All the while, his watery blue eyes impaled her.

"Can't your attorney subpoena the information that you need? Why come to me?"

"It would be better for me this way, Erin. Otherwise I'd never put you on the spot. You know that. But any information that my attorney subpoenas will be sifted through by the prosecution. If they don't know about the information until the time of the hearing, I could get the jump on them. You know, surprise the court, confuse the D.A., perhaps avoid the indictment!"

Erin began to shake her head in a negative sweep. "You're just putting off the inevitable. You can't expect me to take such a chance. I…can't…"

"And I counted on you as a friend," Mitch spat out with a bitterness that chilled the air.

"I—we are friends."

"No, you've got that one wrong, Erin, dead wrong!" he snapped, waving an angry accusatory finger and his cigar within inches of her face. "We were friends when it was convenient for you—when I was your boss, and I could help you. Especially when that jerk of a husband dumped on you and you needed a shoulder to cry on. But now, when the tables have turned, our friendship seems to be wearing a little thin, doesn't it?"

Erin drew in an unsteady and disbelieving breath. "You can't possibly mean what you're implying. You know that I care for you—I always have—but you're asking the impossible!"

"Ha!"

"Mitch…don't…"

"Don't what, Erin?" he taunted, all of his hatred coming to the surface. "Don't overextend your friendship? Don't ask you to help me, after I helped pull you back together during your divorce? Don't ask you to do anything that might endanger your fragile relationship with your new boss?"

"What?" she gasped, but the meaning of his words was clear.

"Don't give me that wide-eyed shocked virgin routine, Erin. It won't work. Besides, it's demeaning. I know that you're Kane Webster's mistress, and that you've been hopping in and out of bed with him since he first set foot in this town!"

All of the color in Erin's face washed away with Mitch's cruel words, and little protesting, choking noises came from somewhere in her throat. But Mitch's vicious tirade wasn't finished.

"You're surprised, aren't you. Well, let me tell you this—it's all over town!"

"No!"

His eyes narrowed evilly. "I never thought you would stoop so low as to sleep with such despicable scum as Webster. But then you've never had very good taste when it came to men, have you?"

"That's enough," she gasped, finding her voice and her purse at the same moment. "I'm leaving!"

"What's the trouble, Erin? Am I getting too close to the truth? I should never have promoted you over Olivia Parsons eight years ago. That's where I made my mistake."

Erin's lilac eyes flashed fire. "I'm sure she would agree with you." She stood and hurriedly pulled on her coat. "I don't know what it is that's making you so bitter...."

"The prospect of prison, Erin. It can be very frightening!"

"I'm sorry, Mitch, but there's absolutely nothing I can do." Her poise was beginning to come back to her. She sighed heavily. "But no matter what, if it's any consolation, I do wish you luck today."

"Sure you do," he echoed sarcastically. "Thanks but no thanks. I don't need your good wishes, Erin. Not now, not ever!"

Erin turned on her heels and didn't bother to say goodbye. Her back was rigidly straight as she marched to the door and never looked over her shoulder. She felt tears begin to pool in her eyes, but she determinedly pushed them backward. She refused to cry over Mitch, not after the way that he had treated her today. She knew that she was trembling and weak-kneed by the time she reached the rain-dampened streets, but she ignored her weakness and the drizzle that collected on her hair and ran down the back of her neck. A queasy, nervous feeling of desperation was churning in her stomach.

How had Mitch changed so much, she wondered. What had happened to the kind and caring man she had once known and respected? And how—how had he guessed about her affair with Kane? Erin's mind was spinning in circles, and her face, now covered with drops of rain, had lost all of its color. Her sleek ebony hair had begun to curl in the rain, and tiny tendrils began to spring out of the tidy black knot at the base of her head. She walked along the rain-puddled streets, absorbed in her own distant thoughts for over an hour. With her head bent against the wind, her small fists thrust into the pockets of her raincoat and her jaw clenched at an angle, she hardly looked her pert business-like self. She felt a burning sense of betrayal that Mitch would stoop so low as to ask her to confiscate bank records secretly for his personal use. How far did friendship reach? How much would he ask of her? Again, she was reminded of Mitch's initials on the chart showing that Erin had possession of a key that she had never seen. Had Mitch, somehow, tried to implicate her in his crime? Was it possible that she had been wrong about Mitch all this time? She stamped her booted foot impatiently on the sidewalk.

Suddenly aware of the passing time, she hurried back to the bank. She was oblivious to the fact that her usually neat appearance was disheveled from the wind and the rain and that her normally clear eyes were clouded and preoccupied. As she rushed into her office, she paused only to pick up her messages and remind her secretary more curtly than she had intended that under no circumstances, other than a telephone call from Kane, was she to be disturbed.

For the remainder of the afternoon Erin holed up behind her desk, and tried to immerse herself in paperwork. But all her concentration seemed to shift to Mitch, and she found it impossible to forget the hollow look of despair on his face or the nervousness of his hands or his eyes, once clear and blue, now gray and pasty. Erin's stomach twisted violently as she remembered him and realized just how suspicious she had become of a man she had once trusted completely. Was she being paranoid, or had she been a fool to trust him in the past? She let her forehead drop to her hand, and hoped to God that the afternoon would slide by without any further complications.

The little yellow car couldn't hurry home fast enough for Erin, and the snail's pace of the late-afternoon traffic as it snarled in the rain only added to her frustration. Maneuvering the Rabbit through the hilly streets of the downtown area of Seattle, she made it to the freeway, but to no avail. Tonight, even the freeways were choked with commuters anxious to get home, semis on their assigned routes and recreational vehicles hoping to get a head start on the wet weekend. As the windshield wipers danced rhythmically before her eyes, Erin sighed, realizing that because she usually worked much later than six o'clock, she had forgotten how difficult and frustrating rush hour could be.

It took her nearly an hour to get home. As she guided her car to a halt she jerked on the emergency brake before racing up the sidewalk and taking the steps to her third-floor apartment two at a time. With unsteady fingers she unlocked the door, hurried into the apartment and switched on the local news. She was too preoccupied to bother shaking the rain from her coat or umbrella.

The sullen-faced newscaster was already making predictions about the upcoming state-wide elections as the television snapped on. From habit Erin began to unbutton her coat, but she never let her eyes waver from the small black and white screen that held her attention. At the next commercial break, she managed to slip out of her coat and toss it next to her on the couch just as the dark-haired newsman began to recount the story that was uppermost on her mind: an alleged case of embezzlement at a downtown Seattle bank.

Erin's eyes were riveted to the set, and nervously she began to bite at her lower lip. As the scene on the television changed to the district courthouse, the eye of the camera sought Mitch and caught him hurrying out of the double doors of the marble courthouse. He was accompanied by a rather short and balding attorney who attempted to protect his client by fending off persistent questions from the group of anxious reporters clustered at the courthouse doors. Mitch, shielding his face with his hands, rushed to a waiting car. Erin only caught a glimpse of her former boss, and she felt a rush of pity for the man as his watery blue eyes darted anxiously back to the attorney before he climbed into the waiting automobile and sped away from the newsmen.

"Yes," the mustached anchorman was stating, "Mitchell Cameron, once considered one of Seattle's most prestigious and trusted bankers, was indicted today on seven counts of embezzlement. If Cameron is found guilty, the maximum sentence…" Erin couldn't listen to the rest of the broadcast. She was too numbed by the chilling realization that Mitch actually had been indicted! Rubbing her temples with her slender fingers, she tried to think rationally—indicted, what exactly did that mean? It took her a few minutes to understand that Mitch hadn't been found guilty of a crime, at least not yet. But apparently there was enough evidence against him to warrant a serious investigation and a trial. Erin sunk onto the sofa, mindless of the water that had started to collect around her boots on the Persian rug.

The TV continued to talk to her. A picture of the bank building, looking somehow more foreboding in the variegated gray tones of the set, flashed onto the screen. Consolidated First Bank stood out in bold letters, while a reporter recounted the bank's recent history along with the fact that, within the last month, the ownership of the prestigious building had changed hands. The smug newsman noted that when the president of Consolidated, Mr. Kane Webster, was summoned by the television station to remark on the alleged embezzlement, Mr. Webster declined. He was, of course, unavailable for comment—supposedly out of the state.

Erin had heard enough, and she clicked off the television with cold, numb fingers. Drawing her knees beneath her chin, she wrapped her arms about her legs and sat on the couch, staring at the black Seattle evening through the window. A loneliness settled upon her and she thought about Kane, thousands of miles away in southern California. The smoky gray drizzle and the heavy purple cloud cover that cloaked the city only added to her gloom. Unconsciously she began to take the pins from her hair, and shake loose the tight, confining chignon. She ran her fingers through her black tresses and rubbed her scalp, hoping to deter the headache that was starting to throb against her temples. If only Kane were here now—perhaps the lonely desperation that was closing in on her would fade....

She must have been staring into the oncoming darkness for quite a while, but she was too lost in her own black thoughts to realize that time had escaped her. The urgent ringing of the telephone startled Erin back to the present, and she rushed into the kitchen to answer its incessant call. As she spoke, she tried to conceal the note of depression that had crept into her voice.

"Hello?"

"Erin?" a concerned voice inquired.

"Oh, Kane!" She sighed, and let her knees give way in relief. Resting against the counter, she found herself overwhelmingly grateful for the thin wire that stretched the length of the West Coast and tied her to Kane.

"Are you okay?" he asked, and she recognized a tremor of concern in his voice.

"I'm fine," she assured him. "It's been a long, hectic week without you. I'm just a little tired, that's all."

There was a weighty pause in the conversation before Kane spoke again. "Have you heard about the indictment?" he asked, and his voice seemed to have become suddenly reserved.

"Yes… I saw the evening news…." She hesitated a moment. Should she tell him about her meeting with Mitch this afternoon and his proposition? Erin knew that Kane would be angry and upset when he found out about it, and she reasoned it would be better to tell him face-to-face. A long-distance call was too short and too impersonal. Too many misunderstandings could occur.

"I know that you care a lot about Cameron," Kane began, wondering to himself why he continued to pursue a subject that only incensed him.

"I did, and I suppose I still do…but, really, it's okay. This is the way it had to be, didn't it?"

Why did he feel that there was a trace of hesitation in her voice? His fist involuntarily balled at his side, and his grip on the telephone receiver tightened until his knuckles showed white. It had been a difficult week for him also. Dealing with his strong-willed daughter had proven to be nearly impossible. And the fact that Erin was alone and over fifteen hundred miles away only added to his irritation and short temper.

"Krista and I will be home late Sunday afternoon," he was saying. "Probably around six. And the moving company has promised to have the bulk of our belongings in Seattle by Monday—or so they claim. What won't fit into the apartment, I'll have stored. Will the apartment be ready for us?"

Erin couldn't hide the disappointment that swallowed her. She had hoped that Kane would be home this evening or, at the very latest, Saturday.

"What? Oh, yes," she agreed distractedly. "Mr. Jefferies moved out at the beginning of the week, and the cleaning people were here earlier today. I'm sure it will be ready by Sunday evening...."

"Good—I'll see you then."

"Good night, Kane," Erin whispered, not wanting to hang up the phone and sever the frail connection that bound her so distantly to him.

"Erin?"

"Yes..."

A pause. "Good night."

Erin felt an incredible loneliness as she hung up the phone.

"Oh, darling!" Kane murmured to himself as he heard her ring off. He slammed the receiver down in mindless frustration and rubbed his hands together anxiously, all the while leaning against the wall and staring at the clean, white telephone in his sister's apartment. How was he going to handle his emotions for Erin? God, had it only been four days since he had last seen—or touched—her?

Somehow he had expected and silently hoped that once he had put some distance between himself and her, the miles would erase the goddesslike image of her body and that her likeness in his mind would fade, cooling his hot-blooded need for her. But he had been mistaken, grievously mistaken, and just the reverse had occurred. Instead of forgetting her, the image of her body was burned savagely on his mind and achingly in his loins. He felt an urgency, a driving *need*, warm and molten, that throbbed against his temples and fired his blood. He had to see her again, and he had to see her soon, or he would surely go out of his mind!

And the lies! Oh, God, how he hated his lies. The duplicity of his situation was eating at him, tearing at him from the inside out. He slammed a powerful fist against the wall. How could he lie to her and to himself? How long could the tense charade continue?

Kane had convinced himself that it would be a good idea to live near Erin, in the same building, in order that he might watch her more closely. But now, as he stood staring at the phone, he knew that it was only his mind playing games with him again. Another lie to justify his urgent need to be near her and protect her.

Protect her? He laughed mirthlessly at himself and reached for the tall glass of Scotch that he had poured before placing the long-distance call. Erin needed to be protected all right, from Kane Webster, from himself! *He* was the one who continued relentlessly and mercilessly to track her down, stalking her like some wild, criminal creature. He was suspicious of her and too much of a coward to admit it for fear of losing her. A damned hypocritical bastard, that's what he was, he conceded to himself.

Kane's hands were shaking from the turbulent emotions that were battling cruelly within his mind. He took a long drink, and groaned as the Scotch hit the empty bottom of his stomach. His thoughts were black and excruciating as he strode into the living room and levered himself down on his sister's uncomfortable floral couch.

Why couldn't he just forget about Erin O'Toole and her crazy connection with the embezzling scam? Why did he continue to torture himself with the memory of the gentle curve of her neck, the slim, feminine contour of her legs or the longing way that her near-violet eyes could reach out and touch him?

Damn it, Webster, his persistent mind scolded, *control yourself! For all you know that woman is just another two-bit thief, and you're letting her rip you to shreds! She's destroying your objectivity! Erin's a witch,* his mind warned, *the less you have to do with her, the better!*

Kane shifted his weight uncomfortably on the prim blue cushions of the couch and took another long dissatisfying swallow of the potent warm liquor. He needed to break away from Erin and the spell she was casting over him, he reasoned.

Then, why the hell couldn't he convince himself to leave her alone?

Chapter 10

Sunday morning dawned as gloomy as the rest of the Seattle weekend had, but Erin felt somewhat lighthearted at the prospect of seeing Kane again. It seemed like forever since he'd been gone. She stretched out on the bed, and discovered that she ached all over. The muscles in her arms and legs seemed to be all knotted and twisted this morning, but she smiled to herself in spite of the pain. In order to keep her mind off Mitch's indictment and Kane's absence, Erin had run out on Friday night and purchased several gallons of paint. That night and all day Saturday she had spent repainting Mr. Jefferies's old apartment and

the massive entry hall. This morning her aching muscles rebelled.

Against the silent protests of her body Erin
got up and showered. The new paint job had
been such an improvement to the building
that she had decided to continue the project.
She had almost finished with the entry hall,
and today she planned to tackle Mrs. Cavenaugh's apartment. Ever since the repairmen
had insulated the flooring and the windows,
parts of the little old lady's apartment had suffered, and a new coat of paint would hide the
dirt and chips of paint that had been loosened
during the repairs. Erin shuddered when she
realized that she had nearly depleted her savings with the insulation and painting projects.
But it just had to be done!

Mrs. Cavenaugh had embraced the idea
of repainting her apartment, and by the time
Erin had swallowed a cup of coffee, looked
over the headlines and nibbled on a bit of
toast, it was only eight-thirty. Yet Mrs. Cavenaugh was already up and ready to help Erin
with the task at hand.

For as long as Erin could remember, she
had never seen Mrs. Cavenaugh in anything
other than a prim housedress and a single
strand of pearls. But this morning the half-

bent figure of Mrs. Cavenaugh sported a garishly loud green-and-purple scarf that was wound tightly over her hair, oversize trousers and tennis shoes that were presumably antiques. She was a comical sight in the outlandish outfit, but her blue eyes sparkled with eagerness, and against Erin's protests, the elderly woman grabbed a brush and began to tackle the job at hand, only pausing to grumble about working on the Sabbath. Erin ignored her complaints and to her amazement found that Mrs. Cavenaugh was handy with the brush and had the endurance of a woman half her age.

"This is a wonderful idea," Mrs. Cavenaugh exclaimed, "even if we are working on the Lord's day." Her blue eyes were carefully checking over some of Erin's work with a practiced eye. Not able to complain about Erin's painting, she continued, "Adds a lot to this apartment, don't you think?" A pleased smile crept over her features. "You really are a dear. You know that, don't you?"

"Keeping up the place comes with being a landlord, especially when I can get some free labor from my tenants," Erin laughed, and smiled at the little old lady's compliment.

"Is the apartment across the hall ready for the new renters? When are they moving in?"

Erin slid a suspicious glance at the old woman, who seemed intent on trimming the windowsill. "As a matter of fact I expect them this afternoon."

"Young couple?" Mrs. Cavenaugh asked, a mischievous twinkle lighting her eyes.

"No…it's my boss… Mr. Webster. I believe you've met?" Erin watched Mrs. Cavenaugh carefully.

"Charming man," the older woman agreed, and paid even more attention to the windowsill. "So he's moving in today?"

"Why do I get the feeling that I'm giving you yesterday's news?" Erin asked suspiciously. "You've already talked to Kane about this, haven't you?"

A smile spread across the wrinkled face. "Someone's got to look out for your best interests."

"And so you just appointed yourself guardian angel. Is that it?"

"Close enough," the little old lady averred. "Now don't you go jumping off the deep end, Erin," Mrs. Cavenaugh cautioned, and wagged a warning finger at Erin. "I just happened to mention in passing that there was an apartment available...."

"In passing! When did you see him?"

Mrs. Cavenaugh's face puckered for a moment. "Now listen here, young lady. I may not be as young as I used to be, but I have a pretty good idea of what goes on around here. I've seen Kane come and go, and I've also got it figured out that, for some reason, the good Lord only knows why—" she threw her hands heavenward in supplication "—you keep running away from him."

Erin began to protest, but the gray-haired lady would have none of it. "It's a mistake, pure and simple, for you to run from him. That man is hopelessly in love with you, Erin. Only a fool would let him slip through her fingers!"

"Oh, Mrs. Cavenaugh," Erin sighed, smiling wistfully. "If it were only that simple."

"It's as simple as you want to make it!" The old lady eyed Erin speculatively, and noticed the resigned droop of her shoulders. "Why don't you call it a day—the apartment looks fine. You go and get ready for your Kane and his daughter. They'll be here this evening, won't they?"

"Just where do you get all of your information?"

"Like I said before, I know what's going on around here!" Before Erin could voice any further questions or objections, the little bent figure hustled her out the door. "And don't you dare accuse me of snooping," she cautioned. "It's just that I care."

"I know you do," Erin replied thoughtfully, "but you do seem to have an uncanny sense about some things...."

"Comes with age, don't you know? My eyesight isn't what it used to be, and my hearing's, well, you know, a little less than it should be. But I can still see love when it stares me in the face. Now you hurry up and change into something pretty and make that man something to eat. I bet he'll be starved by the time that he gets home—the girl, too."

Erin started to protest, but Mrs. Cavenaugh pursed her lips, and balanced the wet paintbrush on one of her hips. "Scoot," she ordered authoritatively, and slammed the door tightly shut.

Several hours had passed, and somewhat reluctantly Erin had taken Mrs. Cavenaugh's well-meant advice, although she doubted that the little old lady downstairs would consider her slim designer jeans and print cotton blouse as "something pretty." But Erin had made dinner for Kane and his daughter, and then, realizing that Krista probably wouldn't be able to manage the two flights of stairs to Erin's loft, Erin had moved the meal downstairs to Kane's new apartment.

She paced nervously while waiting for Kane and glanced at her watch for the sixth time in the space of two minutes. The trying weekend without Kane had made Erin anxious and tired, and she found that her nerves were stretched as tightly as a piano string. How would she react to Kane's daughter, and how would Krista take to Erin? she wondered.

Erin had attempted to bring as much warmth as possible to the small first-floor apartment by bringing down a few pieces of her own furniture. To her credit, the interior did look a little less stark and more comfortable for all her efforts. The creamy new coat of vanilla paint gleamed against the walls, and the few small pieces of furniture, though sparse, added a homey familiarity to the otherwise vacant rooms. Erin had even managed to cover the card table with a linen cloth and centered a basket of freshly cut flowers on it. All in all, she had done a decent job of making the tiny apartment attractive, but she found it impossible to shake the feeling of apprehension that shrouded her.

The sound of feet shuffling in the hall snapped her attention to the doorway. She knew in an instant that Kane and Krista had made it home. Nervously she wiped her suddenly wet palms against her jeans and pasted what she hoped appeared to be a pleasant smile upon her face. The door swung open, and father and daughter entered the room. At the sight of Kane, Erin's heart turned over. How, in less than a week's time, could anyone change so dramatically? He was dressed casually in jeans and a dove-gray sport shirt, but that's where the casual part of his image stopped. Erin could sense the signs of strain that hardened his features, the thin light lines of worry that crowded his forehead, and the somber tilt of his dark eyebrows that were drawn thoughtfully together. His eyes met hers for an instant, and a small flicker of relief and affection lessened the severity of his gaze.

At the whirring sound of the electric wheelchair, Erin's attention shifted from Kane to his daughter. Krista was beautiful in the classical sense: a small, evenly featured madonnalike face was surrounded by thick sun-kissed curls, and her deep-set, perfectly round icy blue eyes held a sparkle and a vibrancy of youth. Krista's cheekbones were high and noble-looking with just a hint of pink on her otherwise cream-colored skin. Even in the awkward stage of adolescence, it was apparent that Krista was an uncommonly beautiful girl. Only the mechanical apparatus of the wheelchair detracted from her wholesome, California-fresh appearance. The presence of the chair served to remind Erin just how difficult the past year of Krista's life must have been for the girl. Krista was much too young to have lived through the trauma of witnessing the death of her mother. Erin felt her heart go out to the attractive young girl in the mechanical beast.

There was a tense, uncomfortable moment as Kane dropped a bundle of blankets that he had carried into the apartment and shoved them into the corner of the room. For a split second Erin faced Krista alone and was surprised at the frigidity in the pale blue eyes of the girl. Uncontrollably Erin shuddered and hoped that she could somehow warm the cool look that hardened Krista's gaze.

After unsuccessfully arranging the pillows

and blankets on the floor, Kane gave up and turned his attention to Erin and his daughter. He seemed to appraise the uncomfortable situation with knowing eyes, and in a minute, he stood near to Erin. He was smiling, but the grin was tight, forced as if it had been slapped on his face out of courtesy. He showed Erin no outward signs of affection, but his stormy gray eyes reached out for hers, and Erin realized that he was asking her indulgence with Krista. It was as if he had expected a confrontation.

"Krista," Kane said softly, and Krista's blue eyes sparked upward to him. "This is Erin. You remember, I told you all about her. She works with me at the bank, and she'll be our landlord until we can find a house of our own."

Krista's eyes skimmed over the interior of the apartment, and from the bored expression on her face, Erin sensed that Krista disapproved of her new, temporary home. The girl remained silent, and for a moment Erin wondered if the child had even heard the introduction. Kane's dark eyebrows melted together at Krista's rudeness, but for the moment, he chose not to reprimand her.

Continuing the stilted introduction, he said more firmly, "Erin, this is Krista."

Erin ventured a sincere smile for Kane's daughter and wondered if the young girl in the wheelchair was just being shy, or if she was purposely giving Erin the cold shoulder.

"Hello, Krista. It's nice to meet you. I hope you like it here." Erin offered her outstretched hand to the girl.

Krista didn't immediately respond to Erin's attempts at warmth or friendliness. In fact, Erin was sure that if Kane hadn't been in the room, the blue-eyed girl would have ignored the greeting altogether. As it was, Krista hesitated and then gave Kane an accusatory glare before finding her manners and answering. "Hello," Krista muttered, almost to herself, and reached for Erin's open hand. Her eyes never met Erin's puzzled gaze.

There wasn't time for a proper handshake. The instant that Krista's smaller fingers touched Erin's open palm, Krista withdrew her hand as rapidly as if Erin's touch were white-hot. Erin found herself standing with her open palm suspended in midair and an astonished expression of disbelief disturbing her features. Was the girl always so rude, or did she just dislike Erin?

Rather than commenting on Krista's complete lack of courtesy, or asking about Krista's negative reaction to her, Erin forced herself to remain calm and hang on to the dwindling amount of control she had left. Excusing herself, she turned her attention back to the kitchen and preparation of the meal. She could hear the quiet reprimand that Kane was giving his daughter, but Erin tried to ignore the tension between father and daughter—tension that she somehow felt guilty about. Perhaps she shouldn't have intruded on the homecoming. It was obvious that Krista would have preferred that she had never met Erin.

As Erin extracted the platter of warm rolls from the oven, she tried to convince herself that she was overreacting to Krista's indifference. After all, the girl was disabled and probably extremely self-conscious about her condition. Aside from the obvious, it couldn't be easy moving away from the only family and friends she had ever known to start a new life with a father she barely knew in an unfamiliar city. It was no wonder that the child was frightened and misbehaving. *Give the girl a chance,* Erin told herself. *It's barely been a year since the young girl witnessed her mother's death.* Armed with a new sense of conviction, Erin decided to ignore Krista's coolness.

As she carried the meal to the table, Erin forced herself to smile and say, "Let's get started. I bet you're both hungry!"

"We ate on the plane!" Krista announced, and Kane threw his daughter a grim reproving glance. Krista ignored it.

"That we did," Kane acknowledged, "but that was several hours ago, and it wasn't particularly good." His steely eyes never left his daughter—it was as if he dared her to act up again. "As I recall, you didn't eat much." The muscle cords in his neck stood out clearly against the collar of his shirt, and Erin could tell that he was holding on to the rags of his patience. He was about to explode. Erin hoped that Krista realized how dangerous the situation was becoming.

Erin tried to steady her rapidly disintegrating nerves as she went back to the kitchen for the rest of the food. She couldn't gloss over it, not even to herself. For some reason Krista was determined to hate her. Erin mentally counted to ten, took several deep breaths, and once again poised, returned to face father and daughter. It took a lot of determination, but she was able to hide her discomfort and take some pleasure in serving the dishes that she had so meticulously prepared, although Krista's discriminating eye took a little of the satisfaction away from her. Though the aroma of the food was tantalizing, and the marmalade-glazed game hens looked delicious as they sat on a platter of steaming wild rice and mushrooms, the meal was tense and uncomfortable. Everything seemed to have soured slightly under Krista's disapproving blue-eyed gaze.

"This looks great!" Kane exclaimed a little too heartily as he helped Erin to her chair. His fingers brushed against her arm, and startled by the intimate gesture, Erin turned her eyes away from the meal to look more closely at him. He seemed more than tired—he seemed weary. She could tell his jovial words were just a cloak for the tension coiling rigidly within him. Although his voice was cheerful, the lines on his forehead, the muscle cords strung tightly at his neck, and the darkness of his gaze betrayed his calm exterior.

"Doesn't this look delicious, honey?" he asked his daughter as he took his seat. Krista remained silent. Kane cleared his throat and rubbed his hands together. "I'm famished!"

He looked at Krista with concern. Her large, liquid eyes met his, but still she didn't speak.

Finally she broke her gaze from that of her father, and stared instead at the napkin in her lap. Kane's forced smile disappeared into a frown. He was obviously distressed by Krista's coolness and lack of manners, but he wisely said nothing, preferring to wait until he was alone with his daughter before having the argument that he knew was brewing between them.

The meal began in silence, and Erin thought that she would scream if some of the icy tension in the air didn't melt. Fortunately the telephone rang, and Kane excused himself to answer it. The conversation was extremely one-sided and uncomfortable.

"Not tonight," Kane argued but was apparently interrupted. "No—it's absolutely impossible! I just got in from California with my daughter. You'll have to handle it yourself!" A pause, and the muscle in Kane's rigid face tightened again. "Can't Jones handle it? No—how about Martin?" Another long pause. "For God's sake, Jim, doesn't anyone down there know what they're doing?" Kane was shaking his head, raking his fingers through the burnished copper of his hair and pacing the length of the telephone cord. "All right, all right! I get the picture. I'll be there in—" he checked his watch "—about twenty minutes!" He slammed the receiver down viciously and uttered a curse under his breath.

"I'm sorry," he apologized sincerely, once he had subdued his temper. His gray eyes pleaded with Erin to understand. "It seems that there are major problems in the computer center tonight. I have to go to the bank for a little while…."

"No…" Krista began to wail, looking frantically from her father to Erin and back again. "Don't go…."

"I'm sorry, honey," Kane responded with a fond pat on her silky blond curls. "But, really, I have to go—just for a little while…"

"No…no…" Krista pleaded, clinging to her father's shirtsleeve.

"I'll be back in a couple of hours. You can stay here with Erin."

"Daddy! No!"

Kane's expression became confused, and for a moment Erin thought that he might reconsider. She fervently hoped so, but when his dark brows straightened again, she knew that the decision had been made. He was leaving Erin with the adolescent girl who obviously hated her.

"Erin, do you mind?" he asked, ignoring Krista's pleading eyes.

"Not at all," Erin agreed, as kindly as she could, and rained a warm smile on Krista. "We'll get along just fine!" Kane's gray gaze was dubious.

"Daddy, *please*, don't go!" Krista cried in a shaky voice. Her frightened blue eyes skittered over to Erin and back to her father.

"Look, honey," Kane answered, taking both of Krista's hands in his. He squatted next to the chair, so that the child could look him squarely in the eyes. "You know I don't want to go, so let's not make it any harder than it already is. I'll be back soon. I promise." He planted a loving kiss on the top of her forehead as if to ward off any further protests. His silvery eyes locked with Erin's for a moment, begging her to understand, but there was something more—the same old sense of wariness seemed to flicker across his face for an instant as he grabbed his jacket and walked to the door. Krista stared at her plate, unable to watch her father leave, but Erin followed him.

Kane stretched into his coat, took Erin's

hand in his and gently guided her out into the semiprivacy of the hallway. "Thank you," he stated and his eyes held hers. Erin could see a question in their steely depths.

"It's no problem," she replied, doubting her own words as she thought about the headstrong blond girl.

Kane looked at her and seemed unconvinced. "You don't have to mince words with me. I know that Krista's a handful!"

"I can handle her," Erin insisted.

"I know." Still he hesitated, and in the dimly lit hallway Erin could sense an uneasiness creep over both of them. It was the same feeling that seemed to keep them from completely trusting each other. He began to reach for her and then let his hand drop. "I'll be back as soon as I can…."

"I'm sure it won't be long," she agreed, knowing that her voice sounded feeble. What was it that was bothering her? Something didn't seem right. "I thought that the repairmen fixed the computer on Friday," she puzzled, shaking her head in an effort to remember the details of Friday afternoon. "Yes, I'm sure that we got a call around five o'clock, stating that all systems were go."

Kane's jaw flexed. "Apparently there have

been additional problems." His voice was strangely devoid of emotion—cold.

"Odd, isn't it?" she murmured. "Oh, well." She lifted her shoulders and managed a sincere smile. "Try to hurry home...."

His sudden and powerful embrace surprised and baffled her. His arms held her closely, tightly, as if he were afraid she might disappear. His strength imprisoned her, and she could hear the hammering of his heart, belying his calm exterior of a few moments before. His breathing was labored and uneven. She couldn't see his eyes as her face was crushed, almost savagely, against his chest. There was anger in his strength and passion in his words. They were torn from him as if his admission were painfully traitorous.

"God, but I've missed you, Erin," he breathed, and the pressure against the curve of her spine increased. "I've had dreams about you, ached for you..."

"Shhh..." Before he could utter another word, Erin checked his speech by placing a trembling finger against the warmth of his lips. "Later," she whispered, cocking her head toward the open doorway to his apartment. "I'd better go inside and check on Krista."

Erin knew that she was shaking from the intensity of his passion, but she controlled the urge to reach up and trace the angled contour of his cheeks with her fingers.

Kane reluctantly let his embrace loosen and an unreadable, agonized expression passed over his face. "I won't be gone long—it should only take a minute...."

"Don't be too sure," she laughed hollowly as she stepped back toward the apartment. "Computer problems tend to be complicated...."

"That they do," he whispered cryptically, and let his eyes rove over her face searchingly. What did he expect to find? Finally he tore his gaze away from her and threw open the door before stepping into the night. If only Erin could guess the *real* reason that he had been summoned to the bank on this black, rain-drenched night, Kane thought sardonically. If only she knew that he was aware of the fact that another three thousand dollars had slipped out of the dividend account during his absence. *Oh, Erin,* he thought as he drove toward the winking lights of Seattle. His grip tightened on the steering wheel, and the tires of the black sports car screamed against the pressure of a corner taken too recklessly. *Why,* he wondered—*oh, God, why?*

Erin straightened her shoulders before she entered the tiny apartment and let the door whisper shut behind her. At the sound of the soft noise Krista stirred and looked longingly at the door with cold disbelieving eyes.

Mentally Erin fortified herself. She could tell that the upcoming evening was going to be a test of will between herself and Kane's stubborn daughter. And although Erin was an adult, and the old Victorian house was "her turf," she felt at a distinct disadvantage to the blond girl who had folded her arms defiantly over her small chest. Erin dreaded the argument that she knew was simmering in the air. Forcing herself to appear more collected than she felt, she walked back to the table and ignored Krista's wounded look as she spoke softly to the child. Erin's voice was friendly but firm.

"Is there anything else I can get you?" she asked the girl, and motioned to a basket of sourdough rolls at her end of the table.

Silence.

Erin gritted her teeth together in frustration and noticed that Krista hadn't touched any of the food on her plate. Once again Erin attempted to communicate. "How about a glass of milk?"

Nothing.

"Krista," Erin said, commanding the girl's attention, and bracing herself for the inevitable confrontation. "I'd like it very much if we could be friends."

Cold fearful blue eyes surveyed Erin as if seeing her for the first time. Pouty pink lips pressed into an insolent line. "I don't like you!" Krista hissed in a trembling voice.

Erin sucked in her breath but bravely continued the stilted conversation. "Why? Why don't you like me? Is it because I'm a friend of your father's?"

"I don't want to like you—and I won't!" Defiance and anger were evident in the tilt of Krista's finely shaped chin.

Erin sighed wearily and sat down in the chair opposite the rebellious girl with the fearful eyes. Their gazes locked and Erin found herself folding and refolding the napkin in her lap, while contemplating a way to bridge the gap that existed between her and Kane's daughter. She took in the challenging look on the girl's face, the proud carriage of Krista's head, and then Erin's gaze touched upon the empty wheelchair. Compassion washed over Erin. Krista was bearing a heavy cross.

"You don't have to like me," Erin stated simply, and a look of astonishment softened Krista's defiant features. "It's up to you."

Once again Erin paid full attention to her meal and hoped it seemed that she was enjoying her food, while all the time her stomach was twisting into knots of revulsion against the meal. It took all of Erin's will to finish the cold and suddenly tasteless meal.

It was several minutes before the silence was broken. Krista's small voice trembled and Erin politely looked at the girl. "They were getting back together, you know!" Krista announced, and toyed with the food on her plate.

"Pardon me?"

"Mother and Daddy. They were going to get married again. Mother told me so!" Krista's face was set for the denial she expected from Erin.

"Were they?" Erin asked calmly.

"You bet!" the girl nearly shouted. "And it would have been soon, too. And...and...we were all going to be a family again!"

Erin listened intently, not knowing exactly how to respond to Krista's outburst. She studied

Krista and saw the turbulent play of emotions that was contorting the beautiful child's face.

"We were going to be together again. We were!" she proclaimed, tears glistening in her round eyes. "If only Mama hadn't died… I know we would!" Her frail voice caught and tears began to flow freely down her cheeks.

Erin's heart bled for the small girl at the other end of the table. Dropping her fork onto the plate, she got up and hurried to Krista's side. She let her hand touch the sobbing shoulders.

"I'm so sorry," Erin whispered.

"No, you're not!" the child sniffed. "If Mama was alive, then you couldn't have Daddy. He loved her! He did!" By this time Krista's body was racked with her uncontrolled weeping, and Erin let her arm reach tentatively around the slim shoulders.

"Don't touch me," Krista screamed. "Don't you dare touch me!" She pushed her chair back from the table and attempted to reach for the wheelchair. Erin knew that the situation was getting dangerously out of control, and she tried to help Krista by pushing the wheelchair in the girl's direction.

"I can do it myself!" Krista declared, and to Erin's surprise, the slender girl braced herself on the table's edge and took a few hesitant steps before falling into her mechanical chair.

They faced each other as if they were opponents on a battlefield. Each one eyed the other distrustfully. Hesitantly Erin drew herself up to her full height, and her lilac gaze rested on her ward for the evening. How was it possible to handle Krista? There was no answer but the obvious.

"Krista," Erin said, and offered the girl a tissue to dry her eyes. "I want you to know that there's no rule stating that you have to like me. All I ask is that you give me a chance, an honest chance. And, for your father's sake, I'm asking you to be, at least, civil to me. Is that so much to ask?"

"I don't want a new mother!" the girl cried, nearly hysterical.

"I understand that, and… I respect it," Erin agreed, still holding the tissue out to the child. "No one has the right to step into someone else's shoes, unless they're asked. I'm sure that your mother was a very wonderful woman, and that she loved you very much, but, unfortunately, I can't bring her back to you. Nobody can." Erin's eyes had begun to fill with tears as she looked into a face that was much too young to understand death. "I hope you know that whatever happens between your father and me, that I would *never* attempt to take the place of your mother—that's a promise!'"

Krista stared silently at Erin for what seemed an eternity before taking the tissue and wiping the stain of tears from her cheeks. Assured that the girl was poised again, Erin turned toward the kitchen and hastily wiped her own tears with the cuff of her blouse. She hoped that Krista hadn't seen her tears or her weakness.

For the rest of the evening, while Erin cleared the table and cleaned the dishes, Krista brooded in a corner of the room, pretending interest in the empty fireplace. Erin offered to build a fire, but Krista had withdrawn back into her shell and didn't respond to the invitation. Therefore, Erin shrugged her shoulders and acted as if it didn't matter in the least to her, one way or the other, before turning back to the task of straightening the kitchen. But she sensed that beneath Krista's cold exterior, the girl had begun to thaw.

Whenever Krista didn't think that Erin would notice, she studied the black-haired woman with interest. So this was the lady that her father was falling to pieces over. Although this Erin creature was very unlike her mother, Krista couldn't help but admire Erin's mettle. Maybe Seattle wouldn't be quite as bad as she had imagined.

It was late when Kane returned to the apartment house. He parked the car and sat motionless for several minutes, just staring into the darkness of the night. He was emotionally drained to the point of exhaustion, and he had the urge to restart the car and head to the closest tavern. He wanted a drink—make that several drinks—and then he wanted to fall into bed and sleep for days. He didn't want to face Krista and endure another fight, and he couldn't face Erin, not now.

He groaned when he thought about the scene at the bank: the evidence, the fear and the anger as Jim Haney explained about the latest development in the embezzling operation. Not only was three thousand dollars missing, but Jim had learned from Olivia Parsons that Erin had met with Mitchell Cameron on the day of his arraignment hearing—the very day the money was transferred from the dividend account. The only good news was that Jim had traced the money's path and it would only be a matter of days before he had sifted through all of the departmental checks to find one that was out of balance with the general ledger. At last the torture of the un-known would end, and Kane realized bitterly that Erin would be caught.

Erin was sitting in a chair, engrossed in a mystery novel, when Kane let himself into the apartment. Her black hair was wound into a loose ponytail, her glasses were perched on the end of her nose, and her legs were curled comfortably beneath her. As Kane saw her he was reminded of the first time he had seen her, dressed much the same and crouched in a pile of legal documents at the bank. He felt the same, now-familiar male response that he had several weeks ago. He wanted to run to her, to scoop her up in his arms, to crush her against him and to bury his head in the soft warmth of her breasts. Even now, suspecting what he did about her and knowing he was deathly close to the truth, he wanted her as he had never wanted another woman.

"Hi," Erin greeted him, and pulled her glasses off her face. She laid the book and the glasses on an upturned box that she was using as a table, stood up and stretched. It was an unconscious and provocative gesture that made Kane's blood heat as he watched the fabric of her clothes mold tightly to her body.

Her eyes found his. "Can I get you anything? There's quite a few leftovers...."

He stood in the doorway, his shoulders drooped in resignation. Though she could tell that he, in his own way, was glad to see her, there was a strange look on his face.

"Are you well?" she asked.

"What? Oh, yeah. I'm fine," he responded, and rubbed the back of his neck.

"Were the computer problems that difficult?"

"The what? Oh, no, the computer is fine. But you know how it is, one problem seems to lead to another, and before you know it, the half-hour that you planned to be gone has stretched into three." His voice was vague, distant, and Erin wondered if he was trying to tell her something.

"How's Krista?" Kane asked, and dropped to the floor. He grabbed a loose pillow for his head and patted the floor next to him, inviting Erin to sit next to him on the floor.

"We got along fine," Erin replied, and leaned against Kane, who cocked a dubious eyebrow. "Well, it wasn't easy—not at first," she admitted hesitantly. "But we worked things out."

"Did you?"

"Well, somehow we managed to get by...."

Erin's voice drifted off. Kane seemed remote this evening, and she could see the evidence of exhaustion on his face. She hated to add to his problems, but she thought that he should know about Krista. "Did you know that she can walk?" Erin asked in a near whisper.

Kane stiffened. "What do you mean? Did she actually walk while I was gone?" His voice had lost all of its distance, and his fingers dug into her upper arm.

"Not exactly…"

"But you said…"

"I know what I said. Just listen a minute. Krista and I had an argument. It wasn't serious," Erin added hastily, and felt guilty for the lie. "And when I tried to help her to the wheelchair, she wouldn't stand for it. She braced herself on the table and took two—three—possibly four steps until she made it to her chair."

"You're certain?"

"Kane! I was right there—only inches from her! She walked."

"Oh, God," he murmured, and covered his face in his hands. "If only I could believe that she would be able to walk again. If only…"

"Have you spoken to a doctor in Seattle?"

"Not yet… I thought I'd wait until she was

settled into a routine." He rubbed his chin thoughtfully. "The tutor comes on Tuesday for her evaluation, and then I thought I'd call the doctors that were referred to me by Krista's doctor in L.A."

"Good." Kane was weary, and now disturbed. It had been a long, tiring day for both of them. Erin stood up and tightened the thong around her hair. "Krista went to bed at ten. She wanted to wait up for you, but the poor thing was exhausted. Maybe you should go in and let her know that you're back...." Had he even heard her suggestion? He was looking at Erin intently, but for some reason, she felt that he was light-years away from her. "Well... I'd better be getting upstairs," she said, and then added more lightly, "Work tomorrow, you know. And my boss is a very punctual person."

"Don't go," Kane breathed, ignoring her joke and reaching for her wrist. "Stay with me tonight...." His face seemed so earnest, his gray eyes so intent, that Erin had trouble resisting him.

"I'd like to stay, you know that." She hesitated. "But I can't..."

"Why not? Erin, I need you."

"Oh, Kane. You know the reason why I

can't stay with you—she's sleeping in the next room. You're the one who said she needed a more normal family existence," she reminded him, and lovingly touched his forehead. "What do you think she would do if she knew that you and I were sleeping together? You said yourself that her paralysis is psychosomatic, and now we know for sure—because she walked tonight!" Erin was on her knees, placing both of her hands on his cheeks. "Oh, Kane—perhaps the doctors were right, maybe she did need a change to get her motivated to walk. But…we, you and I, we mustn't do anything to blow it with her. We can't take the chance and set her back, don't you see?"

Kane's eyes agreed with her, although he cursed his frustration.

"Damn!" he spat. "You're right," he conceded, "but just how long do you expect me to keep my hands off you?"

"It's not what I want, and you know it. But I think that we, both of us, need to give Krista some time for adjustment."

"You're right," he sighed, and taking her hands in his, pulled the two of them upright. The passion in his eyes simmered for a minute, and he dropped her hands. "Thanks for staying with Krista. I'll see you tomorrow at work." He seemed calm, only his clenched fists gave any indication of the restraint he was placing upon himself. "I'll be in late, because of Krista and the moving company, but when I get to the office, I... I think that we should have a talk."

"Oh?"

"You and I have a lot to discuss."

She smiled up at him and tried to ignore the unreadable expression in his eyes. "I'm glad you're back," she whispered. "I missed you."

He started to respond, but stopped and closed his eyes for a second before rubbing his temple. "I'm glad to be back," he admitted, trying to rub away the deep ridges of concern that were creasing his forehead. Erin thought that he had finished speaking.

"Good night," she called over her shoulder, but his voice whispered to her and stopped her as she started to ascend the steps.

"Erin?" he beckoned.

"Yes?" Her face turned to him, and even in the semidarkness he knew it was the most beautiful face he had ever seen, the most incredible woman he had ever made love to.

"You would tell me, wouldn't you? I mean,

if you were in any trouble, you would tell me about it so that I could help you?"

"Of course I would. Honestly! Don't you know that?" She couldn't hide the smile that played on her lips.

"Sure," he agreed absently, as if totally unconvinced.

"Good! Then trust me!" She laughed, and shook her hair loose from the ponytail as she sprinted up the two flights of stairs. What was Kane talking about so seriously? Sometimes, she admitted to herself, he was a bit overly dramatic.

As Kane closed the door to his apartment, he leaned heavily against the cool hard wood. Erin's final words echoed and reechoed in his ears. "Then just trust me...trust me..."

Chapter 11

Several days had passed, and Erin found it nearly impossible to spend any time alone with Kane. Even the meeting at work had to be postponed indefinitely. During the days at work, whenever their paths would cross, it seemed that there wasn't any time for the lengthy discussion that Kane had alluded to on Sunday evening. Most of the staff was still out with the flu, the computer was working erratically, and the general disorganization of the office kept Erin from seeing Kane. Also, Kane was in and out of the office, dividing his time between the office and home, hoping to get Krista settled. Fortunately for him,

Mrs. Cavenaugh had been more than willing to be with his daughter when it was impossible for him to be at home. But the strain of the situation was wearing on him; Erin could see it in his eyes.

In the evenings, although Erin would eat with Krista and Kane, there wasn't much time spent relaxing. Kane's things had made it up to Seattle Tuesday afternoon, and after dinner each night for the next four days, Erin would help him and Krista get the apartment organized. It was a nearly impossible task. Although Kane had most of his belongings in storage, it still seemed to Erin that he had overstuffed the apartment with furniture, books, clothes and whatever else he could imagine. For the first time she realized how different Kane's lifestyle in California must have been. The expensive leather furniture, an endless wardrobe of clothes, everything he owned spoke of money.

Although Kane seemed to become more tense with each passing day, Erin decided it had to do with the added responsibilities of being a full-time father. All in all, Krista seemed to be adjusting better than Kane to their new life together in Seattle. Slowly Krista was coming out of her shell. She adored Mrs. Cavenaugh and had even accepted Erin. It was difficult, but the girl had begun to take hesitant steps in her father's presence, and at those times, all of the tension would drain from Kane and he would relax. The brooding sense of distrust in his eyes would die, and he would seem to enjoy life again.

The hectic week passed quickly, and Erin let a sigh of relief escape from her lips at six o'clock on Friday when she could forget about the flu, the computer, and the inheritance tax auditors. She grabbed her coat and hurried out of the bank building. Knowing that Kane was working late this evening, she hadn't even bothered to knock on his office door to let him know she was leaving. Tonight she had special plans.

She hurried along on foot for several blocks before locating the pet shop that she had found just this week. As promised, the owner had kept his store open the extra ten minutes that Erin needed.

Erin entered the little building and tried to keep her nose from wrinkling at the pungent odor within. Several fat puppies yipped to get her attention, and longingly she patted a black fluff of fur with sparkling eyes. The puppy's entire rear end was set in motion and a long pink tongue licked Erin's fingers.

"Oh, Miss O'Toole," the bearded shopkeeper smiled. "Have you changed your mind and decided on a dog?" He held up the fat black puppy, who responded by washing the shopkeeper's broad face.

"No, unfortunately, I don't have the space for a puppy." She wavered a moment, and then shook her head resolutely. "No, I think a kitten is a better choice. It's a gift for a friend."

The round shopkeeper held his hands out helplessly and shrugged his broad shoulders. "If you're sure. Just give me a couple of minutes. I know which one you picked out earlier." He hurried to the back of his store and came back with a tiny black and white kitten that couldn't have been more than six weeks old. "This is the one, right?" he asked.

Erin held out her hands and petted the warm powder puff of black fur. The kitten began to purr noisily and scratched its tiny paws against Erin's jacket. "She's perfect!" Erin breathed, raising the kitten to eye level and inspecting it.

The shopkeeper tugged on his beard. "That one's a male—is that acceptable?"

"It doesn't matter. This is the one I want!"

Erin couldn't hide her excitement as she tapped lightly on the door to Kane's apartment. The little cat was perched contentedly on her arm as she called through the door. "Krista? Mrs. Cavenaugh?"

"Where have you been?" Mrs. Cavenaugh scolded as she opened the door. "Kane's already called twice. Finally decided to leave a message with me...say, what's that you've got there?"

Erin breezed into the room, looking for Krista. "What does it look like, Mrs. Cavenaugh?" Erin asked in a whisper. "He's a surprise for Krista."

"Oh-ho," Mrs. Cavenaugh said, shaking her head, but reaching a tentative hand out to pat the kitten's soft, downy fur.

The whir of the electric wheelchair caught Erin's attention as Krista came into the room. The defiant look of rebellion had left her features several days ago, and for the first time since their meeting, Erin was sure that Krista was glad to see her.

"Oh, there you are. Look!" Erin announced with a wide, infectious grin as she proudly held up the black and white kitten for Krista's inspection. The blond girl let out a squeal of delighted excitement at the sight of the small cat. "I brought him home for you—you do like cats, don't you?"

"Oh, Erin," Krista stammered, wheeling more closely to the object of her delight. Erin placed the black ball of fur on Krista's lap. The kitten stretched and curled into a sleepy ball, purring contentedly. "He's...beautiful...." Krista's sparkling blue eyes swept from the drowsy kitten to Erin. "Thank you."

Erin smiled back at the girl and was surprised to feel a lump in her throat. "You're welcome, Krista," she murmured, and for a moment her breath caught. Erin kneeled next to the wheelchair and stroked the dozing kitten. "Now, if you decide to keep him, you'll have to take care of him. Feed him, take him outside...."

"I will," Krista agreed hurriedly. "Does he have a name?"

Erin shook her head. "That's for you to decide, unless Mrs. Cavenaugh has any suggestions...." Erin looked at the elderly lady and caught the gray-haired woman taking in the scene before her with teary eyes.

"What? Me?" Mrs. Cavenaugh coughed back her tears. "Oh, no. I've never been much of a cat person myself."

"Then it's up to you, Krista," Erin said. She cocked her head and stroked her thumb against her chin as she studied the cat with feigned thoughtfulness. "What do you think?"

"How about—Figaro. You know, like the cat in Pinocchio?" the bright-eyed girl asked, and Erin realized that for the first time since they had met, Krista had asked for and needed her opinion.

"I think Figaro's a great name," Erin agreed. "Now," she said as she stood up and adjusted her skirt, "I'll hurry upstairs and change my clothes before I cook us all some dinner."

Mrs. Cavenaugh and Krista exchanged knowing, conspiratorial glances. "Don't bother," Mrs. Cavenaugh suggested. "Krista and I are going to eat a pizza and watch *The Late Show.* I suppose the cat will, too. Remember I told you that Kane called earlier. He wants the two of you to go out alone."

"I don't know...." Erin looked pensively at the blond girl in the wheelchair and the cat nestled comfortably in her lap. "Are you sure that Kane wanted only me? I thought he wanted to spend some time with Krista."

"It's already been decided," Mrs. Cavenaugh stated firmly. "He called a few minutes ago. It was his idea. You're supposed to meet him at a place called The Tattered Sail or some such nonsense. I think he said that it's on the waterfront."

"Are you sure?" Erin still wasn't convinced. "He didn't say anything to me about dinner…."

Mrs. Cavenaugh clucked her tongue and interrupted, "That's why he called. He missed you. He'd been in some sort of a meeting with a fellow from California, a Mr.…."

"Haney," Erin supplied.

"That was it. Anyway, by the time he got out of the meeting, you had already gone." Mrs. Cavenaugh noted the puzzled expression on Erin's face. "Now, don't ask me any more questions, because I don't know anything else."

Erin turned her attention to Kane's daughter. The girl had managed to take a few steps on her own and flop down on the couch with the cat. Krista's progress was encouraging. "Krista, wouldn't you like to join us?"

The girl rolled her head negatively against the back of the couch and playfully scratched the kitten's belly. "Naw—not tonight. I think I'd rather stay here with Figaro. Besides, we've already ordered the pizza, and the movie is going to be great!"

Erin glanced at Mrs. Cavenaugh, who lifted her shoulders. A tiny hint of a smile pulled at the corner of the wrinkled mouth. "Well, if you're sure, but somehow I feel that I'm the innocent victim of a conspiracy."

"No one could accuse you of a lack of imagination. Conspiracy, ha!" Mrs. Cavenaugh rejoined, but her wise old eyes brightened. "Now, you'd better get going. You don't want to be late. Kane said he'd meet you at about eight o'clock."

Convinced that both Mrs. Cavenaugh and Krista were satisfied with their plans for the evening, Erin made her way up the stairs and began changing for her dinner date with Kane. She couldn't hide the feeling of excitement that surged within her. It seemed like an eternity since she had spent some time alone with him. It wasn't that she begrudged him the time he shared with his daughter, it was just that Erin missed the intimate and quiet times she had shared with him in the past. He had seemed so remote lately.

The cool amethyst silk dress that she chose for the date slid easily over her body. It was simple, smart and understated with its modest

V-neck and long sleeves. The slit that parted the hem added just the right amount of flair to be called sexy in a discreet manner. Erin eyed herself speculatively in the mirror and was pleased with her reflection. Her ebony hair cascaded in loose curls to her shoulders and brushed against the neckline of the dress. Her skin was already rosy with the blush of excitement and only a few touches of makeup were necessary to add to the effect. She reached for her coat and purse and headed out the door.

Just as she had closed the door, the telephone began to ring insistently. Erin was late already, and she considered letting the maddening instrument ring, but she couldn't. It might be something important, possibly Kane rearranging their hastily made plans. Reluctantly she threw her coat over the arm of the couch and hurried to the kitchen to answer the relentless ringing.

"Hello?"

"Erin! I can't believe that I finally got through to you. I've been trying to get in touch with you for days. You never called me, you know," the male voice accused, and Erin could picture the pouting lips and hurt expression in Lee's boyish blue eyes.

"I'm sorry, Lee. I did try, but there wasn't any answer."

"You could have tried again."

"I... I decided that it probably wouldn't be wise."

"What if it had been an emergency?"

Her conscience felt a twinge. "It wasn't, was it?"

"No...but it could have been!"

Erin leaned heavily against the wall, and let her head fall backward. Why tonight? Why was Lee calling again? "Look, Lee," she whispered. "I'm in a hurry for an appointment. Was there something that you wanted?"

There was a heavy pause in the conversation before he replied. "I just...wanted to see you again...."

Erin bit at her fingernail. "Bull!"

"I need to talk to you," he pleaded, and his image flashed in her mind's eye: wavy blond hair, cut-off jeans, old tennis shoes, a grass-stained football jersey that she had given him for Christmas one year.

"So talk," she managed, her voice unsteady.

"Can we meet?"

"I told you I've got a date...." She glanced at her watch.

There was silence, then a deep, theatrical sigh. "Is he someone special?"

"Yes, Lee. He is. Very special. But what do you care, after all these years?" She blinked back the tears that threatened to spill.

"Believe it or not, babe, I've always cared about you."

"Don't lie to me, Lee. I've heard it all before. I don't think this is the time to go into all that. Not now."

"When?" he demanded.

"Oh, Lee, don't you understand? It's over for us. It's been over for a long time—probably before you met Olivia."

"Okay, Erin," he retorted testily. "I deserved that. I was a louse and I admit it. But can't you believe that I want to see you again?"

"No."

"Erin, I have to."

The tears she was choking back began to slide down her cheeks. "No!"

"But, babe…"

"And don't call me that! Just what is it you want, Lee? Money?"

Silence. Incriminating silence.

"Look, Lee, do us both a favor and don't call back—ever! We've been through this scene too many times, and I for one won't repeat it ever again. It's too hard on me and it's too hard on you."

"Erin, baby, listen to me…"

He was still talking when she hung up the phone. Hastily she brushed back the tears and attempted to recapture the sense of exhilaration she had felt before she answered the phone. Why did he insist on calling? There was only one reason, the same one that she'd heard in the past: money. Damn! How could she get him out of her life once and for all?

Erin pushed her wayward thoughts aside and dashed out to her car. Soon she would be with Kane alone. Soon everything would be all right, as it should be, and she would be able to forget about Lee, the telephone call, the past.

The Tattered Sail had a reputation for being one of the best restaurants in the Northwest for fresh seafood, and tonight Erin found the rumor to be true. Once in the intimate old, barnlike structure, Erin could feel herself beginning to relax. The atmosphere was smoky and dark, and Erin was sure that if she listened closely, above the light contemporary music and the quiet chatter of the patrons, she would be able to hear the waters of the Sound lapping quietly against the pier that supported the restaurant.

The succulent house specialty, fresh Dungeness crab in a tangy sauce, was superb, and the sparkling bottle of chilled champagne that Kane had ordered added just the right touch of elegance to the otherwise casual Pacific Coast cuisine. The dimmed lanterns, the massive ship's rigging that covered the walls and ceilings and the view of the inky water of Puget Sound all served to enhance the romance and intimacy of the evening. Erin ate quietly, entranced by the setting and her powerful feelings for Kane. His eyes, two dark silver orbs, never left her face, and the smile on his face spoke more clearly than words of the depths of his feelings for her.

Somehow he seemed to have shaken off the tension that had been boiling within him for the past few days. All the heavy undercurrents that were usually evident in his eyes had disappeared, at least for the night. The dinner was a thoroughly enjoyable experience, and Erin found herself unwinding as she hadn't since the weekend in the San Juans. They talked little and spoke mostly with their eyes, but Erin did mention that she had brought

Krista the kitten, and Kane seemed more than pleased when he heard about his daughter's affection for the little black cat. The tender light that illuminated his face when he spoke of Krista touched Erin's heart.

The romance of the evening extended past dinner, and as they drove home together in her small car, Erin was overwhelmed by just how desperately she had grown to love the man sitting next to her. She couldn't deny to herself that she loved him with an unspoken passion that was consuming in its intensity. For the first time in weeks she wondered if, indeed, she and Kane and Krista might have a future together. Everything seemed to be falling into place. Perhaps someday, given enough time and affection, Kane could learn to love her. The little car climbed the hill that supported the Victorian apartment house. Its broad-paned windows winked cheerfully in the night.

As she shut off the engine, Erin felt the warmth of Kane's hand when it covered hers. "Let's not go in, not just yet," he suggested in a husky voice.

"But Krista..." The protest was feeble. Already she could feel the heat of desire beginning to warm her.

"She's fine," Kane assured her, and pushed a wayward wisp of her hair back into place. "She and Mrs. Cavenaugh planned to sit up and watch old movies all night long."

"But don't you think we should check on her?"

"In a minute," he insisted, and his face moved closer to hers. The warmth of his breath, laced with the clinging vapors of champagne, whispered over her face. "I'd just like to spend a few more minutes alone with you..." His fingers reached out and traced the curve of her cheek, the length of her throat, the neckline of the dress. Erin's breath began to constrict in her chest, it became ragged as she breathed. His hand found the slit in her dress and moved gently, heatedly against her inner thigh.

"Kane," she gulped, seeing the undying passion in his gaze. "I...we...can't possibly, not here...."

"Shhh..." he commanded, and rimmed her lips with his tongue. She was melting in his embrace, feeling herself begin to blend with him. "Walk with me," he suggested intimately. "The night's warm, and so am I."

His lips found hers, and he nibbled at them gently, persuasively. His hand moved in sensuous circles against her thigh. "Well," she agreed, her eyes closing, "a walk…a short one…"

He was right, she thought raggedly as they walked together in the clear October evening. Was it the night itself or Kane's presence that made it seem so special, so eternal? The cool nip of fall was in the air, and yet, under the stars winking in the ethereal moon glow, Erin was warm despite the season. Even in the half light, she could see the spiraling vapor of Kane's breath as it mingled with the chilly night air.

He held her hand tightly, as if he were afraid that his grasp would slip and that he might lose her in the shadows. It was a wonderful, exotic feeling; his magnetic touch and the magic of the night wound together. Erin felt drugged as together they made their way to the gazebo in the backyard. It was old and in sad disrepair. But against the backdrop of the clear night, its flaws hidden by the darkness and the stand of fir trees near the worn steps, it seemed intimate and regal with its undisturbed beauty of another era. Silently Kane helped her up the two weathered steps, and she felt herself begin to tremble.

"From the first time I saw this place, I knew that I wanted to make love to you here," he stated. The silver moon glow was reflected in the intensity of his gaze, and his head bent down slowly and seductively to find her chilled lips. He crushed her against his chest with a savage urgency that seemed to be ripping him apart. "Make love to me, Erin," he pleaded. "I don't think I can stand another moment of this agony. Touch me, love me!" His lips wet a trail of desire leading from her lips down her throat, to nestle hotly against her partially exposed breast. Once there he paused to moan, "God, I want you!" Her breathing began to come in short, uneven breaths in the cold night air. Kane fell to his knees and continued to press the warmth of his face against the frail fabric that covered her abdomen. "Love me," he commanded as his hands moved in circular seductive movements against her hips, and she felt the smooth fabric of the silk dress sweep gently upward to brush against her thighs.

"I want you, too," she whispered huskily, and her hands wound themselves in the thick strands of his hair. "Oh, Kane. I need you so much!" she confessed.

"I know," he murmured. Erin felt the cold shudder of autumn pierce her skin as the zipper of her dress was lowered and the silky fabric parted to expose her back and shoulders. The dress slipped to the floor of the gazebo, and Kane's gentle hands and mouth caressed her exposed skin, raining hot moist kisses against her flesh. He dragged her down to lie beside him and tentatively touched one rounded breast with the delicacy of a sculptor. An animal growl escaped from his throat as he watched her, and in wet, heated strokes, his tongue found the ripeness of her nipples.

His mouth seared against her skin, and his tongue licked and pressed hot moistness against her body. She felt the warmth of her desire spread from her innermost core through all of her body. Rivers of passion ran in her veins, and desire, hot and molten, pounded against her temples. She felt tides of feverish passion wash over her until she wanted to drown in its molten embrace. Despite the cool of the evening, a dusting of perspiration covered her body. On their own, without conscious thought, her fingers found the buttons of his shirt, the zipper to his slacks, the proud hardness of his desire. She arched her body heatedly against his, aware only of her agonizing love for him.

His lips teased and satisfied her, toying with her until she thought she would go mad, only to arouse her to still-untouched heights. His eyes, smoldering in the night, took in all of her: the look of yearning in her large luminous eyes, the way her provocative tongue continued to flick against her lips, the full, rounded breasts with nipples proudly erect, and her soft, sensuous hips, inviting him to explore her more intimately. He thought he would lose all control in the instant she arched against him, and he wanted to give in to his virile male urge to take her. God, he'd waited so long, and he felt a need, strong and inflexible, to make love to her, but he forced himself to wait, somewhat impatiently, caught up in the heat of his lovemaking, until he was certain she was ready for him.

Erin wondered if she would fall apart and crumble into fiery bursts of passion as Kane lowered himself onto her. With a sigh of long-denied pleasure, she wound her arms and legs around him, entrapping him and tempting him to make love to her. He could resist no longer.

"Oh, God, Erin. You're so beautiful, I need you…"

His words trailed off into the night in an unspoken confession as he found his way to her. In the shadow of the gazebo, his hot pulse at war with the cool night, he watched her as he loved her, and he saw the heat of desire blossom into the ecstasy of satisfaction. Together they found a love so exquisite that he knew it could never be recaptured. Only his own traitorous duplicity marred the perfect enchantment that he knew as he fell against her and felt the warmth of her breasts flatten against his weight.

It was several minutes before he spoke, as if he were unable to break the peaceful spell of enchantment that covered them. When at last he broke the silence, it was to murmur her name over and over in the night, as if trying to impress her memory upon his lips. It was so difficult to say all the things that he wanted so urgently for her to know. And the questions that had to be asked plagued him. He knew that it was time for explanation and discussion. Too much was at stake to continue to hide behind the truth. He needed her so desperately, yet his duplicity was eating at him. The fear of losing her gripped him more savagely each day. It was time for something to be done.

"What is it?" Erin asked suddenly, staring at the dread in his eyes. Once again she sensed the wariness had appeared, and the knowledge frightened her. She had hoped that all Kane's reservations had melted away. Shivering more from Kane's obvious apprehension than from the coolness of the night, she felt the same cold doubts crawl up her spine. He noticed the chill, rolled off her and pulled his jacket lightly over her shoulders.

His hands trembled as they pressed against her face. "Marry me, darling," he whispered in a voice dry with emotion. For a moment Erin's heart turned over. Her first impulse was to throw her arms around his neck and confess the depth of her love, but something in his face made her pull the reins in on her excitement.

"What?" she asked quietly, looking deeply into his eyes for the trace of love she hoped to find.

"I'm asking you to marry me. Now—as soon as possible," he clarified, and pressed her fingers against his lips. "We need to be together."

She wanted to accept his proposal, to take part in the elation that was beginning to burst in her veins. But there was the strong scent of accusation that hung between them and made her pause.

"I would love to marry you," Erin breathed,

trying to think rationally. The stars, the moon, the wind of the night were all closing in on her, and she found it difficult to concentrate on anything but the feelings of love that were swelling in her veins. "You must know that…."

"Then, get packed. We'll fly to Reno tonight—or early in the morning. The sooner the better." He began to slide into his pants in his urgency to persuade her.

"We have time…."

"No!" he nearly shouted. And then, in a somewhat calmer voice, he continued, "No—we don't have any time."

"But, Kane," she argued, fearing the continuation of the discussion, but unable to stop herself. "You have to put certain things into perspective. We have to take Krista's feelings into consideration—surely you can understand that. And the bank—"

"Erin!" He grabbed her shoulders roughly, and forced her to look up at him. His grip tightened on her forearms, and his face was a harsh mask of determination. "It's got to be soon. You know that."

"Why? We have the rest of our lives…"

"No, we don't!" he snapped. "Don't you understand?" His eyes were shadowed by the darkness of the gazebo, but Erin could feel the pain and torture of his words without being able to probe his desperate gaze. Why was he so insistent? A cold strange feeling passed over her, transferred from him by the urgency of his forceful grasp on her upper arms.

With an unsteady voice, she asked, "Kane, just what is it that you're trying to say?"

"I'm asking you to be my wife, pure and simple. Is that so difficult to understand?"

She wasn't convinced. "There's more, isn't there? Has it got something to do with Krista, because she's already made it plain to me that she doesn't have room in her life for a 'new mother.'" In the blackness Erin tried to read the expression on Kane's face. Hoping to find love, she was disappointed. A cloud passed over the moon, and once the pale light was restored, she found his eyes torn with an emotion she couldn't understand. She tried to draw away from him but still he held her desperately, passionately.

Slowly the grip on her forearms relaxed, and resignation covered Kane's features. "Get dressed," he commanded softly. "And then I promise you we'll talk."

Hurriedly she did as he instructed her, running her pantyhose in her hasty efforts. Was it the chill of the night that made her shudder, or the cold look of determination heightening the masculine angles of Kane's face that cooled her blood?

As she was smoothing the silk dress over her hips, he began to speak in a distant voice that was dry with dread.

"When I was in California," he started, stepping away from her and pacing the length of the gazebo, "some more money was embezzled from the dividend account...three thousand dollars to be exact." He whirled to face her, and his guarded eyes found hers. The expression on her face was one of confusion.

"I don't understand—I thought that Mitch was the suspect...."

He cut off her conjecture. "Of course he's the prime suspect, but it's become apparent that he has an accomplice in the department!"

"No!" she gasped.

"Yes!"

Her voice was faint, barely a whisper. "But who?"

"Why don't you tell me?" he suggested, his voice taking on the quality of a smooth courtroom lawyer.

"But I don't know."

"Don't you?" Accusation singed his words.

"No... I can't imagine...." She was so taken aback by his supposition of an accomplice for Mitch that she hadn't noticed the suspicion in his eyes, the way his arms crossed over his chest, the grim hard angle of his jaw. But now, after the shock of his statement had dissipated, she knew what he was thinking.

"You're not...you couldn't be," she was stammering, but she couldn't control herself. Slowly she stood up and watched the play of emotions that rampaged over his face. "I don't believe that you would think I could somehow be involved. You wouldn't be suggesting anything like that...would you?" Before the anger took hold of her, disbelief and agony tortured her eyes.

"Why don't you explain..."

"No!" She stamped a bare foot on the thin floor of the gazebo. "I don't have to explain anything to you...." Tears burned in her eyes, but she tilted her head defiantly in spite of them. As they began to flow slowly down her face, they caught the moonlight in tiny rivers of outrage. "Are you accusing me of embezzlement?" Her voice was as chilling as the wind that rustled the leaves overhead.

"Erin," he said in a calm voice devoid of emotion. "I just want to know the reason for certain facts...."

"Facts? You mean evidence? I don't believe it. You don't have any evidence—you couldn't, just an overactive and suspicious imagination!"

He tried to interrupt, but she wouldn't let him. "I wondered, from the beginning, why all the questions about Mitch, why all the vague insinuations and especially why you would look at me the way you did. But I must have been a fool, a damned idiot, not to have put two and two together." She took a gasp of cold autumn air, only to find that her entire body was quivering with rage and betrayal. "How can you stand there and accuse me, after all that we've shared together? Oh, Kane—why?"

"If you could just be reasonable."

"Reasonable?" she shrieked, and then laughed from the tension that was capturing her in its angry claws. "Reasonable? How can you expect me to be 'reasonable' after you ask me to marry you and accuse me of a crime I didn't commit?"

"Erin, don't make this any harder than it already is," he pleaded, and leaned against a beam that supported the roof. "I can't ignore the facts, as much as I'd like to. I know that you need money—the employee loan application states as much—"

A protesting sound gurgled in her throat, but he ignored it.

"And your ex-husband, Lee Sinclair—" the name came out in a snarl of disapproval "—you loaned him money once, and he's back in town."

"How?"

"It doesn't matter." He shook his head, and continued in a flat, dry voice. "And there was the securities key discrepancy. You were one of the people who had access to the bearer bonds that were taken, and suddenly, somehow, you find the money to paint the apartment house and fix it up for the winter. An odd set of circumstances, wouldn't you say?"

"Exactly that, circumstances," she commented indignantly.

"That first morning in the bank I found you alone in your office. You had the perfect opportunity...."

"Enough!" she stammered, and started down the two weathered steps of the gazebo. "I've heard enough." She paused for a minute, her hands supporting her weight on the railing. "What I don't understand is why, if you suspected me from the start, you didn't tell me—or ask me? Didn't you have the decency to respect my innocence and ask me about all those 'facts'?"

"It doesn't matter, not now," he said with a rush of enthusiasm. "We can get married, and I'll find a way to replace the money." He strode over to her and captured her wrist. "Don't you see, no more money will be taken, and all the cash that's missing since Mitch left the bank will be replaced."

"Just like that?" she asked incredulously. Her eyes narrowed and she surveyed the hand on her wrist suspiciously. "You really think that I was a part of this, don't you?"

"Erin," he sighed disconsolately as he tilted her face with his thumb. "I know that you met Mitch on the day of his arraignment. I also know that the money was taken on that day...."

"You bastard!" Before she could think, her free hand arched upward and slapped Kane's cheek. The loud smack echoed in the night, and Kane's eyes grew black with suppressed fury. His jaw clenched, and for a moment Erin wondered if he was going to retaliate and hit her.

His voice, suddenly soft, reached out to her. "Erin…"

"Don't! I don't want to hear anything more! Not ever again. I'll… I'll hand in my resignation tomorrow…and I think it would be best for all of us if you would move out of the apartment as soon as possible. You…you can…have two weeks…." The sobs that she was quietly withholding began to rack her body, and she felt as if she were about to be torn in half by his betrayal. At the pressure from Kane's hand on her shoulder, she drew away as if wounded and started stumbling toward the house.

"Erin, wait!" Kane ordered, but she ignored his plea. "You can't resign. If you're innocent, you can't resign. It will appear more incriminating!"

Whirling to face him, nearly tripping on the exposed root from a nearby fir tree, she replied bitingly, "I'm quitting. I… I don't want anything more to do with you…or your bank!"

"Erin, don't!" He was beside her in a minute, and his features had softened. "Don't you understand? I need you, I want you… I love you!"

"Love? You don't have any idea what the

word means. And, as for *needing* and *wanting*, I think you're getting them confused with *using.* Because that's what you did to me, wasn't it? You used me—tried to get close to me so that you could 'look into my darker, private side.' Isn't that how you phrased it? I didn't know what you meant, not at the time, but I know now, don't I? You wanted to get inside my head and find a way to incriminate me for a crime that I had no part of...."

"Please try and understand...."

"Just leave me alone!" Her eyes met his, and even though they were filled with tears, he could see that she meant every word she was speaking.

"I don't want it to end this way."

"There isn't any alternative. You took care of that!"

"I'm sorry."

"Not good enough, Kane, not good enough." Her words were colder than the autumn wind that pushed her black hair away from her face, and highlighted the proud, near-perfect oval with its fine cheekbones and luminous violet eyes.

"All right, Erin. If that's the way you want it."

"That's the way it has to be," she sighed,

and stepped aside to let him pass. She watched him silently as he walked toward the front of the house and disappeared around the corner. When he was finally out of her range of vision, she let herself slump against the tall fir tree near the gazebo. "You are a fool," she muttered under her breath. "And he is a bastard!" The tears started to flow again. How could he even think that she would stoop so low? How could he have misjudged her so? And how, in God's name, how could he be so gentle and caring one minute and so ruthless the next?

It was past midnight when Erin found the strength to return to the loft that she had once shared with the man she still loved.

Chapter 12

An insistent, impatient knocking awoke Erin from a night whose fitful sleep had been interrupted by dismal nightmares. The dull ache in her head increased with each knock on her front door. "I'm coming," she groaned, running her fingers through her tangled hair and hoping that her response would stop whoever it was from making any further racket.

Jerking on her peach-colored terry robe, she cinched the belt tightly around her waist and glanced haphazardly into the mirror over the bureau. The reflection that stared back at her was disheartening—the long, anxious night had taken its toll on her face. Large blue circles under her eyes intensified the pale, washed-out complexion of her face. The large eyes that had always sparkled seemed lifeless, and her black hair hung in tangled curls against her neck.

The pounding started up again. "I'm coming," Erin repeated loudly, and wondered who would be calling so insistently at seven in the morning. The knocking subsided for a minute. Erin half expected to see Kane when she opened the door and braced herself for whatever confrontation might occur when she came face-to-face with him. "Just a minute," she called through the wood panels, and tugged the door open.

What she hadn't expected to see on her doorstep—not in a million years—was Lee. His blond hair was meticulously combed and his blue eyes were as brilliant as ever, perhaps even more so. He was perched atop the polished wood railing of the landing. One arm was bent around a carved banister to aid his balance. His casual slouch, accented by faded jeans and a lightweight sport shirt was a theatrical display of relaxation by design, belied only by the tiny muscle that worked constantly near the back of his jaw.

"Hi, babe." He greeted her with a wink and

gave her a long, suggestive head-to-toe appraisal. "Rough night?" A smile, boyish yet sinister, curved his thin lips.

After the initial shock of seeing him, Erin regained her composure and propped her shoulder against the doorjamb, keeping a careful distance between them. Without conscious thought, she tugged on the belt of her robe and pulled it more tightly around her slim waist.

"I'll ignore your insinuations for now," she replied with a plastic copy of his smirk pasted on her face. "What are you doing here?"

Hopping off the railing in a lithe movement, he responded, "I couldn't seem to get through to you on the phone. So I decided if Mohammed wouldn't come to the mountain...."

"I get the gist," she retorted coldly. She could feel an uneasy caution tighten the muscles of her back. "That doesn't explain why you're here, banging on my door loudly enough to wake up the entire neighborhood at seven in the morning. What do you want?"

"How about a cup of your coffee, for starters. From there, who knows how far our relationship can progress?" There was another long, suggestive look.

"I'm sorry, Lee, but as you already guessed, I did have a rough night last night. I'm tired and I'm not up to playing word games with you. Why don't you just tell me what it is you want? Then you can leave." She crossed her arms over her breasts to shield herself from his gaze. Lee made her uncomfortable, but she did her best to hide her apprehension.

"Why are you always so suspicious of me?" he asked in a low voice that was meant to be hypnotic.

"Because I know you."

"Erin, baby," he cooed, coming more closely to her. Involuntarily she shrank back. "What's happened to you? Let me make you feel better."

"And just how do you think you could do that?" she asked wryly, a grim smile twisting her lips and her black brows cocking nervously.

"We used to get along just fine," he suggested smoothly, and his hand reached out to trace the neckline of her robe.

Jerking away from him, Erin glared at his bemused face. "Look, Lee, just say whatever it is you think you have to say to me and then leave." She paused for a moment, and then continued. "What is it? Do you need money again?"

Sandy-blond eyebrows shot up with undisguised interest. "Ah, well, that's not the main reason that I came over here, but now that you mention it, I could use a few bucks." He smiled his most winning smile and shrugged his shoulders. Erin was surprised at her reaction, total disinterest in his most becoming grin. "You know how it is—I had a run of bad luck."

"Haven't we all?" she muttered under her breath, and raked her fingers through her tangled black curls.

"Ah, come on, Erin. Don't give me that. The way I hear it, you're loaded."

"Is that the way you hear it?" She laughed tightly, despite the headache that was pounding relentlessly in her ears. "I guess you've got the wrong information."

"What do you mean?" he asked, a sudden seriousness killing his smile. *He looks old,* Erin thought to herself. The sunny college-boy looks only survived when he smiled.

"What I mean, Lee, is that I'm out of a job," she explained, her words a little less caustic than they had been. "I'm sorry. I can't loan you any money. I just don't have it."

"You? You've got to be kidding!"

"I'm not!" She shook her head to emphasize her point.

"You must have a savings account—*something!*"

"Not much," she admitted. "And anyway, I don't feel that I owe you any favors. That might sound a little cold-blooded, but it's the way I feel."

Lee began to bite his lower lip, and his eyes darted around the landing. "Look, babe, I'm desperate. I need to get my hands on some bread, and fast!"

"Why don't you get a job?" she asked, and hated herself for the acidic sound of the sarcasm.

A stricken expression covered Lee's face. "A job? I've been looking for a job night and day. It's…just that the right…opportunity hasn't presented itself."

Erin rubbed her hands against her temples and gave Lee a final sorrowful expression. "I'm sorry about that, too," she said honestly, "but if you don't mind, I'm tired, and I'm going back to bed." He must have misinterpreted her feelings, because as she reached for the handle of the door, Lee was against her, his body molding tightly to hers. She tried to wriggle out of his embrace, but there was no escape.

"Erin, baby," he growled. "Why do you enjoy teasing me?"

"What? Lee, let go of me. What are you doing?" She felt the power of his body push against her and force her rigidly against the cold, hard wood. His hands reached for the knotted belt of her robe, and she could feel his long, cold fingers probe against the flimsy fabric of her nightgown. A shudder of fear stiffened her spine.

"Let me go," she hissed, but his lips, dispassionately cool, descended on her open mouth. A sinking sensation of fear swept over her as his tongue pressed ruthlessly against her gums. With all the strength she could gather, she lifted her bare foot and hoisted her knee sharply upward, but Lee had anticipated the move and dodged the misplaced blow.

"So you want to play rough," he growled, and pulled her hands over her head to pin them cruelly against the door frame.

"Lee! Stop this. You're acting like a lunatic," she asserted, but the command in her voice was diminished by the fact that her words were trembling.

"Let her go!" Kane's voice commanded

from the lower landing. At the sound Lee turned.

"What?" Lee studied the source of the noise. The man, tall and dark, was stripped to the waist, wearing only faded jeans as he began to slowly ascend the stairs. "Hey, look, mister," Lee said guardedly. "Why don't you mind your own business? This is my wife...." Lee jerked his head in Erin's direction. "We're just having a little disagreement...."

"I don't think so." Kane mounted the stairs and stood only a few feet from Lee. His gray eyes glinted like steel, and though his voice was outwardly calm and solicitous, his clenched fists and hardened jaw reinforced his words. "Do you have a hearing problem?" he asked. "I told you to let her go!"

Reluctantly Lee stepped away from Erin and glowered menacingly at Kane. "Just who the hell do you think you are?" he snapped, while Erin crumpled in the doorway. The smell of a fight was in the air.

"I was just about to ask you that same question," Kane's calm, hard voice rejoined.

"I'm her husband!" Lee snarled, tossing a look of red-hot anger and rage toward Erin.

"Ex-husband," Kane corrected. "And what

sort of power does that title give you? The right to rough up the lady?"

"I wasn't…"

Kane's fury snapped and his eyes sparked disgusted fire. "Don't bother with any of your explanations. Just get out before I throw you over this railing!" Kane's voice had risen with his anger, and Erin saw Lee gulp and hesitate, casting a final threatening glance in her direction.

"I'd just like to see you try," Lee warned back to Kane. A light of grim satisfaction warmed Kane's face. Lee saw the reaction and slowly, carefully backed down the stairs.

"And just one more thing, Sinclair," Kane cautioned with an evil smile. "If I ever so much as hear that you've been bothering Erin again, I won't wait for you to show up. I'll come looking for you!"

Lee hastened down the remainder of the stairs, the front door crashed closed, and for a few seconds there was silence. Only the feeling of electricity crackling in the air disturbed the tranquillity of the moment until the noise of a racing engine split the silence as it roared angrily down the hill. Erin sighed as she realized that Lee was finally gone.

"I can't say much for your taste in husbands," Kane commented dryly. The grim set of his jaw hadn't relaxed.

"He's not so bad," Erin replied uneasily, as if convincing herself. "Not really, he's just had a run of bad luck…."

"Bad luck?" Kane threw his hands over his head in exasperation. "That gives him the right to come in here and force himself on you?" He regarded her ruefully, since she looked so small and vulnerable this morning. "Erin, you are incredibly naive! What is it with you anyway?"

"What do you mean?" she asked, feeling herself start to bristle, partially because she knew that he was close to the truth.

"I mean, first, Mitchell Cameron—you defend him to the hilt when he's an A-1 jackass—"

"Now, wait a minute," Erin gasped.

"No, you wait a minute! And now your husband, pardon me, your unfortunate ex-husband who's had 'a run of bad luck,' so he takes it out on you by almost…" His pause was effective, and Erin's face flooded with color. "Erin, don't you see? Sinclair's a bastard, a loser. You should know that better than anyone. As far as I can see, so far you've had a pretty poor track record of picking male companions!"

"Is that a fact?" she fired back at him, her temper sparking. "Does that include the latest man in my life? You remember him—a wonderful guy. I trusted him completely only to discover that he thinks I'm a crook!" Sarcasm flavored her words with bitterness.

Kane looked as if he'd been slapped. The stunned expression on his face and the sudden dead look in his eyes tore at Erin's heart, but she proudly held her ground. It would be too easy to forgive him, too easy to let him back into her heart.

His shoulders relaxed, the firm muscles slackening. "So that's how it stands, does it? You won't let me help you?"

"I don't need any help. I'm innocent," she maintained defiantly.

"Would it make you feel better to know that I believe you?"

"Ha! Then why did you accuse me of thievery last night? Why did you wait all this time? Why didn't you just ask me what I knew about the embezzlement and the fact that there is supposedly an accomplice? Why did you wait," she asked, her voice quaking, and her eyes meeting his with accusation, "all the while silently condemning me with your eyes!"

"Oh, God, Erin," he groaned. "I'm so sorry— I was hoping that maybe you had changed your mind...."

"No!" She shook her head firmly, but her voice softened. "Look." She reached out to touch his arm, but he jerked away from her. "I want to thank you for helping me with Lee. He...was...getting a little out of hand."

"Erin," Kane's voice was steady and low. He stood half-supported by the railing, his head drooping down and facing the lobby two stories below him. "I want you to marry me. I need you to be my wife, and Krista needs a mother. Perhaps I judged you too quickly, but it was only because I was afraid of the truth. I wanted to talk to you about it earlier." His eyes rolled heavenward and his voice became husky. "God, how many times did I try?" He shook his head disconsolately and continued to stare blankly ahead of him. "But I just couldn't."

"Because you didn't trust me. You couldn't find it in your heart to accept my innocence," Erin added in a flat, dead voice.

"There are other possibilities. The accomplice has to be in the legal department...."

"But I was the most convenient choice. The easiest target, right?"

His silence was as condemning as the pained droop of his shoulders. "Oh, God, Erin. Just believe that I love you!" he pleaded.

"I guess you and I have a different meaning for the word," she replied, her voice broken by emotion. "Goodbye, Kane," she whispered as she slipped through the door and listened to the sound of his footsteps retreating heavily down the stairs. Biting back the tears that were struggling to fill her eyes, she hurried to the bedroom and pulled out her worn leather suitcase. She tossed it recklessly on the bed. "You're a coward," she snipped at herself, "running from the truth that you love him, and no matter what he's done, the one thing that you want most in life is to be his wife." Her tiny fist balled up and crashed down on the suitcase. *Damn! Why am I such a fool?* For an instant she thought about running after him and throwing herself into his arms, but her pride forced her to restrain herself. He thinks you're a thief, she reminded herself, and the feeling of cold betrayal once again settled upon her. Hurriedly she tossed the rest of her things haphazardly into the suitcase and snapped it shut. She looked around the bedroom to see if she needed anything else but found that she had to get out of the room.

It was too crowded with memories, gloriously happy memories of making love to Kane in her bed.

With shaking, unsteady hands she dialed the phone and made reservations for the week. Then, as calmly as possible, she wrote down the phone number and address of the hotel and placed it in an envelope before sitting down near the window and waiting. It wasn't long, maybe only ten minutes, but it felt like an eternity to Erin before she saw Kane walk out toward his car. Fortunately Krista was with him. Erin managed a smile through her tears as she saw that Krista was able to walk to the car with her father's assistance. Although she leaned heavily on Kane, the girl stumbled only once and he was able to catch her. The playful little kitten followed along. There appeared to be a slight argument of some sort, and Erin guessed that it had to do with the cat. Kane was shaking his head, but in the end, the black ball of fur was allowed to tag along for the ride.

After Kane's car was out of sight, Erin hurried out of her apartment and sprinted down the stairs to knock on Mrs. Cavenaugh's door. Erin tapped lightly against the wood, and the door was opened in an instant. The little old woman was up and dressed, as if she were expecting company.

"Good morning," the gray-haired lady said cheerily, her wise blue eyes flicking from Erin's distressed face to the suitcase in her hand. "Good morning, Mrs. Cavenaugh," Erin replied. "I… I've got to leave town for a while…."

Mrs. Cavenaugh's gray eyebrows shot upward and her mouth pursed into an expression of distaste. Erin continued. "Urgent business… I'll be gone for a week, maybe longer. In this envelope is the telephone number and address of the hotel where I can be reached in case of an emergency…."

"Erin," Mrs. Cavenaugh's calm voice broke into her chatter. "You know that I hate to pry, but what's the matter? Did something happen between you and Kane?" Kind, concerned blue eyes probed Erin's rigid face.

"What…what do you mean?"

"I mean 'leaving town because of urgent business' is a trifle overused." A wry smile twisted the wrinkled face. "Honestly I would have expected something with a little more imagination."

"Well, it's the truth," Erin maintained.

"And you're a terrible liar."

"Mrs. Cavenaugh, I'm not lying, honestly. Something has come up, something I can't deal with. I need a little time and distance in order to sort things out."

Mrs. Cavenaugh's knowing smile broadened. "Well, at least you're opening up a little. I understand that you might need a little space, isn't that what they say these days? I can't argue with that, but…"

"What?"

"Well, don't let your pride come between you and something you really want."

Erin sucked in her breath. "You mean Kane, don't you?" she sighed dismally and broke eye contact with her elderly tenant.

"He's a man who loves you dearly. And his daughter!" The old lady threw up her hands and shook her head at the incredulity of the situation.

"Krista? What about Krista?" Erin asked, her voice full of concern.

"Oh, nothing other than the fact that she worships the ground you walk on."

"Be serious!"

"I am—I've never seen the likes of it! Oh, at first, I'll grant you she was determined to hate you. But can you blame the child—losing a mother the way she did? All she had left was her father, and she didn't want to share him. But now—" Mrs. Cavenaugh moved her head thoughtfully "—that poor girl can talk of nothing but you—except for the kitten of course."

The lump in Erin's throat began to swell, and some of her firm resolve began to be chipped at. Mrs. Cavenaugh was working on her; Erin knew it, but she couldn't help but hope that there was just a sliver of truth in the sweet old woman's words.

"I'm sorry, Mrs. Cavenaugh," Erin managed, looking hastily at her watch, "but I've really got to run. Now, promise me that under no circumstances will you tell Kane where I am!"

"I don't know if I can do that," the older woman replied honestly.

"You have to! I *need* time to myself."

"Well, if you're so dead set against it, I'll give you my word," Mrs. Cavenaugh unwillingly agreed.

"Thanks," Erin sighed, kissing her friend lightly on the cheek. "I'll see you soon."

"Dear," Mrs. Cavenaugh said, placing a bony hand on Erin's sleeve. "Do be careful."

"I will," Erin promised, and turned to leave the apartment building. She could feel Mrs.

Cavenaugh's kind eyes boring into her back as she walked to her car, but she didn't have the heart to turn and wave. It took all her strength to hoist her suitcase into the car, start the engine and race down the hill toward the city and the waterfront.

Once back in Deer Harbor on Orcas Island in the San Juans, Erin realized what a disastrous mistake she had made in returning to the island where she had had such a carefree and loving existence with Kane only a few weeks earlier. Although she was far removed from the rustic cabin that they had shared together, memories of the small town still burned in her brain, and it seemed that she couldn't walk anywhere without coming face-to-face with memories of Kane. The pain in her heart didn't disappear.

The seasons had changed in the past weeks, and each day was as gray and cold as the Pacific Ocean. Wind and rain deluged the coastal town, and although Erin tried several kinds of outdoor amusements, she found that most of her days were spent inside her tiny hotel room staring vacantly at the television or brooding about the turn of events in her life. Knowing that her attitude was as discouraging as the somber, gray rain-washed days, she attempted to pull herself out of her depression, but found it impossible. Nothing seemed to work. And thoughts of Krista and the fact that she hadn't even bothered to say goodbye to the lonely girl only made Erin more miserable and guilt-ridden. While the island had once been a haven, now it seemed like a prison, but Erin elected to continue her confinement until she could no longer afford it. How could she possibly go home to an empty house and no job?

It had been over a week, and the depression still clung to her like a heavy shroud when she picked up the Seattle newspaper to look through the classified advertisements in search of employment. As usual, the openings for legal assistants were few, and Erin faced the fact that it would be more difficult than she had first imagined to find a decent position. Disinterestedly she perused the rest of the paper and stopped at the financial section. A photograph of the bank building with a caption concerning the embezzlement caught her eye. With more interest than she had felt for days, she began to read the article. As the meaning of each sentence in the column became clear to her, Erin began to feel her stomach churn with emotions of rage and disgust. According to the article, Mitchell Cameron had in fact worked with an accomplice—a woman with whom he had shared responsibility for years—Miss Olivia Parsons. The article explained the scam more fully and the fact that the scheme was so elaborate that it had taken the auditing staff and the president of the bank a lengthy amount of time to prove the guilt of the parties involved.

Erin felt a growing nausea as she read the article, and when she had finished, she tossed the newspaper into the wastebasket near her bed. Never would she have suspected Olivia of doing anything illegal. Just like Mitch, Olivia seemed far too professional to stoop to thievery. The delight that Erin should have experienced as she realized that she was no longer under suspicion of the crime seemed to have soured as she thought of Mitch and Olivia, two respected members of the banking industry who had tossed away their careers and possibly their lives for greed. Erin wondered what could have caused their joint journey into crime.

Two days later Erin began preparing for her trip home to Seattle. She had been gone far too long already, and her money was running

out. She realized that she couldn't run away
from Kane and her love for him, and there
was really no reason to linger on the island.

Just as Erin began to pack her things, the
telephone jarred the stillness of the hotel
room. For several seconds Erin just stared
at the telephone, wondering who would be
calling her. Kane? Unlikely. A wrong number? Perhaps. Her heart began to thud wildly
in her chest as she reached for the receiver.

"Hello?" she inquired, and felt a welling
sense of dread when she recognized Mrs.
Cavenaugh's unsteady voice.

"Erin—Erin, is that you?" the old lady demanded.

"Yes, it's I… What happened?" Erin asked,
convinced that Mrs. Cavenaugh wouldn't call
unless there was an emergency of some sort.
Nervously she bit at her thumbnail.

"Oh—I know that he told me not to call,
but I knew that you would want to know. It's
just awful—I really don't know what to do.
Dear Lord in heaven!" The little old lady continued to ramble in endless circles of words
and phrases that meant nothing to Erin. Ap-
prehensively Erin interrupted.

"Mrs. Cavenaugh! What's wrong? Try and
pull yourself together and just tell me what's

the matter." The hairs on the back of Erin's neck began to stand on end.

"It's Krista," Mrs. Cavenaugh moaned in a voice so low that Erin thought perhaps she had misunderstood.

"Krista?" Erin echoed. "Oh, God, what's happened to her?" Erin's heart leaped to her throat and her pulse began to race. Tiny droplets of perspiration moistened her skin, and she felt her knees give way as she sank against the bed.

"Oh, Erin, it's so awful. Ever since you've been gone, Kane, well, he hasn't been himself—in a terribly foul mood." Erin swallowed hard and tried to press back the feelings of guilt that assailed her. "And Krista, well, she didn't fare any better. She…withdrew. You know. You remember what she was like when she first arrived in Seattle…." Erin gasped, and the little lady reassured her. "It wasn't nearly that bad, you understand, but still she just wasn't her cheery self. I'm afraid that she's missed you terribly."

Erin closed her eyes and leaned her head against the headboard of the bed for support. "She didn't stop walking, did she?" Erin held her breath.

"Thank goodness—no." Erin let the air

escape from her lungs in a rush. "However, she was distracted, wouldn't eat, was thoroughly depressed." Erin felt as if a knife were being slowly twisted in her stomach. How could she have been so heartless as to have left Krista without explaining anything? Mrs. Cavenaugh continued. "And then, late this morning…well, Krista was chasing that little kitten of hers, and it scrambled up the stairs. She tried to follow it but fell. She hit her head on the bottom step."

"Oh, no," Erin gasped, the color draining from her face. "Is—is she seriously injured?"

"Well, that's just it. No one seems to know for sure. She's still in the hospital for observation, been there all day as far as I know. I think she regained consciousness, but I'm not really certain." The elderly woman's voice had begun to quake, and Erin felt herself shiver.

"Mrs. Cavenaugh, where is Krista?"

"Virginia Mason Hospital on First Hill, but you shouldn't go there. Kane's there and he specifically instructed me not to tell you."

Erin stifled the sob that threatened to belie her calm words. "Don't worry about Kane. I can handle him—I'm leaving as soon as possible. I'll see you when I get home."

"Good."

"Oh, and Mrs. Cavenaugh?"

"Yes?"

"Thanks for calling."

"I knew that you'd want to know," came the somber reply.

Erin stripped her things out of the closet and dresser. As hastily as possible she threw them into her case, paid the hotel bill and rented a small boat back to the mainland. It wasn't easy to find someone who was willing to take her out in the stormy weather, but fortunately she found a young sailor with a sense of adventure who loved to make a quick buck.

The rain washed down in torrents and the small craft rocked and lurched against the rough whitecapped waters of the Sound. Several times the boat rocked so crazily that Erin was sure that they would capsize, but the steady hand of the dark-complexioned young man kept the tiny craft miraculously on course. The wind tore at Erin's face, pelting it with cold rain, and whipping her long black hair away from her neck. But she continued to watch the shoreline and prayed that Mrs. Cavenaugh had exaggerated Krista's condition.

"Hey, lady," her companion called to her

over the roar of the boat's engine and the howl of the wind. "Would you like something to drink? I've got a thermos of coffee, or… something stronger, if you like rye whisky."

Erin shook her head. The thought of something in her already-knotted stomach made her want to gag. "No…thank you. I'm fine."

"You sure?" he asked, not convinced. The young woman was pale and scared, and deep lines of concern creased her otherwise beautiful face.

"Yes, really," Erin asserted, and managed a wan smile. The young man lifted his shoulders and turned his attention back to the sea. The remainder of the trip was made in silence. It seemed an eternity before Erin was on solid ground once again.

Virginia Mason Hospital stood out starkly white against a threatening charcoal-gray sky. Inside, the corridors were hushed, and the white walls were only made more severe by the garish splotches of color in the modern-art prints that hung on the walls. The bustling, white-uniformed staff, the mechanical groans of the elevators, and the overall oppressive silence gave Erin a strange sense of impending doom.

Room 538 was easy enough to find, and

Erin braced herself to enter the white cubicle just as a portly nurse in a neatly starched uniform approached her.

"Looking for someone?" the nurse asked in a professional voice. There was a calm smile on the broad face that spoke of authority and efficiency. "Can I help you?"

"I hope so. I'm a close friend of Krista Webster. I just found out about the accident today, and I hurried over here as quickly as I could." The disapproving brown eyes of the nurse studied Erin, and for the first time she realized what she must look like in her rain-drenched clothing and wet hair.

"You're not a member of the family?"

"No…not exactly." Erin shook her head.

The nurse placed a friendly hand on Erin's arm. "I'm sorry, but only family members are allowed to visit Miss Webster. Perhaps you would like to wait in the lobby? There's a coffee machine and some magazines…."

Erin refused to be brushed off. "Can you at least tell me how she is? Will she be all right? I… I have to know!"

"I understand," the nurse replied, and Erin felt that those wide, brown eyes and large, kindly face wouldn't lie. "Krista had a very bad fall and suffered a concussion, but Dr.

Sampson is caring for her and the prognosis is very hopeful."

"But...what does that mean, exactly? Will she recover? Will she be able to walk again?"

The nurse was steering Erin toward the waiting room. "Don't worry. Dr. Sampson is a very capable doctor, and he has the entire staff of the hospital to support him." With that, the nurse excused herself to answer another patient's call, and Erin found herself alone in the clinically clean waiting room with its ancient magazines and battered plastic furniture. She waited impatiently, staring out the window at the gloomy city, and ignored the stacks of outdated magazines that cluttered the table, while she sipped bitter coffee from a machine that looked as old as the hospital.

The sound of a familiar voice startled her, and she pulled her gaze from the dismal gray sky and the gathering dusk into the direction of the deep-timbred sound that made her heart leap. For several seconds she found it impossible to move or to speak as she studied Kane, his face lined with concern. He was speaking in low tones to a short, balding man with heavy glasses. The identification tag indicated that he was Dr. Sampson. The conversation was short and one-sided, with Dr. Sampson explaining Krista's condition in medical terms. Although the doctor seemed optimistic, Kane's entire bearing was a slouch of resignation and grim defeat. Erin felt her eyes burn with tears as she saw the pain and confusion in Kane's normally clear gaze. *He loves Krista so much,* Erin thought, *and he is hurting so badly.* She felt the urge to run to him, to comfort him, to love him, but she restrained herself.

Dr. Sampson excused himself, and Kane stood transfixed in the waiting area. He hadn't noticed Erin yet; he was too preoccupied with his own black thoughts. Suddenly she felt very out of place, an intruder. How would he feel when he finally saw her? How could she explain how she felt about him and his daughter, the love that was smothering her in its encompassing grasp? He had instructed Mrs. Cavenaugh not to call Erin. Perhaps he truly didn't want to see her. What would he do?

Her conjecture was cut short as Kane whirled to face her. It was as if he had sensed her presence and her uncertainty. His expression was cold, guarded, and Erin felt her heart stop as her eyes clashed with his brittle gray gaze.

"Erin?" His dark brows drew together. "How did you know?"

"Mrs. Cavenaugh told me."

"That woman can't keep a secret to save her soul!" He bit out the words and Erin wondered once again if she had made a grave mistake by intruding into his private grief. She took a step toward him and stopped. There was so much to say, so great a misunderstanding to bridge, and she wondered if it was at all possible.

"I'm sorry about Krista," she whispered, and the pain in her eyes was undeniable.

She saw him hesitate for a moment. He closed his eyes and seemed to give into the pressure that was battering against him. When he opened his eyes, they were clear once again, and in swift strides, he was by her side.

"I'm glad you came," he admitted, his voice rough from the strain of the day.

"Didn't you know that I would?"

"Erin, I don't know anything, not anymore!" His confession was a sigh of disgust.

"How—how is Krista?"

Lowering himself onto the edge of the plastic orange couch, he rubbed the tension from the back of his neck and ground his jaws together. When he spoke, it was in a monotone. "Dr. Sampson seems to think that she'll be fine, even taking into consideration her previous problem. She's got a concussion, but supposedly it's not serious, or at least not too serious. She was unconscious for a while, but she came to. Now she's resting. They gave her something—a sedative. The doctor thinks she'll wake up soon and that I can see her. God, I hope so. This waiting and not knowing is driving me up a wall." His long fingers raked deep gorges in his thick chestnut hair.

Erin sat next to him, not knowing the comforting words that would soothe him. They sat only inches apart, and yet Erin felt as if it might have been miles. Kane's eyes remained closed as if he were frighteningly weary and unable to face the trauma that was in store for him.

At the sound of Dr. Sampson's clipped footsteps Kane's eyelids flew open, and he was on his feet in a moment. "How is she?" he asked.

The pudgy doctor smiled. "You worry too much, Mr. Webster. Krista is going to be just fine. As a matter of fact, she's coming around now. You can see her if you like."

Erin couldn't keep up with Kane's swift strides as he nearly ran back to Krista's room.

The frail figure in the hospital bed brought back Erin's earlier feelings of apprehension and dread. Krista's complexion was nearly as white as the stark bedsheets that draped her, and the bandage on her head only seemed to add to her fragile appearance. A colorless fluid dripped into Krista's arm from a suspended I.V. bottle positioned near the bed. The tiny arm was secured to the bedrail by a strip of gauze.

Krista's eyes fluttered open after what seemed like hours, and a look of utter confusion and fear crossed her small face as she called to her father.

"Daddy?"

Kane's voice cracked with emotion as he responded. "Krista, honey, I'm right here." His fingers reached out and touched her cheek. "Oh, sweetheart, you don't know how good it is to hear your voice," he sighed.

Krista tried to lift her head, but her small face cringed in pain. "Oooh, where am I?"

"You're in the hospital, honey. Remember you hit your head while chasing the kitten?"

"Figaro? Where is he?" she asked with childish concern.

Kane smiled despite his tension. "Don't worry about him, honey. He's in good hands.

Mrs. Cavenaugh promised to take care of him until you get home."

Krista's eyes moved around the room until she spotted Erin. A smile brought back a little of the color to her face. "You're back!" Krista's enthusiasm shined in her eyes. "I knew that you'd come back!"

"You were right," Erin choked out, stepping nearer to the bed. "You should have known better than to think that I'd ever leave you."

"I did. I knew you wouldn't go without saying goodbye. See, Dad, I told ya she'd be back!"

"That you did," Kane whispered, and his eyes locked with Erin's questioning gaze.

Dr. Sampson came back into the room with his usual quick, short stride. "Well, little lady—so you did decide to wake up after all. About time, I might add! Your father here, he was beginning to worry." The little man's expert fingers probed Krista, and his knowing eyes studied her as he talked.

"That's okay. Dad always worries."

"Is that so? Well, maybe next time you'll be more careful on those stairs," the doctor reprimanded teasingly. When his examination was over, he studied Krista with feigned concern. "I think you should get some rest, young lady, before I send down for a special dinner for you. I'm going to send your dad home for a while, but he can come back and visit you later—what do you say?"

Disappointment crowded Krista's fine features, but she gave in. "All right," she agreed, and turned her attention back to her father. "But you will come back tonight, won't you?"

"You can count on it, pumpkin," Kane said huskily.

"And you, Erin?" Krista asked, her sky-blue eyes searching Erin's face.

Erin cast a quick glance at Kane and then smiled tenderly down at the child. "Sure, Krista. I'll be back," she promised.

As they stepped out of the room, Dr. Sampson gave Kane a quick report on Krista, assuring him that the little girl was responding well to treatment, and Erin felt a tide of relief wash over her. Kane, too, seemed visibly encouraged by the news. They walked out of the hospital together, and Erin wondered what their futures would be—together or apart. Kane was lost in his own thoughts but shook his head when Erin offered him a lift home.

"No, thanks," he said, "I've got my own car." Disappointment shattered Erin, but she tried not to show her feelings. "I have to stop off and talk to Mrs. Cavenaugh. I know she's worried about Krista."

"Will…will I see you later?" Erin blurted, unable to restrain herself.

"Do you want to?"

"Of course I do!" She shook her head in frustration. "I've missed you so badly."

"Shhh," he held her close to him for a moment, and she could hear the clamoring of his heart. "I'll meet you back at your place in an hour," he promised. "It's important that I speak to Mrs. Cavenaugh—you understand that, don't you?"

"Of course," she whispered as he walked away from her.

The hour stretched out to two, and Erin found herself nervously pacing the floor of her apartment. Where could he be? Was he even coming at all? She had tried to fill the time by taking a hasty shower, unpacking and finally brewing a strong cup of tea. The minutes ticked slowly by. What was he doing?

When at last he arrived, she steeled herself for the rejection that she knew was coming. Too much had happened—too many bitter words had been lashed out—it was just too damned late.

She didn't bother to get up when he opened the door and came into her antiques-filled loft.

"I'm sorry I'm late," he apologized, but didn't move to take off his jacket. "I've spent the last two hours driving in circles, wondering how on earth I can say the things that have to be said."

"I know," she whispered.

"I appreciate the fact that you came to the hospital."

A wry smile curved her lips. "You don't have to thank me. I had to come. Krista means a great deal to me."

"Erin." She let her eyes melt into his as he spoke her name. "I feel as if I owe you this incredibly large apology about the embezzling."

"Oh, Kane, not tonight, not after everything that's happened to Krista. It...doesn't matter."

"Damn it, Erin! The least you could do is let me explain. Then, if you want to throw me out of here, I'll go." Kane walked into the living room and sat on the small antique coffee table, positioning himself directly in front of Erin. She found it impossible to take her gaze from his. She was compelled to listen to him.

"After our last fight, I began thinking about

alternate suspects in the embezzlement. You were right and I feel like a fool admitting it, but I was so blinded by my love for you, so afraid that you were the culprit, that I couldn't see the facts correctly. It was an unforgivable injustice to you."

Erin started to protest but he ignored her. "Just let me finish," he commanded. "I started putting some of the pieces together and discovered that Mitch was having an affair with Olivia. It really wasn't all that difficult to see, once I knew you were innocent. Olivia was the one person who seemed to know too much—everything about you, the securities key, the meeting with Mitch on the day of the arraignment. She was clever and subtle, but she took great pains to mention that you and Mitch had always been friendly, and Cameron, the bastard, didn't deny it."

Erin shook her head in disbelief as Kane continued. "At the point that I began to suspect Olivia, I was inhibited because of Krista's depression. I'm sorry, Erin, if you can only guess how really sorry I am that I thought, even for a moment..."

"It's okay," she whispered, and reached to touch his arm.

"No, it's not!" He closed his eyes and shook

his head. "And what makes it worse is the fact that I fell in love with you the moment I saw you sitting in the office on the floor with all those books spread around you, and still I thought that you were involved with Cameron. I must have been out of my mind."

Erin's head was reeling with the magnitude of Kane's confession. He had said it over and over—that he loved her. Was it really possible?

"I want you to know that it doesn't matter, not anymore. When I heard about Krista from Mrs. Cavenaugh, I realized that nothing matters—nothing except for you and Krista," she admitted, smiling into his face.

His eyes opened slowly. "Erin, just what are you saying?" he asked quietly.

"I'm saying that I love you, and the only reason that I wouldn't marry you before was because I didn't think that you loved me."

"How could you have been so blind?" he asked, reaching for her and crushing her to him. "It was so evident!" He didn't wait for an answer. His lips came crashing down on hers with a fiery passion that was soon exploding in her veins. "I'll never let you get away again," he vowed. "We're getting married as soon as Krista is out of the hospital."

"You haven't heard any disagreements from me, have you?" she asked.

"Thank God for small favors!" He sighed, and let the weight of his body fall against hers.

* * * * *

Get 4 FREE REWARDS!

We'll send you 2 FREE Books <u>plus</u> 2 FREE Mystery Gifts.

Harlequin Special Edition books relate to finding comfort and strength in the support of loved ones and enjoying the journey no matter what life throws your way.

FREE Value Over **$20**

Get 4 FREE REWARDS!

We'll send you 2 FREE Books plus 2 FREE Mystery Gifts.

Harlequin Romance Larger-Print books will immerse you in emotion and intimacy simmering in international locales— experience the rush of falling in love!

FREE
Value Over
$20

Get 4 FREE REWARDS!

We'll send you 2 FREE Books plus 2 FREE Mystery Gifts.

FREE Value Over **$20**

Both the **Romance** and **Suspense** collections feature compelling novels written by many of today's bestselling authors.

YES! Please send me 2 FREE novels from the Essential Romance or Essential Suspense Collection and my 2 FREE gifts (gifts are worth about $10 retail). After receiving them, if I don't wish to receive any more books, I can return the shipping statement marked "cancel." If I don't cancel, I will receive 4 brand-new novels every month and be billed just $7.24 each in the U.S. or $7.49 each in Canada. That's a savings of up to 28% off the cover price. It's quite a bargain! Shipping and handling is just 50¢ per book in the U.S. and $1.25 per book in Canada.* I understand that accepting the 2 free books and gifts places me under no obligation to buy anything. I can always return a shipment and cancel at any time. The free books and gifts are mine to keep no matter what I decide.

Choose one: ☐ **Essential Romance**
(194/394 MDN GQ6M)

☐ **Essential Suspense**
(191/391 MDN GQ6M)

Name (please print)

Address   Apt. #

City   State/Province   Zip/Postal Code

Email: Please check this box ☐ if you would like to receive newsletters and promotional emails from Harlequin Enterprises ULC and its affiliates. You can unsubscribe anytime.

Mail to the Harlequin Reader Service:
IN U.S.A.: P.O. Box 1341, Buffalo, NY 14240-8531
IN CANADA: P.O. Box 603, Fort Erie, Ontario L2A 5X3

Want to try 2 free books from another series! Call 1-800-873-8635 or visit www.ReaderService.com.

---

*Terms and prices subject to change without notice. Prices do not include sales taxes, which will be charged (if applicable) based on your state or country of residence. Canadian residents will be charged applicable taxes. Offer not valid in Quebec. This offer is limited to one order per household. Books received may not be as shown. Not valid for current subscribers to the Essential Romance or Essential Suspense Collection. All orders subject to approval. Credit or debit balances in a customer's account(s) may be offset by any other outstanding balance owed by or to the customer. Please allow 4 to 6 weeks for delivery. Offer available while quantities last.

Your Privacy—Your information is being collected by Harlequin Enterprises ULC, operating as Harlequin Reader Service. For a complete summary of the information we collect, how we use this information and to whom it is disclosed, please visit our privacy notice located at corporate.harlequin.com/privacy-notice. From time to time we may also exchange your personal information with reputable third parties. If you wish to opt out of this sharing of your personal information, please visit readerservice.com/consumerschoice or call 1-800-873-8635. **Notice to California Residents**—Under California law, you have specific rights to control and access your data. For more information on these rights and how to exercise them, visit corporate.harlequin.com/california-privacy.

STRS21R

Get 4 FREE REWARDS!

We'll send you 2 FREE Books plus 2 FREE Mystery Gifts.

Harlequin Heartwarming Larger-Print books will connect you to uplifting stories where the bonds of friendship, family and community unite.

FREE Value Over $20